Books by G.A. McKevett

Savannah Reid Mysteries

Granny Reid Mysteries

Published by Kensington Publishing Corporation

G.A. McKEVETT

Hide and SNEAK

A SAVANNAH REID MYSTERY

KENSINGTON BOOKS
www.kensingtonbooks.com

KENSINGTON BOOKS are published by

Kensington Publishing Corp.
119 West 40th Street
New York, NY 10018

All Kensington titles, imprints and distributed lines are available at special quantity discounts for bulk purchases for sales promotion, premiums, fund-raising, educational or institutional use. Special book excerpts or customized printings can also be created to fit specific needs. For details, write or phone the office of the Kensington Special Sales Manager: Kensington Publishing Corp., 119 West 40th Street, New York, NY, 10018. Attn. Special Sales Department. Phone: 1-800-221-2647.

Kensington and the K logo Reg. U.S. Pat. & TM Off.

ISBN-13: 978-1-4967-0088-9
ISBN-10: 1-4967-0088-0
First Kensington Hardcover Edition: May 2018
First Kensington Mass Market Edition: April 2019

ISBN-13: 978-1-4967-0087-2 (e-book)
ISBN-10: 1-4967-0087-2 (e-book)

10 9 8 7 6 5 4 3 2 1

Printed in the United States of America

Acknowledgments

Thank you, Leslie Connell, for your encouraging words when I need them most, for always being my "first reader," and for your many years of service to the Moonlight Magnolia team. I am so grateful to you, dear lady.

I also wish to thank all the fans who write to me, sharing their thoughts and offering endless encouragement. Your stories touch my heart, and I enjoy your letters more than you know. I can be reached at:

sonja@sonjamassie.com
and
facebook.com/gwendolynnarden.mckevett

Chapter 1

"Oh, for heaven's sake. Of course, I can babysit for a couple of hours. I'm the oldest of nine children. Hightail it over here with that little red-headed punkin. Auntie Savannah's been aching to get her hands on her."

Words uttered so blithely with such conviction, such confidence, with only the best of intentions.

They were words that came back to haunt a person. Not unlike: "For better or for worse." Or in Savannah Reid's former life as a police officer, "Hey, only five more minutes to the end of my shift; what could happen now?"

As Savannah stood in the bathtub, letting the hot shower water stream over her exhausted body, washing baby urp out of her hair and rinsing even more from between her breasts, she pulled the shower curtain aside a few inches and peered down at her unhappy charge.

The less-than-angelic pixie lay, squalling, in her

makeshift cradle on the bathroom floor, snugly tucked into what had been, only moments before, a towel drawer from the linen closet.

If the drawer had been lined with prickly pear cactus instead of Savannah's softest Egyptian cotton guest towels, Miss Vanna Rose's yowling couldn't have been louder or more piteous.

The sound reverberated around the room, bouncing off the tiles and straight into Savannah's heart. "I'm so sorry, kiddo," she told her tiny niece as she applied a second application of shampoo. "But I'm sure you'd pitch an even bigger hissy fit if I was to bring you in here with me."

The child responded with another plaintive wail that threatened to peel the rose-spangled paper off the walls.

"Lordy mercy, that kid can holler!" Savannah marveled at the sheer volume, not to mention the vibrato that would do a mezzo-soprano proud.

Suddenly, the bathroom door flew open, startling Savannah. She jumped and dropped the shampoo. It hit her big toe. Yelping, she danced around, while grabbing for the closest weapon of opportunity—a bar of her husband's favorite soap on a rope.

Not that she was likely to fight off an intruder with a half-gone bar of soap, but the pain from her mashed toe had shot all the way up her body and into her brain, so she wasn't thinking clearly.

It was simply shocking how heavy a bottle like that could be when nearly full. Whoever had invaded her sanctuary, burglar or babynapper, they were about to become the first person to be slaughtered with a chunk of Old Spice.

Fortunately, it was her husband who rushed inside.

Detective Sergeant Dirk Coulter stood there, taking in the scene. His wife. Her head covered in lather that was streaming down into her eyes. Eyes filled with shampoo, pain, and fury. Her hand upraised, brandishing his soap. The cherub in the drawer on the floor, mouth wide open, screaming, her cheeks red with rage.

Dirk wore his own look of alarm, along with an unsettling amount of blood on his face, his shirt, arms, and hands.

While a typical day in the Reid-Coulter household could hardly be called "mundane" or "hohum," Savannah had to admit, this was a bit unusual even for them.

Her anger quickly turned to concern as she watched him peel off his bloodstained shirt.

Tossing it into the hamper, he said, "And here I thought *I'd* had the worst day."

"Oh, sugar," she said, fighting down the fear every police officer's spouse suffers daily. "Are you wounded?"

"Naw. It's all Loco Roco's. We tussled, I clocked him a good one on the nose, and the dude sprung a leak."

"Roco's out of jail?"

"Not anymore. Apparently, in the state of California knocking over a liquor store is a violation of a guy's parole. So's assaulting a police officer. Go figure."

He knelt beside the angel in the drawer and, leaning down with his face close to hers, he said, "I'm sorry, Curly-locks, but I can't even touch you, let alone hold you till I get every drop of ol' Roco's bodily fluid yuck offa me."

He stared at Savannah, the shampoo bottle in one hand, the soap still in the other. "You're taking a shower *now*," he asked semi-indignantly, "with my birthday present soap? Funny time to treat yourself to a luxurious bath routine, when you're supposed to be babysitting my favorite girl here."

Savannah scowled. "I thought *I* was your favorite girl."

"No. Kitty Cleo's my favorite," he said with a grin. "At least, she was, until this little beauty came along. But don't worry. You've always been a solid second. Actually, now you're third, but at least you're still on the podium."

He gave his wife a wink. She stuck out her tongue, responded with a loud, rude raspberry, then ducked back into the shower. "Just for that, I'm not going to jump out of here, like I was fixin' to when I saw you all bloodied up. Figured you'd be anxious to get in. But now I'm gonna take my time and 'luxuriate,' as I've been accused of doing. Might even condition my hair, exfoliate, and shave my legs, too, while I'm at it."

"Fine," he replied. "I'll go downstairs." He looked around and shuddered. "This bathroom always gives me the heebie-jeebies anyway. Flowery walls, lacy towels, perfumey candles. Girl crap everywhere."

Ducking his head closer to the baby's, he spoke to her in the softest tone imaginable—the one he used for cats, dogs, and children. Occasionally for Savannah as well, but only if they hadn't been arguing about such things as overly feminine bathrooms and him leaving the toilet seat up. "Don't you cry, little darlin'," he told the child. "Uncle Dirk will make it up to you as soon as I get out of the shower, and that'll be before Auntie Savannah. While she's still shaving that first leg, you and me'll be all comfy in her big chair downstairs, reading a book."

The baby stopped crying and stared up at him, big blue eyes bright with interest, as though she understood every word and was intrigued by the prospects.

"It won't be no pansy, princess book neither," he added as he stood and walked to the door. "It'll be a good one with some bears or a big, bad, pig-eatin' wolf or two in it."

Savannah watched him, enjoying the blissful silence from the drawer on the floor, while experiencing just a tiny jab of jealousy that he could comfort her niece far better than she.

"Hey, since you have such a quieting effect on her," Savannah said, "why don't you take her downstairs with you and let me finish my shower in peace?"

Dirk looked positively scandalized. "And let her see a grown man shower? *Naked*? No way! That's just . . . just . . . *wrong*. She'd be scarred for life."

Savannah rolled her eyes and sighed. "Oh, for heaven's sake, Dirk. She's two months old. I assure you, she'd never even register it, let alone remember it."

He grinned and waggled a blood-streaked eyebrow at her. "But *you'll* never forget the moment *you* first laid eyes on the Big Monty."

He ducked as a net bath scrubbie sailed past his left ear, then chuckled as he left the room and closed the door behind him.

Savannah could hear him whistling the theme to *The Godfather*, loudly and badly, as he walked down the hallway, heading for the staircase and the more gender-neutral, less female-foo-foo bathroom downstairs.

Actually, she couldn't remember her first sighting of the much ballyhooed "Monty." Undoubtedly, it was years ago when she had still been a cop and they had been partners. It was probably during a stakeout when she had inadvertently caught a glimpse of him "draining the dragon" onto a roadside sage bush. But she knew better than tell him she had no distinct recollection of the momentous event.

Personal experience had taught her that men didn't take such news well.

For the sake of domestic tranquility, she decided to revise their love story, creating a version more in line with his. She decided that her initial glimpse of such manly glory and her subsequent swooning at the sight occurred on their honeymoon night.

What the heck, she thought, mentally dismissing the whole subject. *Where's the harm in a bit of revisionist history, as long as everybody lives happily ever after?*

Anticipating a renewed series of protests from the juvenile on the floor, Savannah quickly rinsed away the last bit of shampoo, turned off the shower, and stepped out of the tub. After a quick "lick and a promise," as Granny Reid would say, with a towel, she slipped into her fluffy terrycloth bathrobe.

In the drawer at her feet, her tiny niece appeared to have been temporarily distracted from her fit-pitching and seemed moderately mollified by the brief, but pleasant, encounter with one of her favorite people, Uncle Dirk.

The baby gave her aunt an enchanting half smile and cooed adorably as she waved her tiny fists.

"Yeah, I know, you like him better than me," Savannah said, scooping her up and cradling her against her chest. "So does Cleo."

Savannah tweaked the tiny rosebud mouth with her fingertip. "That's perfectly okay. I understand."

Savannah pressed a kiss to the child's cheek. Little Vanna squinted as one of her aunt's wet, dark curls fell down onto her forehead.

The baby's tiny fingers tangled in the hair and tugged.

It hurt, but Savannah didn't even notice as she gazed into eyes as sapphire blue as her own. Squalling fits and upchucked milk were forgotten as the bond between the two Reid females tightened yet another notch. Two hearts, forever entwined with Love's soft, but ever-enduring chains.

"I plum adore you, Miss Savannah Rose. You'll never know how much," the former cop, present private detective, all-around tough gal whispered to her tiny namesake as they left the bathroom and headed down the stairs. "I have a lot to teach you.

Especially about men. Most of it you won't need to know for a long time, but for right now, let's discuss deep voices. Us gals are suckers for a deep voice, like your Uncle Dirk's. Women are always just hurling themselves at his feet, and all because of that voice of his."

As they reached the bottom of the staircase, Vanna gazed up at her aunt with a slightly doubtful look.

"Okay," Savannah clarified, "not *all* women. To be honest, the vast majority of them don't really like him very much, deep voice or not. Mostly, it's just you, Cleo, me, and sometimes Diamante—if he's feeding her off his plate. It's a pretty small fan club, when you come right down to it."

Vanna cooed, expressing agreement and adding her own opinion on the subject.

"Yes," Savannah replied. "You're absolutely right. He *is* a good guy at heart. The barking and growling are mainly just when he's hungry."

They passed the bay window, where Diamante lay drowsing in the sun, a glossy black panther-ette soaking in some rays.

Normally, Di's sister, Cleo, would have been curled next to her, enjoying the day's last bit of sunshine. Life-giving, bone-warming, soul-uplifting, California sunshine.

But Dirk was in the shower, which meant that faithful, brave Cleo would be standing just inside the bathroom door, staring, terrified, as once again the daily horror unfolded before her eyes. Every muscle in her sleek, feline body would be taut, quivering with anticipation, ready to make the ultimate sacrifice. If necessary, she would leap into that shower and at least attempt to rescue poor "Daddy," should he be overcome by all that vicious water raining down pitilessly on him.

Yes, Cleo adored Dirk and had since they'd met, back when she was a six-week-old kitten. It had been love at first sight for both of them.

She had decided that his lap was the most comfortable and his petting the most satisfying of any human anywhere, including Mom's. She would abandon Savannah and her caresses the moment Dirk walked into a room—much to Mommy's consternation.

Back then, he had even shown his devotion by changing his bank password from "BROKE1" to "MYCLEO."

Diamante, on the other hand, was far more practical. While she would have fought a rabid Rottweiler, fang and nail, to prevent it from harming her beloved mom, she was perfectly willing to let any human being, even dear Mommy, die a hideous death if they were foolish enough to step into a cubicle where water poured down on them. As far as Di was concerned, anyone who did such a dumb thing was just asking for it and deserved whatever they got.

Diamante scrambled down from her window and followed Savannah as aunt and niece passed into the kitchen. Savannah took a small glass bottle, filled with Tammy's breast milk, from the refrigerator.

"For heaven's sake, do *not* microwave it!" Her friend Tammy had instructed her with what Savannah considered an overly enthusiastic admonition that bordered on Maternal Mania. "There's no telling what nutrients those waves might destroy or alter in some horrible, unnatural way."

"O-o-o-kay," Savannah had replied with an ever-so-slight eye roll.

"No! Not o-o-o-kay!" was Tammy's passionate response. "I know what that means when you say that and roll your eyes. That means you think I'm being silly, and you're going to do it your own way. But you better not! I'm the mom around here, and when it comes to my baby, what I say goes!"

Savannah had been taken slightly aback, given that Tammy was usually such a gentle, acquiescent soul.

But when Waycross added, "Better do it, Sis. She's got all those postnatal hormones roarin' through her bloodstream, and she's liable to slap ya neckid and hide your clothes if you don't abide by what she says."

Savannah promised, Tammy was convinced, and the topic was discussed no more.

A promise is a promise, Savannah reminded herself when she passed the microwave on the way to the stove. *Especially one made to a woman whose hormones have run amuck.*

She looked down at Vanna Rose and said, "It'd be just my luck that, if I snuck it on the sly, the first words out of your little mouth wouldn't be 'Ma-ma' or 'Da-da.' They'd be, 'Hey, Mom. Guess what? When you weren't looking, Auntie Savannah microwaved my bottle.'"

Vanna watched with a slightly concerned frown crinkling her forehead as Savannah placed the bottle into a shallow pan of water to heat.

"Don't you worry your pretty little noggin," Savannah told her. "I'll get it right. I'm actually a very good cook, as you'll discover in a few years. Your mommy will probably raise you up on celery sticks and carrot puree, but what happens at Aunt Savannah's house *stays* at Aunt Savannah's house. Yessiree. Over here, you'll get introduced to the wonders of homemade ice cream and chocolate chip cookies. If you're lucky and I'm ambitious, maybe on the same day."

Once the milk was heated to precisely the right temperature, Savannah offered it to the child and sauntered back to the living room.

Savannah decided to forgo her own cup of coffee or steaming cocoa with whipped cream, peppermint crumbles, and chocolate shavings. Vanna had quick-action piston leg kicks to rival the Rockettes. There was no point in taking a chance with a hot beverage.

As they settled into the rose chintz-covered, comfy chair—a cushion at Savannah's back, her feet on the overstuffed ottoman—Savannah adjusted the bottle in the infant's mouth and continued her sage instruction. "As a baby, who'll be a girl and then a woman someday," she said, with a tone of great gravity, "you have to remember a very important thing about the males of our species. Here it is. Don't ever forget it: men . . . if you keep 'em fed and comfortable, for the most part, they're darned near tolerable."

Vanna spit out the bottle nipple and cooed a question.

Savannah listened with utmost attention, then gave a solemn nod. "Women, you ask?" She sighed and drew a deep breath. "Well, that's a different situation all together. As it turns out, us females are a mite more complicated."

Chapter 2

Half an hour later, Savannah emerged from the kitchen, a tray of predinner snacks in hand, to find her favorite chair occupied by her favorite husband, who was holding her all-time-favorite niece.

"I leave the room to round up some treats, and this is the thanks I get. I lose my seat," she muttered as she placed the tray of assorted cheeses, crackers, sliced apples, and pears on the coffee table. "If you can tear yourself away from what you're doing," she told Dirk, "dig into this here. I got some of that stinky cheese you like so much."

"Not now," he told her with a dismissive wave at the food. The first dismissive wave she had ever seen him perform in the presence of edibles. "My girl and me are right at the good part of the story."

As promised, Dirk was reading a small children's book to Vanna—the ageless tale of *The Three Bears*. The baby stared up at him with eyes wide, a look of deep concern on her sweet face, as he described the discovery of the golden-haired child by the bears.

Being Dirk, he was embellishing in typical, pseudo-tough-guy fashion. "Miss Goldilocks, you are under arrest!" he pronounced in his best Papa Bear voice—if Papa had worked for the San Carmelita Police Department and had spiked his porridge with half a cup of testosterone powder that morning.

Then, in a tremulous little-girl voice, Dirk squeaked, "What for? What for? Why are you arrestin' me? What did I do? What did I do?"

Dirk turned to the baby and said, "They always ask that. Even when they know damn—um, I mean—darned well what they did. It's really annoying to us law enforcement professionals. Of course, I know *you* won't ever say anything like that, because *you'll* never do anything wrong. Not in your whole life."

Savannah stifled a giggle as she helped herself to the least-stinky selection of cheese and some fruit. Then she settled onto the sofa near Diamante and Cleopatra, who were sitting on the footstool with their backs to Dirk and the baby. They were staging a not-so-subtle protest about their demotion to Spoiled Rotten Babies Second Class. A ginger-haired, fairy fey had taken their place.

As a result, life was hardly worth living for the felines of the household.

Cleo was particularly miffed, and who could blame her, after she had risked life and limb performing "shower duty"?

Savannah offered them a nibble of Dirk's stinky cheese, and they perked up. Okay, so life might be worth living. But only a little and only for a moment.

Dirk kissed Vanna on the top of her head, which for a two-month-old, was lushly covered with curly fuzz. Then he continued his action-packed story. "Miss Goldilocks," he said, channeling Papa B. again, "you picked the wrong house to vandalize. I happen to be a part-time, volunteer, auxiliary cop, and I am hereby charging you with first-degree malicious trespass and—"

"*Malicious* trespass?" Savannah asked with a snicker. "That seems a bit harsh."

He frowned. "You tell the story your way, and I'll tell it mine."

With a shrug, she added, "Doesn't matter anyway. Miss Goldi Prissy Pants'll lawyer up, and the public defender will finagle it down to third-degree loitering."

"An-n-nd," Dirk interjected, ignoring her, "the additional charge of felonious, heinous, and cruel vandalism of domestic furnishings."

Vanna squealed with delight, waved her arms, and kicked her legs joyfully.

"See there?" Dirk said. "She likes her colorful uncle's version best."

"'Colorful' is one word you could use to describe him," Savannah replied under her breath. "Now, how's about you vacate my chair and give me that young'un back while you tie into these goodies?"

As she watched a rapid succession of conflicting facial expressions cross his features, reflecting a major war raging within his soul, she knew which would win.

Even food couldn't compete with the charisma of a two-month-old who adored you.

"I'll stay put," he said. "But you could load up a couple of those crackers and cram them in my mouth, if it's not too bigga strain."

She began to do as he asked, but no sooner had she commenced the task than she heard a brief knock on the front door and then the sound of a key in the lock.

"It's us," Tammy announced from the foyer.

"We're back," shouted Savannah's younger brother, Waycross. "If you're teaching our daughter to play poker, you'd better put the cards and chips away."

"We finished the poker and billiard lessons an hour ago," Savannah said when a beautiful, statuesque blonde glided into the living room, accompanied by a grown-up, male version of Vanna. "We've moved on to darts. She keeps wanting to chew on them, though. I reckon that'd fall in the same category as zapping the milk in that nasty ol' microwave."

"Ha, ha. Aren't you funny?" Tammy said as she walked over to Dirk and started to take the baby from him. But she paused when she saw the storybook, then lingered a moment, taking in the tender scene.

Even Savannah had to admit, they were a pretty cute twosome—a big, rough-around-the-edges, sunburned bruiser like Dirk, with a lily-white, carrot topped angel in his arms.

Who would have thought a streetworn police detective would prove to be the perfect babysitter?

Savannah knew, of course. Unlike most people in Dirk's personal and professional circles, she was quite familiar with his softer, sweeter side, and she was enchanted and endeared by it.

But Tammy had seen far more of the cranky, difficult aspects of Detective Sergeant Coulter's personality, so Savannah wasn't surprised that the new mother was awed by this seemingly miraculous transformation in the man when he was holding her infant daughter.

Dirk moved his feet off the ottoman and made room for Tammy. She sat down and began to gently stroke her baby's downy curls.

Savannah watched Tammy, her dearest friend, now sister-in-law, as she whispered to her child, asking her about the bears and if she had enjoyed Uncle Dirk's story.

But for all the sweetness of the scene, Savannah felt that something was wrong.

Yes, something was definitely wrong with Tammy.

For days, Savannah had watched her friend changing before her eyes and had been unable to do anything about it. Their bubbly, positive, energetic, California golden girl was gradually turning into a tired, dispirited, dull and colorless version of her former self.

Glancing over at Waycross, she saw that he, too, was watching his wife, an expression of equal concern on his freckled face. Normally, her little brother was like Tammy in temperament, both happy to grasp and enjoy every moment of the present, fully embracing life as it came.

But not yesterday or the day before, and even less today.

Reaching over to snatch up the tray from the coffee table, Savannah said to her brother, "I'm gonna go load this up again. Would you give me a hand in the kitchen?"

"Sure," he said, after a brief glance at his little family. "I reckon Uncle Dirk's got this here situation in hand."

With Waycross, Diamante, and Cleo following close behind, Savannah walked into the kitchen, where she pretended to busy herself with cutting a Honeycrisp apple into thin slices.

Di and Cleo began to make furry black figure eights around her ankles. "These miscreants think they're starving, as usual," she told her brother. "Would you mind pouring some of that awful-smelling kitty vittles into their bowls, before they tangle me up and take me down?"

As Waycross hurried to do as she asked, she lowered her voice to a whisper and said, "Your honey seems a mite droopy. I thought you two were going to enjoy a nice, romantic afternoon while I was babysitting. Figured that'd perk her up a bit."

He shrugged as he slid the cat food back into the upper cupboard. "It might've, if we'd spent it being romantic."

"But you didn't?"

"Nope. Spent it scrubbin' the bathroom floor that didn't need scrubbin' and cleanin' out the garage that didn't need cleanin'. Then we washed the windows, inside and out, that were already so crystal clear we've got birds crashin' into 'em."

Savannah didn't have to ask why they were on this extreme cleaning spree. Both Tammy and Waycross were known for their fastidiousness. Tammy with the house and Waycross with the automobiles and yard. At any given moment, open-heart surgery could have been performed atop her washer and dryer or on the floor of his garage.

Ordinarily, Savannah would have thought this extreme scouring to be strange. But she was pretty sure she knew the reason why, and it troubled her.

"When exactly are they arriving?" she asked him.

"Shortly. In just a few hours. Boy, howdy, this day sure arrived quick. It was on us before we could turn around twice," he replied with a Georgia drawl that was even thicker than hers. She had lived in Southern California twenty years, while he had been only recently transplanted.

Savannah looked into his eyes and saw a deep sorrow there that surprised and saddened her. Usually, Waycross's ruddy, freckled face was alight with joy—joy for what he considered his charmed life. He couldn't have been happier if he had won a record-breaking lottery. He had been lucky enough to marry the love of his life, and she had given him a beautiful little daughter.

Waycross was still in awe and wonder that an exquisite, perfect creature like Tammy Hart, now Tammy Reid, had chosen him, of all people, to love. A dirt-poor, wrong-side-of-the track kid from a rural Georgia town that was little more than a wide spot in the road.

Even before the birth of their baby, Waycross

had considered himself blessed. Now he figured he was in bliss.

It was all a fairy tale that was too good to be true.

Looking into her brother's eyes, Savannah could see that he was afraid his storybook life was about to crumble around him.

"The bad part is," he said, "no matter how much she cleans, it ain't gonna be enough for the likes of *them.*"

Savannah reached out her arms and folded him to her. "You don't know that, sugar," she told him. "Never underestimate the difference a wee one brings to a situation like this."

"Even if they like Vanna, they've already made up their minds not to like me."

"Their sweet little granddaughter is half you. One look at her will tell them that. They'll love her to pieces, and that's gonna spill over onto you. You just wait and see."

Waycross gave his sister a squeeze, then kissed the top of her head. "But what if it don't—spill over onto me, that is?"

Savannah thought it over for a moment, deciding whether to give him the brown sugar–coated version or just speak the truth. As she almost always did, she decided on the truth. "If after meeting you and getting to know you, darlin', they still don't approve of you, that's on them. You're a fine man. You're plum crazy about their daughter. You're a wonderful husband to her, and a fantastic father to their grandchild."

Waycross gulped. "They had dinner with the governor of New York last Saturday night."

"Okay. We had dinner at Granny's. Her fried chicken and rhubarb pie ain't nothin' to sneeze at."

"On Sunday, they went to see some fancy opera at a place called the Lincoln Center in New York City. After the show, they went backstage and drank champagne with the stars of it. I was guzzlin' a beer and watchin' NASCAR."

"Okay, but I'll bet your favorite driver won, while the hero of that opera they were watching probably stabbed or strangled himself to death or some such hooey. Those things always end bad."

Waycross laughed. A little. "Thank you, Sis."

"You're welcome," she said, ruffling his copper curls. "Don't you forget that you come from good stock, too."

He gave her a sad half smile, and she knew he was thinking about their less than upstanding parents.

"Shirley and Macon Sr. aside," she continued, "Granny Reid is as fine a person as ever walked the earth. The same can be said of Grandpa Reid. So, if anybody has a mind to make you think you're less than them, you remember that. Waycross Reid takes a back seat to nobody. Hear me?"

He nodded, but she could tell that her admonition hadn't gone very deep into his psyche or soul. He'd be back to dithering in moments.

But she knew how to cheer up a Reid.

She walked to the refrigerator and took out a tin covered with foil. "This here's what was left over from Gran's rhubarb pie," she said, shoving it into his hand. "There's homemade vanilla bean ice cream in the freezer to go with it. You polish it off in here by your lonesome and nobody'll be the wiser."

The familiar smile returned to her brother's face.

When the ice cream was presented, his eyes shone with their usual love-of-life gleam.

Yes, Savannah knew her business well.

It was the unofficial family motto. "If you wanna perk up a member of the Reid clan, shove some good food under their nose."

Worked every time.

Except with Tammy.

As Savannah was strolling back into the living room, mulling over possible ways to light a fire under the lackluster Tamitha, she heard her phone buzzing in her sweater pocket.

She answered it, and within a minute, all thoughts of personal family drama had been set aside—at least for the time being.

Holy Aunt Betty's cow, she thought as she listened to the worried caller explain a troublesome situation.

She had always been amazed to see how quickly a day could turn around, for better or for worse. While she sympathized with the parties who were in trouble, she had to be honest and admit that, as far as she was concerned, this was definitely "for the better."

Glory be! She had a case!

Chapter 3

E *than Malloy! Ethan Malloy! What a delicious dis-*
traction from family drama, Savannah thought
as she drove south along the Pacific Coast Highway on her way to Malibu, home of the stars.

Thanks to her friends Ryan Stone and John Gibson, who had recommended her to yet another of
their celebrity acquaintances, she would soon be a
guest at a wonderful mansion owned by none
other than *the* Ethan Malloy.

Well, not exactly a guest. Apparently, the gorgeous, Academy Award–winning actor found himself in need of a reliable private detective to
handle a delicate and highly personal issue.

When John had called her that morning, he had
asked with his aristocratic British accent, "Would
you mind terribly, love—if you have the time and
are so inclined—calling on a dear friend of ours?
You may have heard of him. A lad by the name
of Ethan Malloy. He lives in a simply charming

Norman-style chateau, perched on one of the highest mountains in north Malibu. Admittedly, 'tis a fearsome drive up those treacherous canyon roads, but you'll find it well worth your while for the view alone."

Did she mind? Not a bit. In fact, she had forced herself not to dance an Irish jig at the thought.

The view, indeed!

Though she was certain that the scenery John was referring to would be the magnificent coastline, nestled against a gently curving mountain ridge, she was looking forward to getting an eyeful of Mr. Malloy in his glorious flesh-and-blood person.

Ethan wasn't just one of her own personal favorite movie stars. Since his debut in a blockbuster "sword and sandal" gladiator film six years ago, he had been the darling of the international film community. Especially its female members. Since then, he had played period heroes from every chapter of human history, and incited love and more than a little lust the world over.

Whether he was a pistol-packing sheriff dealing out justice in the Wild West, or a dark and brooding Gothic hero who rode his black stallion across the moors of Cornwall at midnight, Ethan—along with his broad shoulders, six pack, thick dark hair, and stunning blue eyes—was the subject of more women's fantasies than any male star in decades.

Savannah considered herself one of Ethan Malloy's most ardent admirers. So ardent in fact that, as a married woman, she would have felt a bit guilty about her obsession if she hadn't frequently witnessed her husband risking life and limb to race from the kitchen to the living room, just to catch a glimpse of his beloved Catherine Zeta-Jones on the television.

Savannah was no dummy, and she hadn't been a detective for years without learning a thing or two. No doubt about it. Her dear, darlin' hubby suggested they watch *Chicago* far too often for a manly man who, otherwise, positively loathed musicals.

Though, besotted as Dirk was with Ms. Catherine, Savannah doubted that he donned any special type of apparel to watch her roll around atop a grand piano while belting out "All That Jazz."

But Savannah had "dressed" for this occasion.

To her shame.

Not the "hang your head and stare at the tile on the floor for hours" shame that caused a gal to feel like a fallen woman, cook her husband's favorite meal, or treat him to an especially exciting and illegal-in-some-states sex act on a non-birthday night.

No, it was just one of those niggling notions that one was doing something a tad naughty.

To her discredit, when she had gotten dressed, in anticipation of the auspicious appointment to come, Savannah had put on her newest, sexiest Victoria's Secret underwear. She had also shaved her legs. Extra close.

She wasn't proud of it.

She firmly believed that a happily married woman should never put on her best black lace underwear with red satin ribbon trim for a meeting with a married man who wasn't her husband.

If for no other reason, it seemed like a "two-bit hussy" thing to do. Something Savannah's Hussy-

First-Class sister, Marietta, would stoop to. Although Mari's knickers would be purple leopard print, and she would be sure to adopt some unladylike pose during the course of the visit to make certain that the man in question got an eyeball full. Whether he wanted his eyeball filled or not.

Savannah supposed she herself was a wee bit classier in her hussy-ness.

Funny, how a gal could rationalize just about anything if she tried hard enough.

It doesn't matter anyway, Savannah thought as she drove her vintage red Mustang south along the Pacific Coast Highway, drawing ever nearer to Malibu and Ethan Malloy. He was never going to see her knickers. Not in a million years. Unlike her sister, she wasn't into exhibitionism and wouldn't be, even if she wasn't married to the sweetest grouch on the West Coast.

But after watching Ethan for hours on the screen, with his ripped muscles and those pale blue eyes that could smolder with passion one moment, flash with temper the next, and then soften with incredible sensitivity when least expected, Savannah wanted to look her best. All the way down to her freshly shaved legs.

Ethan would never know that they were smooth and silky, but *she* would.

That was all that mattered.

She consoled herself with the thought that, if Dirk was going to meet Catherine Zeta-Jones, he wouldn't have put on a pair of underwear with Swiss cheese holes in it.

Though, being Dirk, he might have.

All thoughts of shaved legs, sexy lingerie, and

shabby briefs left Savannah's mind the moment she saw the iconic road sign that welcomed her to MALIBU, 27 MILES OF SCENIC BEAUTY.

No matter how many hundreds of times she had seen that sign, the thrill never faded. Malibu might be a town known for having pristine beaches, glorious sunsets, and island views. But it was no ordinary seaside village. The magnificent houses that lined the beach to her right and the opulent estates scattered among the mountains and canyons to her left housed some of the world's richest, most famous, and occasionally infamous, personalities.

More than once since moving to California, she had gone on the Internet and found maps that identified the "Homes of the Stars" living along those twenty-seven miles. She had always been amazed to see how many celebrities, people whose names were household words, could be so densely packed into one area.

But the beauty of the place, along with its convenient proximity to Hollywood and the movie and television network studios, explained why each square foot of Malibu property was such a precious commodity.

Savannah allowed herself the luxury of sightseeing as she drove down the curvy, difficult-to-navigate highway. At least today it was free from rock slides and there were no plumes of smoke or lines of ominous red flame snaking their way down the mountain slopes, endangering those beautiful mansions.

For all its picturesque grandeur, the seaside home of the rich and famous was not without its challenges. A day without mudslides, brushfires, or an earthquake was a pleasantry, indeed.

Since Ethan Malloy's mansion was located in northern Malibu, Savannah began to watch for landmarks once she had passed Mugu Rock. The enormous rock with its one distinctive flat side sat on the edge of the highway. It was said the rock formation, over twenty feet tall, had once been a beautiful Indian princess who, brokenhearted over a philandering husband, had thrown herself into the sea and turned to stone.

But after a bit of research, Savannah had discovered that the rock, so frequently featured in movies, television shows, and car commercials, had actually been formed when a road, cut for the Pacific Coast Highway, had been blasted into the mountainside in the late 1930s.

Even knowing the true origin of the strange rock, Savannah could never pass it without thinking that the beautiful Indian princess should have spared herself and tossed her unfaithful husband into the surf instead.

With the rock in her rearview mirror, Savannah began to watch for the next major landmark. "As soon as you pass the Malibu Tennis & Riding Club, look for a narrow, rugged road on your left," John had told her. "There's a sign, but it's nearly covered by a cluster of red bougainvillea, even larger than over your door, climbing a rusty, open gate."

Soon, she saw it on the left side of the highway, a tangle of thorny vines and crimson blossoms. Barely visible inside the foliage, a simple sign read VALLE DE FUEGO. Just on the other side of the sign was a small, nondescript road leading up a mountain canyon.

Having traveled that road more than once, Savannah steeled herself for the next part of the journey. "As crooked as a dog's hind leg" was the quote that crossed her mind as she turned the Mustang off the highway and onto the rugged, pothole-pocked, and cracked pavement.

Even in an area known for its notorious canyon roads with hairpin turns and five-hundred-foot cliffs, Valle de Fuego Road was a challenge. As beautiful as the view might have been, Savannah couldn't imagine living in one of the luxury estates that dotted that mountain and climbing that dangerous, challenging stretch daily.

She could feel the Mustang struggling with the rapid ascent as she urged it up the ever-steeper road. No, this was definitely not a route designed for vintage automobiles. She forced herself to keep her eyes on the road and avoid sideways glances at the magnificent ocean view, and even more tempting, the precarious cliffs, the edges of which began mere inches from the pavement on either side.

Here and there, flimsy metal railings had been installed to prevent all-too-frequent tragedies. But noticing how bent they were and striped with various colors of paint from numerous wayward vehicles, Savannah didn't find the barriers particularly comforting.

Yet, as formidable as the path might have been, she couldn't help noticing that the higher she climbed, the more opulent the estates perched on the hillsides became. Most were Spanish-style with plastered walls that ranged from glistening white, to cream, to gold, and roofs with terra-cotta tiles.

But after a series of particularly harrowing switchbacks, Savannah glanced up to the top of the mountain and saw a home that looked more like a fairy-tale castle than a Malibu mansion.

With stone walls, a steeply pitched roof, and even a round turret tower with a conical top, the chateau was both imposing and intriguing, evoking childhood memories of stories with kings and queens, enchanted beasts, fire-breathing dragons, and evil witches.

"You'll know the house when you see it," John had told her with far more enthusiasm than was considered acceptable for a proper British gentleman like himself. "You'd have to travel to Normandy to view its like. You'll not be surprised if the door is answered by a butler wearing a suit of armor."

Savannah parked the Mustang on the cobblestone driveway, got out, and walked to the oversize arched doorway made of rough-hewn timber. When she knocked, using the cast-iron knocker—the ferocious face of a snarling bear with a ring through its teeth—she could hear her summons echoing through the chambers beyond.

She thought of John's joke about an armor-clad butler and prepared herself for anything as the door swung open with just the right number of atmosphere-producing creaks and groans.

When she saw the person who had come to greet her, she was quite taken aback. No butler in full livery. No housemaid in a short black dress with white frills.

It was the master of the chateau himself.

Savannah didn't know which shocked her most: the fact that the movie star heartthrob, object of millions of women's love and lust, was dressed as casually as any guy walking down any street, or that he was far more handsome in person than on screen. His crumpled T-shirt looked like he had slept in it, his uncombed hair was a bit longer than was the current fashion, his jeans were tattered, and his feet bare.

He fixed her with eyes so intense that in an instant, she felt his troubled, grieving soul all the way through her own. They were blue, but unlike hers, which were dark sapphire, his were so pale as to almost appear white. Rimmed with thick dark lashes, they would have been breathtakingly striking, except that now they were swollen and red-rimmed from weeping.

Savannah's heart went out to him immediately. She had seen too many people who were experiencing the worst moment of their lives not to know that this was one of those unfortunate individuals standing before her.

Ethan Malloy was in emotional hell, and no doubt, it would be her job to help him find a way out of it.

"Mr. Malloy," she said, "I'm Savannah Reid, a friend of John Gibson and Ryan Stone. I believe they've spoken to you about me."

"They have, with great respect and affection," he said with a slight drawl that she recognized as Southern, but not Georgian like hers. "You come highly recommended, Ms. Reid."

"Savannah, please," she told him as she offered him her hand.

He was an enormous fellow, and when his hand closed around hers, enveloping it in a firm shake, she was struck by the size and strength of the man.

If anything, he appeared even larger and more like a "superhero" in person than he did on screen.

At that moment, Savannah was dismayed to discover, so late in life, that she had developed multiple personalities. In the recesses of her somewhat muddled brain, she could hear a giddy little girl screaming, "Oh! Oh! Oh! I don't believe it. I'm actually touching Ethan Malloy! I'm doing it! I'm never washing this hand again. Not even after cleaning the litter box!"

Meanwhile, a far calmer and far more collected voice—that of a former cop—detailed the evidence at hand.

His palm was dry, not sweaty. His skin neither clammy nor feverish. His handshake firm but not bruising.

Nor was he shaky. She could detect no sign whatsoever that he was nervous about meeting her. The only emotions she sensed emanating from Ethan Malloy were fear and great sorrow.

"Please, come in," he said pulling the door wide open and ushering her inside. "I'm afraid my manners aren't the best right now," he admitted. "I don't know how much you've been told about my situation, but I have a few things occupying my mind."

"Actually, I know very little about your problem," she said. "Only that it's 'personal, confidential, and highly sensitive.' Those were the words John used when we talked this morning."

She walked into the foyer of the great house and allowed herself a moment to take in the splendor of it all: the beamed ceiling that was at least thirty feet high, ancient but still brightly colored

tapestries hanging from the walls, a highly polished suit of armor holding an enormous battle-ax
in one hand.

But it was a large bronze statue in the very center of the foyer that caught and held her attention.
Without a doubt, the image was one of the more
frightening works of art she had ever seen.

A dragon with the eyes of a serpent, cunning
and wise in a diabolical manner, watched her enter
the room. Its silent snarl revealed fangs, as sharp
and deadly as its claws, and the scales that covered
its reptilian form resembled chain mail. Though
Savannah couldn't imagine any battle fierce enough
that this ghastly creature would require protection.

"Don't mind Nidhogg," Ethan said with a dry
chuckle. "He's harmless as a puppy dog."

"Nidhogg?" Savannah asked.

Ethan shrugged and shook his head. "That's the
sort of thing you get when you give a decorator full
rein. He's Norse. A rather unpleasant fellow who's
constantly gnawing on the roots of the Tree of
Life, trying to bring about the end of the world.
And as if that isn't bad enough, he eats the corpses
of people who've committed murder, adultery, or
the worst of the worst—those who've broken an
oath."

"Oh yes, those darned oath breakers. They plum
beat all," Savannah said with a slightly sarcastic
tone.

"In Norse mythology they do," he assured her.
"You can get away with tickling kittens until they
cry or tugging on a puppy dog's ears, but break an
oath and—"

"You not only die, but your corpse gets eaten by this hideous fellow."

"That's right, and don't you forget it."

They shared a moment of companionable levity, but the smile on his handsome face quickly faded, replaced by the grim expression he had worn when first greeting her in the doorway.

"Would you like to talk in the library?" he asked her. "It isn't the fanciest room in the house, but it's quiet and a bit cozier than some of the bigger ones. I like it better."

"Wherever you're most comfortable, Mr. Malloy, is fine with me," she replied.

He nodded. "This way then."

She followed his lead down a hallway with dark wainscoting and cream plastered walls. To their left, a row of mullioned windows looked out upon the driveway where she had parked.

As they neared the end of the walkway, approaching a small, arched doorway, a movement outside caught her eye. She turned and saw a silver Jaguar pull beside her Mustang and stop. A fellow, perhaps in his late forties, with a slight build and thinning blond hair stepped out of the vehicle and walked to the mansion's front door.

Savannah wondered if his arrival would put an end to her interview with Malloy, even before it had begun. She expected the newcomer to knock on the door and Ethan to answer it, as he had for her.

But, although she was pretty sure the master of the house had noticed his new visitor, he continued toward the small door at the end of the hall.

"This way, Ms. Reid," he told her as he took a key from his pocket and unlocked the door.

As he stood aside for her to pass into the room, he said, "May I offer you some tea or coffee or something to eat?"

Savannah took a couple of extra seconds to answer, because she was occupied, mentally filing away the fact that Ethan Malloy found it necessary to lock his library door. Had it been a bathroom, or even a bedroom, she wouldn't have found a keyed lock out of the ordinary. But she couldn't recall when, if ever, she had seen someone lock the door to their library.

"I'd love a cup of coffee, if it isn't too much trouble," she replied, while reminding herself that she didn't know many people who actually owned a library. Bathrooms with books and magazines tossed into a basket near the toilet didn't really count.

"No trouble at all," Ethan replied, as he walked over to an intricately inlaid antique desk and picked up a phone. "Amy, could we please have coffee for two in the library? Yes, thank you."

Savannah saw him give her a quick sideways look, glancing up and down her figure. She wasn't sure how to interpret his brief perusal. Usually, when someone noticed her ample shape, their reaction registered either lust or disapproval, depending upon their own preferences and prejudices.

She was pleased to see neither expression on the actor's face, only a look of what she might call "casual acceptance."

"Uh, Amy, do we have any of those cinnamon rolls left over from breakfast?"

Cinnamon rolls? The words floated deliciously through Savannah's brain. *Really? God bless that man.*

"Great," he was telling the angel named Amy, the potential bearer of not only coffee but, apparently, cinnamon rolls as well. "Then bring some of those, too, if you please."

Savannah decided, then and there, that no matter what she might hear about this new case in the next half hour, Ethan Malloy would be her favorite actor for life.

No doubt about it, she told herself. *Move over, Sir Anthony Hopkins.*

Chapter 4

When Ethan Malloy had finished ordering refreshments, he waved an arm toward a seating area near the windows. "Please, sit yourself down and linger a spell," he told her with a smile, as he infused his words with a liberal Southern accent to match her own.

Savannah half expected the sarcastic expression that was usually worn by those mocking her Dixie-rich speech. But instead, his eyes were kind and playful when he said, "Sorry. I couldn't resist. I've always had a soft spot for a Southern accent."

"You did a fine one yourself onstage, when you played Jim Bowie last year in *The Alamo.*"

He chuckled. "That wasn't much of a Southern accent. More of a Texas drawl, which comes easy for me. I was born and raised in Amarillo."

A good ol' Texas boy, she thought. *That explains the good manners.*

"You saw the play in Los Angeles?" he said.

"In Santa Barbara. I enjoyed it very much."

"Do you get to the theater often?"

"I make the effort if I'm a fan of the actors. You made me cry there at the end."

He ducked his head in a modest way that she found endearing. A bit too endearing. So, she quickly added, "It was one of the few plays I was actually able to get *my husband* to go to. He'll only attend productions that could be classified as 'manly.' "

"He sounds like my old man. Let's just say that Dad wasn't exactly thrilled with my choice of occupation."

"Wanted you to grow up and ride bulls, throw calves, and break broncos?"

"He would have been overjoyed with that. But he would've settled for me staying home and running the ranch."

"But he must be proud of you now, with all your success."

Ethan laughed, but there was no humor in it. "He liked the Porsche Cayenne SUV I gave him for Christmas. Other than that, he's still not impressed."

Savannah thought of Tammy, of the success she had made of her life by doing the work she loved best, and of the fear and apprehension she was feeling at having her disapproving parents visit.

So often it seemed parents weren't fair.

But then, it had been Savannah's observation that life was seldom fair. From what she could tell, no one was immune from its inexplicable whims and fancies. Perhaps, by being less than perfect themselves, parents were doing their job by preparing their kids for the real world.

Savannah recalled her earlier conversation with Waycross and their own parents. Unfortunately, some parents did their job a bit too well.

Once again, Ethan waved his hand toward a cozy seating arrangement near a set of bay windows that overlooked a perfectly manicured formal garden. "Please, sit down and make yourself comfortable. Amy will be here any minute with the coffee."

"Then we can talk about why I'm here?" Savannah asked gently, sensing that he was delaying the topic for as long as possible and wondering why.

"Yes," he said softly, as he turned toward the window, avoiding her eyes. "Once Amy's left the room, we'll talk. It's, um . . . confidential."

"So John said." She stepped into his line of vision, forcing him to look at her. "Please don't worry, Mr. Malloy. If I'm known for anything, it's my discretion, and I take pride in that."

He gave her a half smile. "So John said."

Savannah took a seat on a settee with delicate, curved legs in the French provincial style. The small sofa was almost too beautiful to sit upon with its handstitched cushion and back, depicting a dark forest inhabited by colorful birds and a magnificent stag.

"My granny would love this," she said, running her hand over the work of art. "She does needlepoint herself, but of course, nothing like this."

He sat on the edge of an equally fragile chair next to her, his giant body dwarfing the tiny piece of furniture. The delicate, curved legs appeared too dainty to support his weight.

A melancholy expression came over his face as he said, "I asked my wife and her decorator if this one room could look like a man lived here. A woodsy scene instead of roses—that was their idea of a masculine compromise. That and Nidhogg."

Savannah nodded understandingly. "Just this morning my husband was complaining about the rose wallpaper in our bathroom. Reckon it's not easy for you fellas, tolerating such feminine frivolities."

To her surprise, tears flooded Ethan's eyes. He opened his mouth to speak, but at that moment there was a gentle rap on the door.

He cleared his throat with a harsh cough, then said, "Yes, Amy. Come in."

A young woman, whom Savannah judged to be in her mid-twenties, walked into the room. She was pretty in a girl-next-door way with glossy dark hair, pulled back into a ponytail. She wore a simple yellow sundress and no makeup. Her complexion was clear, her cheeks rosy, and her eyes bright with the energy of youth.

However, as she placed the tray on an ancient chest that served as a coffee table in front of the settee, Savannah sensed that Amy, like her employer, was deeply worried about something of importance.

"Thank you, Amy," Ethan said, giving her a wan smile.

"You're welcome, sir," she replied.

Seeing the shy smile Amy sent his way, Savannah also deduced that Amy had a crush on her boss.

Hardly surprising, Savannah thought. *Considering.* She couldn't imagine how she herself would have handled working for such an attractive man at such a young age. She would have been swooning a dozen times a day, which, no doubt, would have interfered considerably with her duties.

Then, there would have been the guilt of lusting after a married man. Having been raised by a woman as righteous and sensible as Granny Reid, Savannah knew that setting your cap for a man with a wife was an express ride down the road to perdition. It was also the fastest way to get your heart broken and—if his missus found out about it and if she was a spirited lady of Southern heritage—your head snatched bald and your front teeth badly loosened. Maybe even relocated altogether.

"Will there be anything else, Mr. Ethan?" Amy asked demurely.

Savannah could have sworn she saw her even give a tiny curtsy.

Yeah, poor little Amy's got it bad, Savannah thought. *Wonder if Mrs. Malloy knows* how *bad.*

"That's all for now. Thank you," Ethan replied.

As Amy hurried to the door, he added, "Oh, Amy . . . I saw Mr. Orman arrive a few minutes ago. I assume you answered the door and let him in."

Amy looked confused. "No, sir. I don't think he knocked. I thought you let him in."

Savannah noted that Ethan seemed moderately

annoyed. "You didn't, I didn't, but he's in the house?"

"Yes, sir. And I don't believe that Luciana let him in either, because she's downstairs, doing laundry."

"Did you see him?" he asked her. "Did he say what he wanted?"

"Yes, sir. He came into the kitchen when I was getting the rolls and asked to see Miss Beth."

Savannah caught it all—the uneasy look the two of them exchanged, the nervous glance that Amy gave her, the tightening of Ethan's jaw.

"Where is he?" Ethan wanted to know.

"I told him, you know, that she isn't home right now," Amy said. "He asked if he could talk to you, so I suggested he wait outside by the pool. I was going to take him some coffee once I was done here with you."

"Good idea." Ethan gave the young woman the briefest of smiles and said, "Thank you, Amy. Go ahead and take him some coffee, but if he tries to start a conversation with you about . . . well, anything . . . excuse yourself. Tell him you're in the middle of doing something important for me. Got it?"

She nodded. "Yes, sir, I do. I understand." With another little half curtsy, she left the room.

No sooner had she closed the door than Savannah turned to Ethan and said, "Okay, Mr. Malloy. We have our coffee, and I'm delighted to say that we even have our cinnamon rolls. But as delicious as the refreshments look and smell, I don't believe

I was invited here today just to sip java and nibble pastries."

Ethan sat quite still, leaning forward with his elbows on his knees, his hands clasped tightly as he stared down at the fine Aubusson rug at his feet.

Finally, he sat back in his chair and took a deep breath. Savannah noticed that he was gripping the armrests of the dainty chair like someone who had just boarded a roller coaster and was dreading the ride.

He looked up at Savannah, nodded, and said, "You're absolutely right, Ms. Reid. When I called Ryan and John this morning, I told them that we might have a very serious situation here. We might need professional help. Or we might not. I don't know."

He wiped his hand over his face and rubbed his swollen eyes, then sighed wearily. "I was awake all night, trying to figure out what's happened, or hasn't happened, around here in the past twenty-four hours. It's either something bad or something horrible. I'm going crazy wondering which it—"

He choked on his words as tears flooded his eyes, then rolled down his face.

Savannah leaned forward, reached out, and rested her hand on his forearm. She gave it a little squeeze, then a comforting pat. "Mr. Malloy, I'm here to help you. Please tell me what you think has happened."

"Beth, my wife, is gone."

"Gone? Gone, as in . . . ?"

"Disappeared. Her and my son. My baby boy."

Instantly, Savannah thought of little Vanna Rose—

tiny, sweet, and vulnerable. "I'm so sorry, Mr. Malloy. But I can tell you that, usually in these circumstances, there's a perfectly reasonable explanation, and everything turns out just fine in the end."

"That's what I told myself all day yesterday and even last night," he said, wiping his eyes on the hem of his T-shirt. "I told myself that at midnight and at one o'clock in the morning. But once the clock in the hallway chimed two, I knew she was in trouble. Yes, we had an argument yesterday morning. I'll admit it was a bad one. The worst we've ever had. And she stormed out of, taking Freddy and Pilar with her."

"Who is Pilar?"

"Pilar Padilla, our nanny."

Savannah pulled a small spiral tablet and pen from her purse and began to takc notes. "What time was this?"

"Just after breakfast. Around nine-thirty, more or less."

"When she 'stormed out,' did she say she was leaving you?"

"She said she was sick of me and my nonsense." He shrugged and blushed. "But she says that a couple times a week, so I didn't take it all that seriously."

"Does she march off in a huff a couple times a week?"

"No. She only does that a couple of times a month."

"You haven't heard anything at all from her since she left?"

"Nothing. I've called her constantly since last night, and she didn't answer. My texts either."

"Is that unusual for her?"

"Yes. She usually answers my texts, if for no other reason than to tell me she's still mad at me."

"Did you try to contact Pilar?"

"Called her. Texted her. Phoned her parents' house. They said they haven't heard from her either. Nothing. It's very out of character for her. They're worried, too."

"I'll need the parents' phone number."

He found the number in his cell phone and gave it to her. She jotted it down.

"Did Beth take anything with her? A suitcase or overnight bag?"

"Just Freddy's backpack. She always takes it with her when she goes out with him. I do, too. It has his toys and snacks. He loves mangos and blueberries and—"

Again, he was overcome and couldn't continue speaking.

Savannah set her notebook and pen aside, and in a soft, gentle voice she said, "Ethan, I can't imagine how hard this must be for you. I'm so sorry. How old is your little Freddy?"

"Twenty-one months. Nearly two. Maybe he'll turn into a Terrible Two, like they say, after his second birthday. But since he was born, he's always been the sweetest little guy, my little buddy. I can't . . . I can't stand it, I—"

He reached over and grasped her hand so tightly that it caused her fingers to ache. But she didn't pull away.

"I can't stand to think that she left me and took him away from me, too. And yet, I have to. I've got to hold on to the hope that's what she did. Because if not, then it's worse. Way worse. If she hasn't actually left me, then she's out there somewhere, unable to contact me. If that's the case . . ."

"No, no, Ethan. Try not to go there. Not yet. My granny's a wise woman, and she always says, 'Don't suffer a misfortune that hasn't befallen you yet. Most folks have their hands full just handlin' the bad luck they've already got.'"

"That's good advice, but when it's your family, it's not that easy."

"I know. But you said that you and your wife had the worst argument of your marriage, right? Then she stomped out."

"Yes. She slammed the door so hard, I'm surprised it's still on its hinges."

"Then she might just be cooling her heels somewhere in a nice hotel, letting you stew in your own soup, so to speak. She wouldn't be the first wife to do that sort of thing. Husband either, for that matter."

He considered her words, then shook his head. "No. Before Freddy was born, she might have. But not now that we're parents. Things haven't been good between us for a while, but she's a great mom. She knows how much that little guy loves me and how much he means to me. She has to know that I'm worried sick."

Savannah searched her mind for an argument, but couldn't find one that she thought he'd believe. She just nodded and said, "I see."

"I do believe," Ethan said, "that if Beth could

have checked in with me last night, she would have. That's why I'm so worried . . . about all three of them."

Savannah hated to admit it, but she believed he was probably right. He knew his wife far better than she. In her experience, those closest to a missing person often made accurate predictions about what had happened to them. The experts on any given person were usually the ones who lived with them— if they were honest.

As Savannah studied those world-famous pale blue eyes, she saw a depth of sincerity that convinced her. Convinced and alarmed her.

What's more frightening than a woman who's inexplicably absent from her home for twenty-four hours without contacting her next of kin? Savannah asked herself. *A woman who's with a second woman who's also missing.* Even if Beth had chosen to remain out of touch, Pilar should have checked in with her parents.

"I wish I could tell you with all certainty that your family's all right," she told him. "But I can't. I won't lie to you."

"I appreciate that," he assured her.

She could see a level of trust in his eyes, and for a moment, the enormity of the situation struck her. Ethan Malloy was placing in her hands the most serious situation of his life.

He was the envy of the world, living in his castle, high above the ocean fogs. The recipient of so much love and adoration, receiving millions of dollars every time he signed a new contract.

Who wouldn't want to be Ethan Malloy?

But, sitting there on the wealthy, successful, beloved actor's antique settee with its beautiful hand-stitched forest scene—a piece of furniture that probably cost more than everything she owned—Savannah wouldn't have traded her life for his.

What did fame and fortune mean, when those you loved most in the world were missing?

Chapter 5

Once Savannah was back in her car and headed north on Pacific Coast Highway toward San Carmelita, she used the new car speakerphone, which Waycross had given to her and installed for her birthday, to call home.

To her surprise, it was her assistant, not her husband, who answered.

"Moonlight Magnolia Detective Agency," Tammy said, employing her breathiest office voice. "May I help you?" Then she must have looked at the caller ID, because she added in a far less sexy tone, "Oh, hi, Savannah. It's just you."

"Yes," Savannah replied, "but why is it *you*? Aren't you supposed to be home, getting ready for your parents' arrival? They should be showing up with bells on in a couple of hours, right?"

Tammy laughed. Slightly. "They aren't exactly the 'rings on their fingers and bells on their toes' type. Mom will probably be wearing one ring on each hand and a Diane von Furstenberg wrap dress. She's been into those ever since I've known her. You know, like my whole life."

"It's a good look, if you have the figure for it."

"Oh, Mother has the figure, all right. I don't think she's gained or lost a pound since the day she married Dad."

Savannah couldn't even imagine weighing the same, decade after decade. Having spent most of her twenties and thirties yo-yo dieting, she had celebrated her fortieth birthday by abandoning the counterproductive practice and deciding to love herself whatever the scale might register. As a result, her weight had stabilized at a number that was greater than society might like, but one that she had initially accepted and eventually embraced.

Now that number shifted only a bit, one direction or the other, in the course of a year. There would be an uptick around the holidays with goodies like Savannah's famous fudge and Granny's divinity in ample supply in the Reid household.

A week of winter flu would usually offset the gain come January.

Overall, it wasn't something Savannah thought about a great deal. Or even a little.

Until she was in the company of someone like Tammy's mother.

She had to admit she wasn't looking forward to meeting Dr. Lenora Hart.

Apparently, neither was Lenora's daughter, because the next thing Tammy said was, "I was going crazy waiting there at home, trying to find one more thing to clean, trying to create space in my closet to hide all the stuff that I know my mom would disapprove of. Waycross told me I should get out of the house. So, I decided to come over here and do something that would occupy my mind before I go completely dingy."

"Oh, sweetie. Every day of the year, your home is clean and cozy and comfortable. It's absolutely lovely, like you."

"But my living room drapes are polyester."

"And so . . . ?"

"Mother's big on natural fabrics. And my kitchen table—"

"Is oak. Does she have a problem with oak?"

"It's veneer, not solid oak."

"Oh, Lordy, and to think I've eaten on it!"

Savannah heard a tiny giggle on the other end. Mission semi-accomplished.

"I can see why you needed an escape. Wanna help me out with this new case?"

"Oh, *yes*! More than life itself. What do you need?"

"I need you to do some background checks. But when I say that this case is top-secret, confidential, and hush-hush, I'm not just being redundant and repetitive. Nobody outside of the Moonlight Magnolia Regulars can hear a word about this. Got it?"

"Got it!"

"Good. You've heard of the actor Ethan Malloy?"

"Heard of Ethan Malloy? Heard of him?" She sighed. "Just between you and me, and not a word to your brother, I've been stranded on a desert island with Ethan Malloy. I've been a female pirate taken prisoner by Captain Malloy, held belowdecks in his private quarters and—"

"Yeah, yeah," Savannah laughed. "Haven't we all. I need everything you can get on him, and I don't mean the tabloid junk either. Real life stuff. And on his wife, Beth. Also on their nanny. Her name is Pilar Padilla."

"We're working for *him*? Ethan Malloy is our client?"

"Sadly, he is. His wife, his two-year-old boy, Freddy, and Pilar are all three missing and have been for over twenty-four hours now."

Savannah heard Tammy gasp, then say, "That's horrible! Has he reported this to the police?"

"I told him he should, and he probably will soon. By hiring us, he was trying to avoid the publicity. Seems she and he had an argument, and she stormed out, taking the little boy and nanny with her. He doesn't want the tabloids to catch wind of it."

"I can certainly understand that. They'd make a huge deal out of it, even if it isn't a big deal at all."

"Exactly."

"If they argued before she disappeared," Tammy mused, "then it might not be foul play after all. It might just be a domestic dispute."

"That's right, and he's determined to guard their privacy and avoid a paparazzi feeding frenzy, if at all possible."

"I'll get on it, all of it, right away. Anybody else you want me to run a check on?"

"Yes, a guy named Orman. Caucasian male, six-foot-two, slender build, thinning blond hair, drives a silver Jaguar that's about a block long. He was a visitor there at the house today, and I got the idea that he wasn't particularly welcome. Also, they have some sort of personal assistant or maid or whatever called Amy. Don't have a last name. Mid-twenties. Long dark hair. Attractive in a whole-some way."

"You want me to check out someone who's wholesome?"

"Are you kidding? Those 'wholesome' folks are the ones you have to seriously look out for."

When Savannah pulled into her own driveway and savored the sight of the quaint, Spanish-style house with its plastered, cream walls and red-tile roof, she almost always felt a surge of heart warmth and self-satisfaction. The front porch with wicker chairs welcomed her with their soft, floral-print cushions that beckoned a body to "relax and sit a spell."

The matching bougainvillea bushes on either side of the doorway, which met and intertwined over the transom, greeted her as well. She had named them Bogie and Ilsa years ago, when they were little more than mere sprouts, stuck in a cou-ple of clay pots. Over the years, in spite of her ne-glect, they had burgeoned into crimson giants that added a lush and gentle beauty to her home.

Like the blue and purple hydrangeas that lent their loveliness to homes, grand and humble, in the tiny, rural Georgia town where Savannah had been born and raised, bougainvillea had no preju-

dices or even preferences. Throughout Southern
California, it graced castillo and hacienda alike.

As was her habit, Savannah reached out and
lightly touched a branch of each when she passed
beneath them, being careful to avoid the thorns.
For her, it was a constant reminder that, as someone wiser than she had once said, "Life is like a rose.
A few thorns don't make it any less beautiful."

Once inside her front door, she placed her
purse on the old, round piecrust table in the foyer,
near the foot of the stairs.

"Is that you, Savannah girl?" a beloved voice
called out to her from the living room.

"Sure is, Gran," she replied, hurrying to greet
her favorite human being on earth, except maybe
her husband. And on days when he slurped his ce-
real, propped his filthy sneakers on her freshly polished coffee table, and left his day-old underwear
hanging from the bathroom doorknob, Granny
Reid scored a solid Number One.

Not only did the sight of her precious grandmother, who had raised her and continued to in-
spire her every day of her life, elevate Savannah's
mood at least fifty percent, but the delicious
aroma of baking apple pie caused it to soar to one
hundred.

Unfortunately, her taste buds were all atwitter
before she remembered that Gran had asked if she
could come to Savannah's house and use her oven
to bake a welcome offering for Tammy's parents.
Savannah's mood tumbled, like a bad day on Wall
Street, when she realized that she was unlikely to

sink her choppers into a single bite of that heavenly dessert.

"Don't worry," Gran told her as she folded her into a warm, tight hug. "There's two in the oven. You don't think I'd use your facilities and not make sure you had a taste, do you?"

Savannah placed a kiss on the top of her grandmother's silver hair and marveled at how, after all these years, Gran could still read her mind.

"Yes, I can still tell what you're thinkin', Savannah girl," Granny said with twinkling eyes. "Let's just say I've had a lot of practice at it."

"You have, indeed," Savannah replied. "If a grandmother's going to stay ahead of nine grandkids, she has to be a bit of a mind reader."

"No mind reading involved. The trick is just to assume that, at any given minute, a young'un's up to no good, and most of the time you'll be right."

"I'm taking all of this in, Granny," Tammy said from the corner of the room, where she sat at the rolltop desk, staring at a computer screen. Baby Vanna Rose was cozy in her mother's arms, nursing vigorously. "I figure if I can learn one percent of what you know about raising children, I'll be able to stay ahead of this one."

Granny chuckled. "Don't even think about trying to stay ahead of a feisty, little puddin' cat like that one there. I can tell you right now, you'll be running for the rest of your life just trying to catch up to her."

Gran gazed up at Savannah, her eyes filled with love and admiration. "Believe me, I know the type o' gal that one's gonna be. Raisin' the likes of her will be the adventure of your lifetime."

Tammy smiled down at the baby in her arms. "I'm looking forward to it. Every minute of it."

Gran whispered to Savannah, "Spoken like a mother who's never found a frog in her underwear drawer. Not yet, leastways."

"I heard that," Tammy replied. "Waycross told me all about that youthful transgression, and he repented of it long ago."

"Oh, he expressed remorse, all right," Gran said. "Young'uns tend to do that when they're doing a jig at the end of a hickory switch."

Savannah suppressed the urge to correct her elder. In fact, neither she nor her siblings had done much dancing at the end of any switch, hickory or otherwise. Gran had applied corporal punishment, but she had saved it for special occasions. Switches and paddles had been reserved for capital crimes. Actually, for only one such transgression. Lying.

Granny's grandkids could have confessed to just about anything short of first-degree, premeditated murder and received little more than a "talkin' to."

Church-going, Bible-thumping Gran firmly believed that any sin that was confessed and repented must be forgiven.

But if a Reid kid committed homicide and then fibbed about it, their hide was in grave danger of being tanned.

As Savannah watched Tammy finish with the nursing, lift her baby onto her shoulder, and gently pat her back, Savannah seriously doubted that little Miss Vanna Rose would be spending a lot of time dancing jigs behind the barn. Any time at all, for that matter.

If this child misbehaved, she would probably pay the price by having to plant a tree, pick up trash on a beach, or paint Earth Day posters. Since she would be doing these things with her playful mother at her side, paying her debt to society would, undoubtedly, be great fun.

Once Vanna Rose had burped, and Tammy had dabbed away the bubbles from her mouth, Tammy handed her to Savannah and turned her attention back to the computer.

"I ran checks on those people you mentioned," she said. "I turned over some rocks that had a few bugs and worms under them."

She shot a sideways glance at her daughter and quickly added, "Not that there's anything wrong with bugs and worms. They're a necessary, important part of nature. They do a lot of good work for us."

Giving Savannah a tired, worried look, she said, "Boy, you don't think about what you say until you're around a young, impressionable child. Then, all of a sudden, everything that comes out of your mouth is important."

Savannah opened her own mouth to reply, to say something like, "Lighten up, sugar. You don't have to be perfect to be a mom, and you don't have to raise a kid all in one day." But she decided to save her breath. Tammy was determined to be the perfect parent, and if anyone on God's green earth could pull it off, she would.

"Tell me about these necessary bugs and important worms you uncovered," Savannah said. "Let's hear it all—dirt still attached."

A timer dinged in the kitchen. As Granny rose from the sofa and strolled in that direction, she said to Savannah, "If you wanted to know the nitty-gritty on a movie star, all you had to do was ask me. When it comes to celebrity gossip, I'm a walkin' encyclopedia. You should know that by now."

Savannah grinned, thinking of the stack of tabloids in the magazine stand next to Granny's easy chair. Just under the Bible, which was always neatly placed on top of the assorted reading materials, one could find at least three months' worth of weekly editions of Gran's favorite gossip rags.

Not only did Granny enjoy the gossip she found printed on those pulp pages, but she considered everything she read from that rack to be the absolute gospel truth.

If a tabloid said that Gran's favorite soap star had been abducted by aliens, she prayed for their safe return. If that star had succumbed to the charms of one of those aliens and was now pregnant with its offspring, she prayed for their immortal soul.

"Soon as I get those pies outta the oven," Gran said, turning the corner and heading in the kitchen, "I'll tell you all about why that young man don't want the paparazzi hangin' round his house. He's got more reason than most to avoid media attention."

Savannah turned to Tammy with a questioning glance. "Have you heard this theory of hers yet?"

Tammy nodded. "Yes, and it's actually worth

considering. Nothing to do with extraterrestrials, or Bigfoot, or the JFK assassination."

Pulling a chair next to Tammy's, Savannah laid Vanna on her lap, the baby's head on her knees, the tiny feet against her belly. She tickled under the infant's chin, then her ribs, and finally, those sweet, baby toes.

Vanna wasn't laughing yet, but she cooed with approval, and Savannah enjoyed every second.

She knew from past experience that the period of time when she could hold her little namesake in this position would be regrettably short. In fact, every stage of her niece's childhood would be far too fleeting and needed to be savored to the fullest along the way.

"Do you have any non-tabloid info for me?" Savannah asked Tammy, who was bringing up half a dozen screens on the computer.

"Of course. You ask; I deliver." She turned and gave Savannah a shy grin. "At least I try."

"You had it right the first time, kiddo. Never, never dilute honest and true words of self-approval. Your heart needs to hear them."

Tammy blushed under the praise, then quickly turned back to the screen. "I checked out Ethan Malloy first, which was the hardest because there's so much about him. He has so many fans, and they're absolutely rabid about him. I found millions and millions of hits. But, of course, who knows how much of it's true."

"With celebrities, you have to figure not much."

"I always do." She brought up a word processing screen where she had made notes and read them to Savannah. "He was born in—"

"Amarillo."

"Okay. You know that. His father was a—"

"Rancher."

Tammy turned in her chair and gave Savannah an offended, annoyed look. "You know how much you hate it when Dirk finishes your sentences for you?"

"But that's because ninety-nine percent of the time, he's wrong. Then he's sure he's right and gets all huffy about it and that leads to a fight. I'm not like him, so it shouldn't bother you."

Her "logic" was met with stony silence.

Savannah shrugged. "Okay, point taken. I'll work on it. What else have you got there?"

Sighing, Tammy turned back to the computer. "Ethan Malloy is his real name. He's thirty-five years old and—"

"That young? Wow. He seems older. In a good way. You know, more experienced, more sophisticated."

When Savannah returned the annoyed look, Tammy chuckled and continued. "Like I said, his fans are rabid. Okay . . . he and Elizabeth Sarsone, otherwise known as 'Beth,' have been married four years. They met on the set of—"

"They met while they were remaking that movie, *The Great Gatsby*," Granny said as she strolled in from the kitchen, carrying a tray with two dishes of apple pie à la mode and a bowl of fresh, sliced strawberries topped with yogurt.

"This interrupting thing runs in the family," Tammy muttered under her breath as she reached over and took her daughter from Savannah. "But is it nature or nurture?"

Gran handed the hot apple pie with its melting ice cream to Savannah and the yogurt to Tammy. "That handsome Mr. Malloy played the main guy in that movie. His name was Mr. Jay Gatsby. A mighty handsome Gatsby that Mr. Malloy made, too, if I do say so myself." She settled onto the sofa with her own plate of pie. "The heroine," she continued, "if you can call anybody in that story a hero or a heroine, was played by Miss Fancy Pants, Candace York. I don't have to tell you, she's a bigtime movie star. Rich as sweet potato pie and pretty as a speckled pup."

"She's rich and she's pretty, all right," Savannah said. "But I've seen her interviewed, and she seemed a little ditsy, not to mention a bit full of herself."

"Not all of us blondes, who seem a bit ditsy, really are, you know," Tammy added softly, as she printed her notes and handed them to Savannah. "That's really just a not-very-nice stereotype."

"That's for sure," Savannah said, giving her a warm, encouraging smile. It hurt Savannah's heart to see Tammy, who was almost always bouncing with happiness and confident as a summer solstice day is long, doubting herself.

"We all have abiding faith in you, Tammy girl," Gran said. "Don't you forget that for one minute these next few days. You hear?"

When Tammy gave her a brief nod, Gran continued, "As I was sayin', everybody thought Candace had Ethan tied up good and tight. But Miss Elizabeth Sarsone was on that movie set, too, playin' Myrtle Wilson—a sorry character who met a sorry end. Some might say she deserved it, but that'd be judgin'. Anyway, the scurrility committed by a certain somebody on that set was downright shameful. Dang near as bad as the shenanigans done by the characters in the movie itself."

"Scurrility? Scurrility and shenanigans were done?" Savannah asked with a grin.

"They sure were. Why that Elizabeth Sarsone snatched Ethan right out from under Candace York. That gal, Beth, wasn't half as pretty as Candace, but she set her cap for Ethan and nabbed him right up."

"Maybe the engagement wasn't a serious one," Tammy offered, always the first to play the devil's advocate in any circumstance. "You know how Hollywood is. People get engaged, married, and divorced all in the course of a week. Sometimes just because their agent tells them it would be good for their career."

Gran shook her head. "No. This was the real thing. Candace was sportin' an engagement ring on her finger. They had a date set, wedding gown ordered, the whole shebang. The diamond in that ring was the size of a doorknob, too. Ethan had to know that a gal like Candace York wouldn't have settled for anything less."

"Maybe Beth was a nicer, sweeter person than Candace," Savannah said. "From what I've heard, it wouldn't take much."

Gran considered Savannah's words thoughtfully, then nodded. "I thank you for pointing that out to me, Granddaughter. I was just goin' along with what I read in my magazines, but you could be right. Maybe he picked the right gal after all.

But either way, there was a major ruckus about it, the fans weighin' in one way or the other. Some said neither Ethan or Beth would ever work in Hollywood again. Especially Beth, since she was considered the *other* woman."

"This is all coming back to me now," Savannah said between bites as she devoured the pie—the cinnamon rolls a fond, distant memory. "I remember seeing those tabloid covers when I was waiting in the grocery store back in the day. A picture of Ethan and Candace being all lovey-dovey, torn down the middle and a shot of Beth stuck in the middle."

"The public took a dim view of it," Gran said. "They were all lookin' forward to a downright royal wedding between Candace York and Ethan Malloy. Then, not only did Beth steal him away, but the two of them eloped to Las Vegas, and we didn't even get a picture of the wedding." She sniffed. "Was probably done in one of those silly, all-night, so-called chapels, and they likely wore jeans and T-shirts. It's shameful how young people don't dress proper for formal occasions anymore."

Tammy giggled. "Jeans and a Vegas chapel would've been an upgrade from my wedding. I was all sweaty and discombobulated, lying on my childbirth bed."

Gran gave her a loving smile. "You were a beautiful bride, child. No matter the circumstances. Better late than never. Like they say: Those first babies can come anytime. After that, it takes nine months."

As Savannah devoured the rest of her pie, she

read the notes that Tammy had printed out for her. "Okay, Amy's last name is Foster. She's been with the Malloys for four months, and her official title is 'Personal Assistant.' "

"No criminal record at all, as you can see," Tammy added. "Super-clean history. Graduated last year from Pepperdine's film school with honors. Wants to be a director someday."

"Then I'll put her near the bottom of my mental suspect list," Savannah said, continuing to read Tammy's notes. "For now, anyway. Unless she does something more sinister than make goo-goo eyes at her boss."

"You go suspecting everybody who makes eyes at *that* man," Gran said, "you'll be busier than a one-eyed cat watchin' nine rat holes."

"You keep talking that way, Gran, and I'll start suspecting *you*," Savannah told her.

"What did I tell you?" Tammy said. "His fans are rabid! Even in this household, it seems."

Granny giggled, but didn't bother to challenge Tammy's assertion.

Savannah came to the next item in Tammy's notes. "Hmmm. That's how Mr. Abel Orman can afford a Jaguar that size. He's Ethan Malloy's manager."

"Not just Mr. Malloy," Tammy told her, "but a bunch of other big stars, too. Keep reading, and you'll see who he just signed last week."

Savannah scanned the list of celebrities represented by Abel Orman, all household names. The last entry on the list caught her eye. Elizabeth Sansone. "Elizabeth? Beth? Ethan's wife just signed up with his manager?" she asked.

Tammy nodded. "I don't suppose it's all that un-usual. If one actor in a family is happy with the way his manager is handling his career, he'd probably recommend his services to another actor, even if it's his wife."

"Yes, I suppose so. But Ethan didn't seem particularly thrilled with the guy when he realized he'd entered his house uninvited."

Gran shrugged. "Unless you're living in a town like McGill where everybody knows one another, I can see why that would bother a body."

"True." Savannah read on. "I see the nanny, Pilar Padilla, has been with the Malloys for nearly two years. Their son is almost two. She's probably been his nanny since birth. Clean record for her, too."

"Not that it matters," Tammy said, "but see the note I made about her having type one diabetes? I found where she'd posted quite a few comments on Internet support sites, trying to help others who have it."

"It would matter if she's somewhere and being held against her will without her insulin," Savannah added. "Let's hope to high heaven that's not the case."

"True," Tammy said. "But mostly, I keep thinking about that little boy." She gazed down at Vanna Rose, fast asleep in her arms. "I can't imagine how Ethan Malloy feels right now, not knowing if his baby is safe or not."

"Must be plum awful," Granny agreed. "About the worst experience a body can go through in this lifetime."

"We have to help him," Tammy said, fighting

back tears. "We have to bring his little one back to him."

Savannah had been feeling the same anxiety as Tammy, but with each passing hour, her stress level had risen. Experience had taught her that the first hours after a disappearance were crucial. If, indeed, bad things were going to happen to a victim, they tended to happen right away.

"Okay, thank you for gathering this," she said to Tammy, laying the papers on the desk. "Now let's look into old flames. Candace York, obviously, and any other significant relationships Ethan might have had. Also, see if Beth has any ex-husbands or boyfriends. Pilar, too."

Granny took the baby from Tammy, and Tammy turned her attention to the computer.

"What would you like me to do, darlin'?" Granny asked Savannah.

"If you don't mind, you can keep an eye on Punkin Little there, so Tammy can work. Also, try to remember anything else you read in those tabloids about Ethan and Beth."

Granny's eyes twinkled. "Oh, *now* you've decided to believe what's in my magazines? Since when? I distinctly recollect you sayin' they're nothin' but a pile o' rubbish."

"Just goes to show you how desperate I am," Savannah replied.

She was going to say more, defending her position, but her cell phone rang. She saw it was Dirk.

"Hey, sugar," she said. "What's shakin'?"

Usually, he would have replied with a breezy quip of a salacious nature, but there was no humor in his voice at all when he said, "I caught a case. A bad one."

Savannah felt a chill run through her soul. "How bad?"

"Real bad. A 10-100, up here in the hills above Oak Grove Park."

Savannah swallowed, so hard that it hurt her throat. "Victim? Victims?"

"A young woman," he said.

"A young woman," she repeated, turning to Tammy, then Gran. She saw the same horror she was feeling reflected on their faces. "Homicide?"

"Not sure yet, but might be."

"Description?"

"Petite. Mid-twenties. Latina."

"A Latina," Savannah said to Gran and Tammy, "deceased."

Tammy gasped, and tears sprang to her eyes. Gran closed her eyes and began to murmur a prayer.

"Got an identity?" Savannah asked, afraid of the answer.

"Not yet" was his reply. "No purse around. I'm just getting ready to check the body."

Savannah glanced at Tammy's notes one more time, then said to Dirk, "Check out her wrist. Would she happen to be wearing a medical alert bracelet?"

She heard him moving about, searching. Then he said, "She does. It says, 'Diabetes on Insulin.' Hey, and her name. It's—"

"Pilar Padilla."

"Yeah. How'd you know?"

"Just an unlucky guess," she replied, her voice

shaking, her knees suddenly feeling weak. "I'll be there in ten minutes."

"You don't need to come, Van. It's not pretty. . . ."

"I have to."

"Why?"

"To help you search for two more victims."

Chapter 6

Oak Grove wasn't the prettiest park in San
Carmelita or the most popular. Those honors
would have belonged to one of the seaside recreational areas—either the park beside the harbor
filled with sailboats, the one with the 1,200-foot-
long pier, used for fishing and romantic strolls, or
the one downtown near the old mission where art
shows occurred on the first Sunday of each month.

On the opposite side of town, the less ritzy side,
Oak Grove was a verdant valley, reaching deep into
the foothills, a secluded area that San Carmelita
folks frequented when they wanted to be alone
and commune with nature, to perform a bit of
yoga beneath the ancient trees, to take a hike
among the waist-high daisies that grew in abun-
dance on the hillsides, to fool around with their
honey under the stars, or occasionally, to dump a
dead body.

Although Savannah and Dirk had done their

share of stargazing tomfoolery in the privacy of Oak Grove, it still wasn't her favorite place. Far from it, in fact.

The discovery of even a single corpse among such natural splendor could turn one off to an area. Permanently. Or so she had discovered.

As Savannah drove the narrow road that stretched from the park's entrance through the arroyo that was lined with old oaks on each side, to the back of the park where the road ended and the hiking trails began, her heart rate steadily increased.

The thought that a young woman, who spent her days caring for a child, was lying dead among those hills, filled Savannah with dread. The thought that the child himself and maybe his mother could have suffered the same fate nearly overwhelmed her with horror.

Experience had shown Savannah Reid that she could bear a lot. In the past twenty years, she had witnessed far more of the evil that one human being could inflict upon another than anyone should see.

It made a person old before their time.

Sometimes she felt like she was forty-something going on ninety-seven.

She tried to steel her heart for what she might find up there among the wildflowers and sage bushes, but she knew there was no point. You couldn't guard your soul from an assault like that.

With each victim of violence that she had encountered in her time as a police officer and then a private detective, Savannah felt she had lost a bit of her humanity, her belief in the basic goodness of mankind.

Granny Reid said you had to keep the faith, you couldn't let the dark deeds of a few overshadow the golden, shining acts of others who chose to do good in the world.

But that was far more easily said than done at a time like this.

Ahead, at the end of the road, Savannah saw two police cruisers parked side by side, their rooftop lights flashing. They appeared identical, but the license plate on one identified it as the squad car that Dirk was now driving and had been since he had wrecked his Buick. Still in mourning over the old Skylark, he was reluctant to replace her with another vehicle. After six months, Savannah had refused to chauffeur him about in the Mustang any longer, so he had finagled a unit from the department.

At least once a week, Savannah had offered to take him car shopping, but since that would require spending money, he always found something more pressing to do. Like sort through his old LPs, or watch a boxing match.

She recognized the license plate of the second black-and-white, as well, and was relieved that it was driven by two of her favorite patrolmen, Jake McMurtry and Mike Farnon. Childhood buddies, they had decided to join the police force at the same time, and although they had only been on the job less than five years, she considered them better than most she had worked with in the SCPD.

She could see that a large area ahead had been neatly cordoned off with yellow police barrier tape. Jake's and Mike's work, no doubt. She was

pretty sure that Detective Sergeant Dirk Coulter
wouldn't have performed such a mundane chore,
with two "underlings" at his disposal.

At least none of the department brass had
shown up yet, and that was just fine with Savannah.
The last thing she needed right now—with a murdered nanny and two of her client's family members missing—was to come face-to-face with the
police department "suits" who had unfairly fired
her from the job she loved.

She parked the Mustang behind a nondescript,
cement block building that served as one of the
park's two restrooms. As far as she was concerned,
the only downside to driving a bright red, beauti-
fully restored classic vehicle was the complete lack
of anonymity it provided—like when she was trying to tail a suspect.

Or hide from the chief of police.

No sooner had she gotten out of the car than she
spotted Dirk, leaving a copse of gnarled, stately oaks
and hurrying toward her. He had a heartsick look
on his face, one she knew all too well. His expression told her that the situation was just as bad as
she had imagined it. Maybe worse.

It bothered Dirk to see a bad guy harmed by another bad guy. He took a dim view of anyone who
gave themselves permission to hurt one of the citizens he had sworn to protect and serve.

But when it was an innocent victim, someone
who had not "lived by the sword" but had nevertheless died violently, Dirk's cynical, street-hardened
heart ached for them and the loved ones they left
behind in a world of grief.

Throughout Savannah's and Dirk's friendship,

he always turned to her when he was in pain, as she had with him. But, since their marriage, it seemed to her that he had become even more dependent upon her during difficult times like this.

He sought her out more quickly, shared more of his grief and frustrations with her, and listened fully and intently to any consolation or advice she offered.

She found it touching and deeply satisfying to have such a strong, self-reliant man turn to her in his time of need.

It felt good to be needed.

She rushed to him and, since there were no other cops standing nearby, she slipped her arms around his waist and hugged him close.

"Sorry, babe," she whispered.

"Yeah," he replied, his voice husky with emotion as he pressed a kiss to the top of her head. "You, too."

She nodded and allowed herself the luxury of resting her forehead on his shoulder. But only for a moment.

Drawing away from him and putting on her best "professional investigator" face, she tried to prepare herself emotionally for what was to come. "Is she over there?" she asked, pointing to the stand of trees where he had been.

"Yeah. I called Dr. Liu. She should be here pretty soon."

"Good. Anybody else coming?"

He knew what she meant, even without her explaining. Her firing had been a blow to both of them. One of those wounds that wasn't likely to heal in the course of a lifetime.

"Not that I know of, darlin'," he said with a sympathetic smile. "Nobody here but us chickens, and Jake and Mike."

"Okay. If the chief or the captain shows up, I'll take a hike, so to speak."

He nodded. "As long as you don't run into a rattlesnake or a mountain lion."

She shuddered. While no relative of Diamante's or Cleo's, no matter how distant or how large, particularly frightened her, like most Southern belles she had a healthy respect for venomous snakes, especially those wearing a set of rattles on their tails.

"Or maybe," she said, "I'll just get in my car and drive off."

"Good idea."

He wiped his palm across his forehead, which was sweatier than the day's temperature warranted. Savannah took his arm and together they started up the path toward the circle of oaks.

"So, how do you know this gal?" he asked.

"I don't know her personally. But do you remember when I told you this morning that John had sent me a new client?"

He gave her a quick, worried look. "Don't tell me this is her, your new client."

"No. But almost that bad. She's one of three people who've gone missing, and my client hired me to find them."

"Damn."

Savannah watched as his eyes scanned the area, as though he half expected to see two other bodies laid out on the hills somewhere.

"Who's the client?" he asked.

"Ethan Malloy," she replied.

"The movie star?"

"None other."

"Wow! Who's our victim to him?"

"The family nanny. She takes care of their little boy—two years old."

Dirk froze, an expression of horror and dread in his eyes. "Don't tell me the kid is one of the three."

"He is." Savannah drew a long, shuddering breath. "And his mother, Ethan's wife."

"Damn," he whispered, shaking his head.

She didn't know what to say, so she gave his arm an affectionate squeeze, then released him and walked on ahead.

It took her only seconds to locate the body, lying on its side, facing the trunk of one of the largest oaks. The bright pink and purple floral print on the woman's dress stood out in stark contrast to the browns and greens of the natural setting.

Pilar Padilla looked as if she could have been asleep, curled into a semi-fetal position, her knees drawn up toward her chest, her hands wrapped around them.

For just a moment, Savannah was grateful that she appeared so peaceful. Then she reminded herself that, until they determined how she had died, tranquil poses meant nothing.

Savannah had seen more than one murder victim who looked as if they were simply taking a nap by the side of the road, in a back alley, or their own bed.

Until you saw the injury that killed them.

"Is there a wound?" she said, more to herself than to Dirk. For a moment, she had forgotten that he was standing behind her.

"Head. Temple area," he replied. "I didn't see it myself at first either, because of all that dark hair."

Savannah leaned forward, her eyes searching the mass of blue-black curls that shone iridescent like a blackbird's feathers in the sunlight.

Then she saw it. As he had said, the injury was to the side of the head, directly over the temple.

"Just a bit of blood," she whispered, again, thinking out loud. "Not as much as you might think, considering that—"

"She's dead?"

"Exactly. Heaven knows, we've seen worse."

"Like that guy that washed up on the beach after five days, and—"

"Don't even start. I'm upset enough as it is."

"Sorry."

Without touching the body Savannah studied the ground around it, looking for a rock or any other hard object. She couldn't help hoping that there was a nonviolent answer to the terrible question: "How did this woman die?"

While it would never bring the dead back to life, an accident was so much easier for a family to bear than the thought that their loved one's life had willfully been taken from them.

But the dirt around the body was smooth and hardpacked from the lack of rain. There wasn't even one discernible footprint, including theirs.

The only rocks were tiny, less than an inch in diameter, not nearly large enough to cause a fatal accident.

"There's no rock or murder weapon that I can see," Dirk told her. "I already checked."

"Of course you did."

For a moment, her eyes scanned the tree bark, searching for blood, scrape marks, or anything unusual. But the old oak appeared as undisturbed as the rest of the scene.

As if reading her mind, Dirk said, "That bark's rough. If she'd hit her head on it, she'd be more gouged up than that."

"True," she admitted. "But when you don't know what you're looking for, you have to keep looking for it."

"Huh? Oh. Okay. Whatever you say."

Savannah returned to the body, knelt on one knee beside it, and studied the victim's hands and arms. "Did you see these?" she asked him.

In an instant, he was kneeling beside her. "See what?"

"Defensive wounds." She pointed to the wrists. "Both are bruised. Just a bit of discoloring on both of them."

"Not much. Wouldn't have been much of a struggle."

"Or maybe it was, but if she died quickly afterward, and the wounds wouldn't have had time to swell."

"One can always hope," he said.

The sorrow Savannah heard in his voice was the same emotion she was feeling. When she turned and gave him a quick look, she could see it in his eyes—the grief a police officer felt when witnessing one of society's worst moments firsthand.

Dirk was a tough guy. No doubt about it. He had

spent most of his childhood in a survival-of-the-fittest orphanage and then, later, had been adopted by a brutal man who worked him like an indentured servant. The few idle hours of his adolescence had been spent on the streets.

But for all his gritty machismo, Savannah knew her husband had a soft place in his heart for victims of crimes. When he had been assigned their cases, he felt a strong responsibility to secure justice for them and their loved ones.

"Yes," she said. "One can always hope it was quick." She turned back to the body, studied it a bit more, and said, "Three of her fingernails are broken."

"Good," he replied.

"Good? Good that she had to fight for her life?"

"I mean 'good' because, with any luck Dr. Liu will get some DNA out from under them."

"Oh. Right."

She hoped that Dr. Jennifer Liu would arrive soon. She didn't have to ask Dirk if he had called the medical examiner right away. At home, he might not be able to find the ice cubes in the ice cube trays or his socks in his sock drawer, but at a crime scene he was all business. A total professional.

Savannah stood, hearing her right knee crack and pop as she did. Rubbing it briefly, it occurred to her, not for the first time, that she wasn't getting any younger. She liked to think she was every bit the woman she had been in her twenties and thirties—even better with all that accumulated experience and wisdom.

But if she was honest, she'd have to admit that with each passing decade, she was getting just a wee bit slower and feeling a few more aches and pains than she had before.

She was discovering that getting older wasn't a heck of a lot of fun.

But it beat the alternative.

Looking down at poor Pilar, she reminded herself that aging is a great honor. One denied to far too many people.

Chapter 7

"When did Dr. Liu say she'd be getting here? How about the CSI unit?" Savannah asked him, trying not to sound anxious as she looked down at the body beneath the giant oak.

"CSI said they'd be here soon. But Dr. Liu . . . not as quick as I'd like. She'd just got called out to Twin Oaks for another one."

When he saw the expression of horror on Savannah's face he quickly added, "Don't worry. It's not one of yours. Some ninety-five-year-old dude passed away in his bed. But he's rich and has a bunch of disgruntled relatives, so she wants to make sure nobody helped him make an early exit."

"Ninety-five is 'early'?"

He shrugged. "It would be if you didn't leave naturally and weren't ready to go."

"True."

She looked around and took in the surrounding area. Other than having fewer trees, it all seemed pretty much the same to her. Daisies, sage, prickly pear cactus, and hills the same tawny brown color as the mountain lions that occasionally roamed them. Just the standard Southern California landscape.

Other than a few weeks in spring, when tropical storms swept across the sea and pounded the area, and the desert hillsides transformed into those resembling the verdant landscapes of Ireland, this was the view.

Savannah enjoyed it, embraced it, felt her soul relaxing and being restored when she was in it.

Unless she was investigating a murder.

"I saw Jake's and Mike's unit when I pulled in," she said, looking around for them on the nearby hiking paths. "Where are they?"

"Don't know. I told them to cordon off the scene and then search the area. Haven't seen 'em since. If they're layin' under a tree somewhere, taking a nap or watching porn on their phones, I'll—"

"I'm sure they're not. Jake and Mike are good cops."

"They only sleep and check out smut on duty when they *aren't* working a murder scene?"

"Exactly."

"Hey, speak of the devil, and he'll appear." Dirk nodded back toward the park, where the dirt hiking trail met the pavement. "It's McMurtry."

Savannah turned to look and was disturbed by the expression on the young cop's face.

"He seems upset," she said. "That's not good."

"No, it's not," Dirk agreed. "'Cause that means I'm about to get upset. And I don't like that."

"I like it even less. Because it means I'll not only have to be upset myself, but I'll have to deal with you being all crabby on top of it."

"Life sucks."

"At the moment, yes, it pretty much does."

Jake came pounding up the hill toward them, his normally ruddy face even redder from the exertion of running.

When he reached them, he had to bend over for a moment, head down, hands on his knees, to catch his breath before he could speak.

Savannah could feel her anxiety level rising by the second. As frequently happened during stressful moments, she felt time slow and her own senses sharpen.

As she waited for what seemed like an hour, but it was actually only a few seconds, she heard birds rustling in nearby bushes, a crow cawing in the distance, and above her head, the great oak's leaves dancing in the hot, dry Santa Ana wind.

Unable to bear the suspense any longer, she said, "What is it, Jake? What's up? Did you guys find something?"

He nodded, still gasping for breath. Finally, he straightened up and wiped the sweat off his face with the back of his hand. "Yeah. Down in the parking lot. By that white Porsche. Between the car and the Dumpster."

"Not a body, right?" Savannah asked, dreading the reply.

"No. It's like a fancy backpack or something. I'm not even sure it has anything to do with . . ." He waved a hand toward the body on the ground, while trying to not actually look at it. ". . . you know . . . her."

But Savannah didn't hear the last part of his sentence, because she was already racing down the path toward the parking lot.

Of course, she was glad they hadn't found another body, but his words still sent a chill through her.

As she ran, she remembered a couple of Ethan's comments earlier that morning.

"Freddy's backpack. She always takes it with her when she goes out with him," and *"He liked the Porsche Cayenne SUV I gave him for Christmas."*

She tried to tell herself that the backpack would contain some careless student's textbooks or a homeless person's hoard.

"Please don't let it be filled with toys and kid snacks," she whispered. "Please, God. I won't ask for anything else for at least a week."

No sooner had she uttered the prayer than she realized she would be breaking her promise before the day was done, asking the Almighty for help in finding that little lost boy and his mother.

Without a doubt, when she was in the middle of a difficult case—a matter of life and death—she uttered more prayers in one day than she usually did in a month.

She asked for more than she gave thanks for. She wasn't proud of it, and she probably wouldn't admit it to Granny Reid, but it was the truth.

When she rounded a curve in the path and saw the big white Porsche in the lot, she wondered how she had missed it when she'd arrived.

She kicked herself mentally for not asking Ethan Malloy the make, model, and plate number of his wife's vehicle. *Rookie mistake,* she told herself. *You know better, girl.*

As she approached the luxury vehicle with Dirk and Jake right behind her, she could see Patrolman Mike Farnon standing just on the other side of the car, a serious expression on his round face.

She continued to berate herself as the license plate came into view. *If you'd only done your job and asked for the plate number,* whispered an ugly, critical voice inside, *you'd know right now that isn't her car, and you'd feel a lot better.*

Another even nastier one replied, *Yeah, sure. Dream on, girl. We'll pretend that we don't know he gave Beth that Porsche when he gave his father one. Let's act like we don't know that some Porsche dealer gave him a heckuva deal last Christmas.*

She reached the car, and in an instant, Dirk was beside her.

"Is it hers?" he asked. "Is that her car?"

"I don't know," she admitted. "I didn't ask. Like a dang fool I didn't think to ask him what—"

"I got it." His face was soft, his eyes kind as he began to dig in his bomber jacket pocket for his cell phone. "I got it, Van. Really. Don't worry."

He punched a couple of numbers, and she heard him say, "Yeah, Coulter here. I need you to run a plate for me."

Savannah left him and hurried over to where Mike stood, guarding their latest find.

It wasn't hard to spot, tossed onto the ground, half leaning against a Dumpster—a bright red designer mom's backpack. It appeared new, and Savannah could tell by the fine, quilted leather that it would have cost more than the average American baby's entire layette.

More than anything, she wanted to grab the pack, tear it open, and see if it contained any ID. But even if she were still a cop, even if she were the investigating officer, she would have to show restraint and avoid contaminating what might very well be evidence.

Instead, she reached into her purse, took out her phone, and reluctantly called Ethan Malloy. It was always difficult to relay bad news to a client.

When the news was especially terrible, she made it a practice to always deliver it in person, if at all possible.

He answered after the first ring. "Hello, Savannah," he said, his deep, theatrical voice shaking. "Did you find them?"

"No, I haven't. I'm sorry, Ethan, but I won't give up until I do. I just have to ask you a couple of quick questions."

He sounded slightly relieved when he said, "Sure. Go ahead."

"You told me what Freddy and Beth and Pilar were wearing when you last saw them. You also told me that Beth usually carries some sort of backpack. Could you describe for me?"

"It's leather. Red. Freddy's favorite color is red. I got it for her last Mother's Day." There was a long pause as Savannah searched for her next words. "Does that help?" he asked, filling the silence.

Yes, she thought, as she stared at the abandoned, red backpack. *It helps like a knife to the heart.*

"It does," she said, trying to sound casual and

not succeeding. "Thank you, Ethan. And another thing—what's the make and model of your wife's vehicle? The plate number and color, too, while you're at it."

"Her car is a Porsche Panamera. This year's model. White."

As he named off a series of letters and numbers, Savannah stared at the car's front license plate, seeing the exact sequence.

She felt her knees go weak as her heart sank.

When Ethan had finished his recitation, he said, "What's this about, Savannah? Why are you asking me about her backpack and her car?"

She closed her eyes, needing to blot out the scene in front of her, at least for a moment. "Those are just routine questions, Ethan," she told him. "I should've asked them this morning."

"Oh. Okay."

She could hear the suspicion in his voice, and she was about to make it even worse. "Is there anyone there at the house with you right now?" she asked.

"Yes. Amy's here. Why?"

"That's good. Someone needs to be there to answer the house phone, if Beth should call."

"But I don't understand. *I'm* here."

"I know. But I need you to come to San Carmelita. I need you to do that now."

"But why?"

"We're going to have to talk to you. In person."

"Who's *we*?"

"Me and my husband."

"Why would I need to talk to your husband?"

Savannah watched in her peripheral vision as Dirk had finished his phone call and walked over to stand beside her.

"He's a policeman," she said, looking up at her husband and feeling a sense of pride, as she always did when making that statement. "He's a sergeant named Dirk Coulter. He's also a detective, Ethan. A very good one, if I do say so myself."

"I'm sure he is. But I told you, I don't want to bring the police into this. Not yet."

"Yes, you do, Ethan. Now."

"What's going on, Savannah?" he demanded. "What's happened? Did you find them?"

Savannah drew a deep breath, chose her words carefully, and said, "I haven't found your family, Mr. Malloy. I wish like all get-out that I could tell you I have. But you need to trust me now when I tell you that you can't keep this a secret any longer."

She waited but there was no answer.

"Ethan, listen to me. I want you to find Amy and tell her that you're going out for a while. Tell her she needs to stay at the house and answer the phone. If she hears anything, anything at all, having to do with the disappearances, she's to call you or me right away. Make sure she's got my number. Are you with me so far?"

She heard a hoarse, "Yes."

"Okay. Then I want you to get in your car and drive straight to San Carmelita. Come to my house. The address is on the card I left with you. Do you have it?"

She could hear him rummaging about for a moment, then he said, "Yes. I have it right here."

"Good. I'm out in the field right now, but I'll head home and be there when you arrive in about a half an hour. Okay?"

"Yeah. Okay, if you say it's necessary, then I believe you."

"Thank you, Ethan. I appreciate your trust."

"Just don't stop looking."

Savannah was only vaguely aware that she was gripping the cell phone far too tightly with her left hand and sinking her nails into the palm of her right when she answered, "I won't stop searching, Mr. Malloy, I promise you I won't. Not until I find them. None of us will. Now go do what I asked, please. I'll see you in half an hour or less."

Savannah tucked the phone back into her purse. Dirk walked closer and put his hand on her arm.

"I'm going to have to talk to him," he said.

"He knows. I told him it was necessary. Didn't say why. But he agreed."

Dirk ran his fingers through his hair and sighed. "But first I have to . . . you know."

"I'm sorry. I sure don't envy you."

"Of all the times I miss having you for a partner, this is the worst."

"Yes, I know, darlin'." She stood on tiptoe and gave him a quick, soft kiss on the lips, not minding, for once, that there were other cops around to see it.

And for once, he didn't seem to mind either.

"Go get it over with," she told him. "I'll see you back at the house."

She squeezed his hand, told Jake and Mike good-bye, walked back to her Mustang, and got inside.

She watched as her husband knelt on one knee beside the red backpack, took a few pictures of it with his phone, then put on a pair of surgical gloves, and began to rifle through its contents.

She knew he would wait until Dr. Liu and the CSI team arrived before he left the scene. She knew him well enough to predict that he wouldn't leave until he absolutely had to.

Because once he did, Det. Sgt. Dirk Coulter would have to do the one thing that most cops found to be the most difficult part of their job.

He would have to inform a family that someone they loved, more than life itself, was gone forever.

Chapter 8

Ethan Malloy pulled into Savannah's driveway exactly twenty-seven minutes after their phone call. She was sitting in one of her white wicker chairs on the front porch, waiting for him.

As he climbed out of the big pickup and walked up the sidewalk to the house, she came down the steps to greet him. From the expression on his face she could tell that he sensed something was badly wrong.

While Dirk's job of informing the family was infinitely worse, she wasn't looking forward to the upcoming conversation she and her client were going to have either. She attempted a bit of small talk to temporarily delay it.

"Nice truck," she said, pointing to the oversized GMC Sierra Denali that dwarfed her Mustang that was parked beside it. "Somehow, I was expecting another Porsche."

He half smiled, then shrugged. "Naw. I'm not a

Porsche kinda guy. At heart, I'm just a good old boy from Amarillo."

"Nothing wrong with that," Savannah told him as they stepped onto the porch. "Good ol' boys are my absolute favorites."

He gave her a sly, sideways look that weakened her knees and said, "Are you married to a good ol' boy, Savannah?"

"Of course. Though he's not from Texas."

"Aw, well. Nobody's perfect."

They shared a companionable, if brief, laugh while she opened the door and ushered him inside.

Other than Diamante and Cleopatra, the house was empty, as it had been when she had first returned home. The cinnamon aroma of Gran's apple pie scented the house most pleasantly. It occurred to Savannah that if, at the end of their conversation, Ethan appeared composed enough to eat, she would offer him a slice.

She glanced at the rolltop desk's empty chair, thought of Tammy, and wondered how she was doing. By now, surely her parents had arrived and they were visiting, preferably drama-free. Savannah hoped Tammy and Waycross might actually enjoy the Harts' visit, but considering all she had heard about Mr. and Dr. Hart, that seemed a bit too much to wish for.

"Wow, what pretty cats," Ethan said, as he walked over to their window perch where they lay, sunning themselves. He gave them each a scratch behind the ear, instantly making two new feline friends.

Savannah decided, then and there, that no Post-it with his name on it would ever appear at the top of her suspect list. Any man who liked cats was a good guy in her estimation.

It was the number one reason why she had married Dirk—or at least in the top five.

"Let me take you to my office," she told him, as she led him through the living room and into the kitchen. "Would you like an iced tea, or soda, or a beer?"

"A beer sounds wonderful, if your good ol' boy hubby can spare it."

"He keeps close count, but I reckon he could turn loose of a can under the circumstances."

She reached into the refrigerator, took out one of Dirk's most prized possessions, and handed it to her new client.

"Thank you," he said, popping the top and immediately downing much of it. After wiping his mouth with the back of his hand, he sighed and said, "It's a bit early in the day for me, but then . . . it's been a pretty lousy day."

She felt a pang of sympathy for him, thinking his day was about to get far worse.

"Let's go out in the backyard," she said. "That's where I usually talk to my clients. My husband should be along pretty soon. He, well, he had some matters to attend to that couldn't wait. But I know he's eager to talk to you."

She escorted him out the back door and across the lawn to a couple of comfortable patio chairs situated beneath an arbor, heavy with wisteria in full bloom.

He sat down, quickly disposed of the remainder of his beer, then set the empty can on a nearby side table. She sat a few feet away in a matching chair, thought of what she had to tell him, and felt her temples start to throb from a tension headache.

"Great office," he said, looking around at her lush flower garden with its rosebushes, statuesque hollyhocks, nasturtiums cascading over stone walls, and then above at the wisteria hanging overhead. "Being a private detective, having meetings with clients in a peaceful, beautiful setting like this, it must be nice."

"It can be," she replied guardedly. "Depending on the case."

"And the outcome of the case?"

"Yes. If it has a happy ending, then I'm glad I'm a PI and not a cowgirl or ballerina."

His pale blue eyes locked with hers. They were filled with pain. "Are you going to be able to write a happy ending to *our* story, Savannah?" he asked, his voice tremulous.

"I sure hope so, Ethan. Really I do." She looked down at her hands, folded demurely in her lap. "But even though I have no idea where Beth or Freddy are, you need to prepare yourself. As it turns out, there *has* been a new development. A most distressing one."

He leaned forward, his elbows on his knees, and stared at her. "I was afraid of that. When you asked me to come here, I . . . What is it? What's happened?"

At that moment, Savannah felt some of what Dirk was, no doubt, experiencing. There was just no good way to deliver horrible news. For the person telling it or the person hearing it.

"Ethan, I regret that I have to tell you this, but we found Pilar."

"You did?"

"Yes. We found her, and, I'm sorry, but she's dead."

He flinched at her words, as though someone had literally struck him. Hard. "Pilar? She's dead?"

"Yes. I'm so sorry."

"No, no, it can't be. Are you sure?"

"Yes. I saw her body myself on a hill above Oak Grove. It's a public park here in San Carmelita."

"I know where it is. It's my family's favorite park. Beth and I drive there all the time and go hiking with Freddy. Pilar joins us, too."

"Thank you for telling me that. It's helpful."

"Pilar is dead?"

He couldn't seem to grasp what she was telling him, and as tears filled his eyes, she found herself thinking that no one, not even an Academy Award–winning actor, could portray shock and grief as well as Ethan Malloy was at that moment.

"No, no, no," he whispered, shaking his head. "Not Pilar. She's so kind. So gentle. How? How did she die? What happened to her?"

"We don't know for sure yet. Dr. Liu, the coroner, will examine the body. Her report should tell us a lot more."

"It can't be foul play. It just can't be. Pilar is a sweetheart. She doesn't have an enemy in the world. Everyone who knows her, loves her." He covered his face with his hands and began to sob. "Freddy loves her," he said. "Beth and I, we all do."

A new expression crossed his face—one of horror. "Her family," he said. "Her poor, poor family. She's an only child. Her parents will be devastated when they find out!"

"That's what my husband is doing right now," Savannah said. "He's informing them."

She reached toward the table next to her chair and offered him the box of tissues she kept there for exactly this sort of occasion. Unfortunately, she had found that tissues were as necessary for a private detective to have around as a cop or a psychologist.

He took some, wiped his face, and stuffed them into his jeans pocket. She waited quietly . . . for it to hit him.

It did.

Three seconds later.

"Oh, my God!" he said, his face growing ashen in an instant. "If she's dead, if someone deliberately hurt her, then maybe that same person—"

Savannah reached over and laid her hand on his arm. "I know it's almost impossible not to go there, Ethan, but try very hard not to. Please wait for the ME's report before thinking the worst, even about Pilar, let alone your family. It could have been an accident. It could have been . . . anything."

Savannah thought of the wound on the side of the nanny's head. Broken fingernails. The lonely seclusion of the area—the perfect place to commit a homicide.

As a rule, she tried not to lie to, or even deceive, a client. But if somehow, by some miracle, there turned out to be an innocent explanation to all that had happened, she hated to see a husband and father suffer even more than necessary, due to an overactive imagination.

As Ethan Malloy attempted to compose himself,

Savannah searched her mind for the next best conversational path to take. Perhaps Pilar Padilla had no enemies, but she had to find out for certain if Ethan or Beth had any who might be capable of kidnapping or murder.

But first things first. The husband or lover of any woman who goes missing is always the primary suspect, as is the person who first reported their absence.

She had to find out if Ethan Malloy had an alibi or combination of alibis for the time period his wife had been gone.

In her experience, she had found it to be a tricky and sticky situation, asking a person for an alibi. Most people had watched enough television and movies to understand the gravity of such an inquiry.

Even among complacent and passive folks, the question, "Can you account for your whereabouts when . . . ?" tended to turn a nice and cooperative person into a guarded, even belligerent one.

So, she made her voice gentle and soft when she said, "I meant to ask you this morning, who was in the house yesterday morning when you and Beth had your argument?"

He thought for a moment. "Beth and myself, obviously. Then there was Pilar and Amy. Freddy and our housekeeper, Luciana. But Freddy was asleep upstairs and Luciana was up there, too, cleaning. I don't think they were aware of what was going on." He looked down and winced. "At least, I hope not. I'd hate to think Freddy overheard his parents arguing. I had enough of that myself, growing up. I wouldn't want it for my son."

"I understand." She plunged ahead. "I know that Beth, Pilar, and Freddy left the house after your argument, but how about the rest? Amy, Luciana, and you. Where were the three of you for the rest of the day?"

There it was. The defensive look. The suspicion in the eyes. Ethan Malloy leaned back from her and crossed his arms over his chest.

"Why?"

"In a situation like this, everyone has to be accounted for at all times. I need to know that you knew where they were all day."

She could tell by his scowl that he wasn't buying it. "And you want to know if *they* knew where *I* was."

"The police will certainly ask—you and them—so we might as well get it out of the way."

"Fair enough." He appeared to relax a bit as he ran his fingers through his dark hair and briefly massaged the back of his neck. "Okay, like I said, I know they were all in the house when Beth and I had our argument. Amy and Luciana were there the whole time that I was that day. Maybe not in the same room with me, but in the house. I could hear Luciana cleaning here and there, and Amy kept popping into the library, bothering me with details about petty social scheduling stuff. I remember because I wasn't in the mood, and I didn't appreciate it."

"I can imagine."

"But I can't say for sure where they were or what they were doing during the time when I left the house to go out and search for Beth."

Savannah felt something like a cold wind blow over her skin. It sent a shiver through her.

"You went out to search for them?" she asked with as casual a tone as she could muster.

"Sure. Later that afternoon, when they didn't come back, and I couldn't reach Beth on her cell, I went out looking. I felt really bad about the argument, and I wanted to make up with her. It's not good to let stuff like that fester, you know?"

"Yes. I agree. Where exactly did you go? Tell me everywhere and in what order. Times, too, as best you can recall."

She reached for a notebook and pen on the nearby table and started to make notes.

When she glanced up from her writing, she saw the guarded expression was back in his eyes. For a moment, she recalled all the posters and ads she had seen for his movies and TV shows—eyes staring intently into the camera, with an intensity that was chilling. The eyes of a potentially dangerous alpha male.

"Do you think I killed my wife? Is that why you're asking me these things, Savannah? Do you?"

"No," she said without hesitation. "I don't. But I won't lie to you. The cops are going to consider you their main suspect, so you need to get used to answering these questions and a whole lot more."

He closed his eyes, shook his head, and groaned. "This is exactly what I was hoping to avoid. I'm a private person. So is Beth. We hate the paparazzi, the way they can take the simplest thing and lie about it, and turn it into something horrible."

"I'm sure that's true, and then innocent people have to live with the stain of those lies for the rest of their days. I can understand why you want to avoid that, and I'll do everything I can to help you in that regard. My husband will, too. Pilar's death—he's caught that case. He'll be the senior investigator. Considering the size of the San Carmelita Police Department, he'll probably be the only investigator, other than the medical examiner and the CSI team members."

He seemed concerned so she quickly added, "But they're very good at what they do, all of them. You don't have to worry. They'll get it right, and by the time they're finished, we'll know what happened to Pilar."

"And Beth? And Freddy?"

"I won't rest until I find them. Neither will my team. We know you want answers, and we're going to do everything we can to get them back, safe and sound."

He sat, saying nothing, for what seemed like forever to Savannah. Then he offered her a weak smile, leaned toward her, and covered her hand with his. Giving her fingers a squeeze, then a pat, he said, "Thank you. I appreciate that, Savannah. I really do. Your best effort is all anybody can ask."

Before she could reply, her cell phone began to jingle. She knew it was Dirk calling, because the song it was playing was the stirring theme of the old television show *Bonanza*.

Apparently, his melancholy task of informing Pilar's parents was finished, she thought, feeling somewhat relieved on his behalf.

When she reached for the phone, which was lying on the side table between her chair and Ethan's, she accidentally knocked his empty beer can onto the ground. She reached for it, but it rolled away from her and under his chair.

"No problem," he said. "I'll get it." He leaned down, retrieved the can, and replaced it on the table.

It was in that instant, when he was bending down, that Savannah saw something that frightened her and made her feel sick in her spirit.

For the briefest moment, as he had leaned down, the neckline of his T-shirt had dropped forward, away from his skin, revealing a few more inches of his neck and upper chest.

She saw them, and as much as Savannah wanted to, she couldn't deny, even to herself, what she had seen.

Scratches.

Deep, red scratches. And bruising.

She tried not to tremble or sound as shaken as she felt, as she reached for the phone and said to Ethan. "Sorry. I have to take this."

"Sure. Go ahead," he said with a dismissive wave.

She looked into his eyes, searching for any sign that he might have noticed what had just happened. He didn't appear to, but her relief was minimal at best.

She jumped to her feet, pushed the answer button on the phone, and tried to appear casual as she walked away from the arbor and toward the house. "Hi," she said into the phone. "I'm glad you called, darlin'. Your timing's perfect, as always."

"I'm just leaving the Padillas' place out here in the East End. Have you got Malloy there with you at the house?"

"I certainly do."

She had reached the back door, but instead of going inside, she turned around and leaned against it.

In a strange, surreal way she was acutely aware of the heat from the sun-warmed wood against her shoulder blades and on down her spine, the hum of insects in the lilac bush nearby, the scent of its blossoms in the air, and in the far distance some kind of siren, screaming out an emergency.

She could see Ethan Malloy, still sitting quietly beneath her arbor, looking troubled, but thoughtful. Such a peaceful sight.

How deceiving, she thought, wondering what he was really thinking behind those famous blue eyes. What secrets weren't being revealed on that handsome face?

"You aren't going to believe what this Pilar gal's parents told me," Dirk was saying. "Of course, they fell apart when I told them that we found her and that she was gone. That's to be expected, them being parents and all. But once they got control of themselves a little bit, they had a lot of beans to spill."

"Oh?" Still stunned from what she had seen, Savannah couldn't think of anything more to say.

"Yeah. Seems their daughter called them yesterday afternoon and told them about the big argument that your boy, Ethan, and his old lady had in the morning. Apparently, it was a doozy. The girl told her parents she had never seen either one of them so mad or heard them carry on like that before. Promised her folks that she'd tell them all about it in detail that night when she got home. But of course, she never got home, so we don't know whatever juicy stuff she was going to tell them."

When she didn't reply, he added, "I'm going to have to talk to your guy there. Probably bring him to the station house and sweat him a bit."

Finding her voice, Savannah said, "You're definitely going to have to take him in. No doubt about it."

"Why? Did you find out something good?"

"No," she said. "Nothing good. In fact, it's bad."

"How bad?"

"He bent down and I saw inside his shirt. He's all scratched up. Something fierce."

There was a long silence on the other end. Then Savannah heard her husband say, "Whoa. That *is* bad."

"Yeah."

"That don't bode well for the missing wife," he said. "Or maybe even the kid."

Savannah felt a sob welling up in her throat. She swallowed it and said, "Don't. I can't stand it. Don't go there. Not unless we absolutely have to."

"Okay. I hear ya. Don't take any chances with that guy, babe. Watch yourself. I'll get there as quick as I can."

Savannah ended the call, then stood there against the door for a few moments more, soaking in the warmth from the door behind her, listening to the sounds of her garden and smelling its comforting scents. As always, she drew strength from these familiar surroundings, a tiny world that she, herself, had created and needed to replenish her soul.

She closed her eyes, reached deep inside her spirit, and found the necessary courage and resolve to take the next crucial steps.

Ethan Malloy wasn't the only seasoned, accomplished actor in her backyard. She'd given more than a few Oscar-worthy performances in her life, too.

With a fake spring in her step, she made her way across the lawn, back to the arbor.

"Everything okay?" Ethan asked as she approached.

"Sure. Don't you worry about a thing. That was my husband, and he's on his way home right now. He'll be here shortly." She gave him her brightest, dimple-deepening, eye-twinkling smile. "Then we'll really get this show on the road."

Chapter 9

As Savannah drove her Mustang behind Dirk's squad car, heading toward the San Carmelita police station, she decided to give her brother a call and see how he liked his new in-laws.

When Waycross answered, he sounded subdued, but happy to hear from her. "Hi, Sis. Looks like you're gettin' the hang of that new speakerphone," he said, semi-cheerfully.

"It's great. Like the guy who gave it to me and installed it," she replied.

"Where you at?"

"Tailing Dirk as he transports Ethan Malloy to the station house. We're about there, so I'll make this short. I'm just wondering how you're doing over there. If you can talk, that is."

"Um, a little bit."

She could hear voices in the background. Voices with an accent she didn't readily recognize.

"How's it goin'? You getting all acquainted with your new in-laws?"

"Do you recollect when the first Colonel met Mrs. Baker?"

"I do, indeed. Gran's petunia patch was never the same after that . . . um . . . rendezvous."

"Colonel Beauregard either."

Savannah chuckled, recalling a memory, permanently seared into the hearts and minds of all nine of the Reid children.

Over the years, Granny had owned numerous generations of bloodhounds. Although she had given them unique first names, every single one had been dubbed "Colonel Beauregard" and all other names virtually forgotten.

The first, Colonel Abraham Beauregard, had been an adorable puppy, a sweet soul, loving to kids, gentle with other dogs, kind to strangers. Totally worthless as a watchdog.

He even loved cats.

Until Mrs. Baker.

The first Colonel had encountered the neighbor's old black-and-white tuxedo kitty, Mrs. Baker, in Gran's flower garden, and the violence committed upon his saggy, baggy, puppy personage had been a sorrow to behold, or so said Gran after the dust had settled.

Their neighbor's oversized, exceedingly grumpy feline had snuck into their yard and ambushed the dog behind the carnation patch. She'd grabbed one of his prominent dewlaps with her left, sharp-clawed paw and held him tightly, while clobbering him mercilessly with her right. She'd landed more rapid-fire blows on his howling little puppy face in twelve seconds than most boxing champions did in twelve rounds.

Subsequently, a wrestling match had ensued that left much of Granny's flower garden in shambles. By the time Mrs. Baker left the petulant pup, vanquished and humiliated, in the dust and sauntered away, the seeds of hatred had been sown.

Colonel Abraham and every subsequent Colonel thereafter had hated cats with a fervor unmatched in the Southern states since the "War of Northern Aggression."

Savannah contemplated what it must be like in the Tammy/ Waycross household, if her brother was comparing their afternoon with Lenora and Quincy Hart to the Petunia Patch Massacre.

"Hm. That bad, eh?"

"Reckon so," he replied.

"You gonna make it through the evening over there without bloodshed?"

"Nothin' a wad of chewed bubble gum and some duct tape wouldn't plug."

"I'd invite you over to our house for supper, but I have no idea when we're going to get home. Once Dirk finishes with Mr. Malloy, I doubt that'll be the day. We've still got a lost baby and its mother to find."

"Thank you for thinkin' of us, Sis, but we've got supper plans already sewed up. Ryan and John done invited us to that fancy restaurant of theirs."

"That'll be nice. You'll have a heavenly meal. Ryan and John are good company—great social buffers. Tammy's folks will wind up having a fine time there, whether they want to or not."

She heard him laugh and thought what a heart-warming sound it was. Waycross had always been the soul of sweetness.

"We're supposed to show up around seven-thirty. Why don't y'all join us? I'm sure Ryan and John wouldn't mind."

Savannah could hear the slight pleading tone in his voice. It wasn't an invitation. It was a cry for help.

"We'll make it if we can, darlin'. Just depends on how long the rest of this takes."

Savannah watched as Dirk pulled onto the station house property and headed for the more private parking lot in the back. Even having seen the scratches on Ethan's chest, she was glad when Dirk had put him in the front passenger's seat, instead of in the rear.

Until they knew for sure what he had or hadn't done, she didn't want to see a picture of one of her clients on the cover of the grocery store tabloids sitting in "the cage" of a police squad car.

"I've gotta sign off, kiddo," she told Waycross. "We're at the station. I'm sorry it's not going well there. You can tell me all about it later, blow-by-blow. If you survive, that is."

"I grew up as Macon and Shirley Reid's kid—the only redheaded boy in a small town, remember?"

She laughed. "Yeah, if you can handle that, you can make it through anything. Toodle-oo."

Again, she could hear him chuckling as she finished the call, so she figured she had done her job as Big Sister Comforter. Half done, anyway. Sadly, sometimes, even Big Sister Superpower had its limitations.

Following Dirk's lead, she drove to the last row of the parking lot and squeezed the Mustang into a narrow spot in the corner that was partially blocked by some overgrown oleander.

As she did so, it occurred to her that, if she was going to keep hiding her awesome car in strange, out-of-the-way places to avoid detection, she should think about hiring Waycross to give the red pony a camo paint job.

She cut the key, reached over, and snatched one of Dirk's old baseball caps off the passenger floor. As she got out of the car, she slapped the hat against her thigh a couple of times to dislodge any surface debris. Then she hurried over to Dirk and Ethan, who were just exiting the squad car.

She rounded the black-and-white, walked up to Ethan, and shoved the cap into his hand. "Here. Wear this."

She turned to see Dirk staring at his hat, which was now sitting on the actor's head.

Her husband was wearing his "deeply disgruntled Dirk" expression.

Anticipating an awkward verbal spat in the making, she told him, "The last thing we need right now is to have your good buddies inside there snapping phone pictures of the 'famous dude we got in the station house' and posting them on Facebook."

Turning to Ethan she said, "Put on your sunglasses."

"I don't have any," he replied.

"You live in Southern California, and you don't own sunglasses?"

"I own some," he replied. "I just don't have any with me at the moment."

"I thought you movie stars always wore sunglasses," Dirk said with a touch of sarcasm.

Ethan shot him an unpleasant look and said, "When your wife told me to get to San Carmelita as quick as possible, I had a few other things on my mind. I wasn't thinking about fashion accessories."

Dirk softened his voice and his expression when he said, "Okay. Just be sure to give me that cap back. It's one of my favorites."

"My husband's wardrobe is limited," Savannah added, handing him her glasses. "Every garment he owns is his favorite."

Ethan gave Dirk's attire a quick once-over, taking in the battered bomber jacket, the faded Harley Davidson T-shirt, the frayed jeans and scuffed sneakers. "Gotcha." He slid on Savannah's shades. "Okay? Am I now incognito enough to enter your police station?"

"You'll do," Savannah replied. "Just don't say anything if you can help it. You've got a distinctive, car commercial–kinda voice."

As the three of them made their way to the back of the station house, Savannah heard Dirk mutter under his breath, "It must suck, bein' a famous movie star with women throwing themselves atcha right and left."

She hoped that Ethan hadn't heard. It was seldom a good idea to alienate a suspect before you even began an interrogation.

But he *had* heard. He stared at Dirk for a long time, and Savannah wasn't sure how to read that look. Sad? Angry? A bit of both?

Then, in a voice that was definitely more dejected than angry, the world-acclaimed, fan-adored actor said, "If you know where your loved ones are right now, Detective Sergeant Coulter, I'll gladly trade places with you."

Savannah sat quietly in an uncomfortable metal folding chair in the corner of the tiny, gray, claustrophobic room and watched Dirk do what he did best. Interrogate.

Although today it wasn't going as well as usual. He and his prime homicide suspect, Ethan Malloy, had gone in verbal circles for the better part of an hour. The "beaten path" around the proverbial "bush" was well trampled, and from what Savannah could tell, little if any progress had been made.

"Believe me, Detective," Ethan was saying for at least the fifth time, "if I'd known that I'd need to furnish you with an alibi, I would've spent the afternoon giving some sort of interview at a local TV station or signing copies of one of my movie DVDs at Walmart, instead of driving up and down the coast, searching for my family."

The two men were sitting across from each other at a small, scarred, and timeworn table. Like everything else in the room, it had been deliberately chosen for its depressing gray color and total lack of charm.

Prime homicide suspects weren't supposed to feel at ease in cheerful surroundings when being interviewed. They were potentially in a lot of trouble and needed to feel as such.

Adapting his usual "grill 'em on high heat" pose, Dirk was leaning far forward, elbows on the table, taking up more than half of the space between him and his subject, and blatantly violating his personal space.

Displaying typical interviewee body language, Ethan was leaning back in his chair, arms crossed over his chest. The look on his face said it all: at that moment, he would prefer to be absolutely anywhere else, with anyone else, doing anything else.

In all the years that she had watched Dirk question suspects, Savannah had never heard any of those express a desire to do it again.

It wasn't supposed to be fun, and Detective Sergeant Coulter made sure it wasn't.

Dirk glanced down at the notebook he had open on the table in front of him, at the scribblings he had made during the interview so far. He picked up his pen and began tapping the paper, making such a loud and annoying sound that even Savannah wanted to reach over and smack him.

"Okay," he said. "I've got this list of all the places you said you drove to. Some of these have closed circuit cameras, you know. I'm going to be able to check them and see if you were really there when you say were."

"Good. Check. I want you to." Ethan's face was pale, his eyes red. He was appearing more frustrated and desperate by the moment. "I wish to God you were doing that right now, instead of wasting time sitting here with me. I told you, Detective, I didn't kill Pilar! I didn't harm my family!

But somebody out there murdered that poor girl, and for all we know, they're doing the same damn thing right now to my wife and child!"

He paused and took some deep breaths as though trying to compose himself.

Dirk didn't give him time. "Then tell me what's really going on between you and your wife," he shot back. "The sooner you're honest with me, the quicker you're outta here, and I'm back on the street, searching for them."

"I *have* been honest with you," Ethan replied. "Every word I've told you was the truth."

"But not the *whole* truth," Dirk insisted.

Ethan threw up his hands in a gesture of utter frustration. "What? What the hell do you think I'm holding back? What do you want to know that I haven't already told you ten times?"

Dirk gave him a small, wry smile—an almost-smirk that Savannah had seen before. One that had chilled the hearts of far more hardened criminals than Ethan Malloy.

"Tell me what you fought with your wife about that morning," Dirk said. "And don't give me any of that 'just regular husband and wife stuff.' That's crap, and you and I both know it."

Instantly, the frustrated expression disappeared from Ethan's face, to be replaced by one of pure rage. His pale skin flushed red as he said, "I already told you, Detective, that's not important, and it's private."

"Oh, yeah. I'll be the judge of what's important and what's not in this conversation. And you can forget about anything in your life being 'private' right now. A young woman is dead. So, your privacy and anybody else's who's got anything to do with this case—they're in the toilet right now. Nothing's private until I find out who killed her and where your wife and kid are."

His words seemed to have found their mark. Ethan nodded, sat quietly for a moment, then said, "You're right. I understand." He took a deep breath. "When we fought yesterday morning—the topic was, well, infidelity."

"Whose?"

"Does that really matter? I'd rather—"

"Do not start with that crap again! Whose infidelity?"

"My wife's. Okay? I found out that she's been seeing her ex-husband again. I confronted her about it, and as you can imagine, it got pretty heated."

"You didn't think that was important enough to mention it?"

"No, I didn't. Neal Irwin's not my favorite guy in the world. But he didn't kill anybody."

"And you know this how?"

"He weighs two pounds. He's afraid of the dark. He cried when a duck bit him."

"A *duck* bit him?" Savannah hadn't said a word since the interview began, but that slipped out before she could stop it.

"Yes," Ethan told her. "He was feeding bread to some ducks in a park. One got rowdy and bit his finger. Beth told me he cried about it for ten minutes. Does that sound like a cold-blooded murderer to you?"

"Good point." Dirk scribbled something on his notepad, then put down the pen. "What else did you argue about?"

Ethan shrugged. "You know how marital spats go. They start off about one thing, then you wind up getting off on tangents that are irrelevant."

"Like your own infidelity?"

Savannah heard Ethan catch his breath, as though Dirk's question had punched him in the gut.

"I haven't been unfaithful to my wife. I have *not. Ever.*"

"That's not what I heard."

"Then you heard wrong."

"Your wife was overheard yelling at you about an affair you're having with Candace York."

Ethan sighed and nodded. "Oh. Okay. That's the problem with eavesdroppers. They only hear half of a conversation, and then they act like they know it all."

"I have it from a good source," Dirk said, "that your wife was upset because she had found out that you've been sockin' it to your old fiancée."

"Your 'good source' would have to be either Amy or Luciana, since they were the only ones in the house with us yesterday morning. They're both kind-hearted, well-meaning women, and I can see why you would believe either one of them. But seriously, truthfully, here's what happened. I found out about Beth and Neal. I confronted Beth. She got all defensive, as you might imagine, and she turned it back on me, accusing me of being with Candace. But it isn't true. It just isn't."

"How did you find out about Beth and Neal?" Dirk asked.

"I got an anonymous e-mail."

"Oh-h-h. An anonymous e-mail. Now there's a reliable source if ever I heard one."

"It had a picture attached." Ethan stared down at his hands, which were clenched tightly in his lap, and added, "An *explicit* picture."

"How do you know it was real?"

Ethan shot Dirk a look across the table that would have withered a lesser man. "I know what my wife looks like naked, Detective Coulter."

"How do you know the picture wasn't taken before you were married? Back when her and her ex were still together?"

"Because when our son was born, my wife had a cesarean section. The scar was clearly visible in the photo." His voice dropped, almost to a whisper, when he added, "Everything was clearly visible in that damned picture."

"I'm going to need to see that photo," Dirk told him. "I'm sorry but—"

"I know. I know. Our little Pilar is dead. There's no such thing as privacy anymore."

"Speaking of your little Pilar," Dirk said, watching his suspect closely, "you haven't asked me how she died."

"I was afraid to," Ethan replied. "I'm very fond of her . . . or, I *was*. I don't think I could stand it if I heard she suffered."

There was a long heavy silence, broken when Ethan finally asked, "Did she? Was it . . . bad?"

"Every killing is bad, Mr. Malloy," Dirk answered. "But we're waiting for the medical examiner's report to find out the particulars."

Dirk closed his notebook, stuck his pen in his jacket pocket, and stood.

Savannah thought he was about to end the interview and dismiss Ethan. But instead she saw him take his small camera from his coat's inside pocket.

"There's just one more thing I'd like you to do for me, Mr. Malloy," he said.

Instantly, Ethan seemed relieved. "Sure, Detective. What's that?"

"I'd like you to remove your shirt."

"What?"

"I'm pretty sure that you heard me, Mr. Malloy. I need you to take off your shirt."

"What is this, a stupid joke? You want a picture you can sell to the tabloids? Are you tired of being a cop and want to retire with a little nest egg to go along with your pension?"

Dirk gave him a level, unflinching glare and repeated quietly, "Take off your shirt, sir. Do it."

"Why?"

"Now."

His face turning nearly purple with fury, Ethan ripped off the T-shirt he was wearing with such violence that Savannah heard the fabric rip. He threw it onto the table.

There they were.

Her heart sank when she saw the scratches, multiple long, deep ones, crisscrossing the actor's broad chest. The marks she had seen earlier were only a small portion of the damage that had been done to him.

Evidence. As damning as she had ever seen.

Dirk turned on his camera, made a couple of adjustments, then held it up to his eye.

But before he could take the shot, Ethan Malloy struck a bodybuilder's pose, accentuating every muscle of that famous chest.

"There you go, Detective Coulter," Ethan said, his voice harsh, his words bitter. "Is that what you want? A flesh shot for your Facebook page?"

Savannah could see Dirk zooming in and knew he was taking close-ups of the scratches—one after another after another.

Finally, he was finished. He scrolled through the photos he had taken, nodded as though satisfied, turned off the camera, and stuck it back in his pocket.

In a manner far calmer than he usually exhibited, Dirk turned to Ethan and said, "Thank you, Mr. Malloy. You can put your shirt back on now."

Ethan snatched his T-shirt off the table and quickly climbed into it. "May I go now? Are you quite finished with me? Because if you are, I'm going to call my lawyer. Then I'm going to go search for my family before something horrible happens to them—if it hasn't already."

"No," Dirk replied. "I won't be releasing you."

Ethan's jaw dropped. "Are you kidding me? Why? I answered all your questions. I—"

"You had a big, nasty argument with your wife yesterday morning, and she hasn't been seen since. You have no alibi for the time when she went missing. You said yourself she's been messing around on you, and some reports say you've been fooling around on her. And to top it all off, you've got deep, long scratches all over your chest, and our victim has broken fingernails. Several of them. Do you really think I'm going to release you?"

Dirk turned to Savannah. "I think we're done here for the moment." He reached over and retrieved his baseball cap from the table.

"What does this mean then?" Ethan asked. "Am I under arrest? Do I need to call an attorney or something?"

"For the moment, you aren't under arrest. You're being detained," Dirk told him. "But if you keep giving me a hard time, you might get under arrest real quick. Just sit there for a while and cool your heels. I'm gonna send an officer in here to deal with you. I'd advise you to do what he says."

As Dirk and Savannah headed for the door, Ethan shouted, "Is this about the scratches? Because if that's what you're mostly concerned about, you don't have to be. I got these two days ago. I was injured on the set. Call my manager, Abel Orman. Ask him, and he'll tell you."

Savannah turned back to her client and saw a man at the end of his emotional tether. He was losing more and more of his sanity, hour by hour. If he was guilty, so be it, but at least for the moment, until proven otherwise, he was an innocent man whose family might be dead.

If she found out later that he had murdered his wife and child, she would hate him. Vehemently. But for now, he deserved whatever compassion she could give him.

She walked around the table and stood beside him, her hand on his shoulder. She could feel him shaking, and she couldn't help wondering what it would feel like to be in his situation—guilty or innocent.

"We'll call Abel, Ethan. We will. If your story checks out, I'm pretty sure Detective Coulter will release you. But either way, our priority right now is finding Beth and Freddy. That's what all of this is about—finding them and the person who killed Pilar. That's what you want more than anything, too. Right?"

She saw his eyes grow moist once again as he nodded and said, "Yes. That's what I want. That's *all* I want. Just do it, please."

"We will."

She squeezed his shoulder, gave it a pat, then left him and joined Dirk beside the door. Together, they exited the room as quickly as possible.

Once outside, she drew a deep breath and said, "He didn't do it."

At the same moment, Dirk said, "He did it."

They looked at each other, both shocked. They usually agreed on such things.

"Reckon we've got a difference of opinion," she said, suddenly feeling exhausted.

"Yep," he admitted. "We sure do."

Chapter 10

When Savannah and Dirk exited the rear door of the police station house, they saw several cops milling about a squad car with a crumpled fender.

"The chief's gonna be thrilled about that," Dirk said. "That's the third unit wrecked this month."

"I feel plum awful about that." She tried to squelch a snicker and failed. "You know how close that man and I are, how dearly we love each other. I hate the thought of him suffering."

"Yeah, right. If he was drownin', you'd toss him an anchor."

"And a set of five hundred pound barbells, just to make sure all that hot air didn't keep him afloat."

"Let's go sit in your car," Dirk suggested, "and make our calls there. I don't wanna be answering no questions about the famous movie star we've got behind bars."

"Detained."

"Whatever."

They cut a wide circuit around the bevy of boisterous cops, who were too busy teasing and tormenting their fellow peace officer, commenting on every wrinkle in his newly crunched fender, to notice them pass by.

Once they were inside the Mustang—Savannah in the driver seat and Dirk riding shotgun—he tossed his beloved baseball cap onto the floorboard and reached into the glove box for his ever-present plastic sandwich bag filled with cinnamon sticks.

Since the day he had failed to chase down a perp who was more fleet of foot than himself and a non-smoker, Dirk had thrown away his cigarettes and gone cold turkey.

But, not inclined to do anything halfway, he was now a hard-core, three-pack-a-day cinnamon stick sucker.

As he poked the end of one into his mouth, Savannah grinned and said, "I love being married to a former smoker—except for when I'm trying to cut back on my sweets."

"You've cut back on your sweets?"

"I have. A few times. It didn't work long."

"What's you flunking out of dieting got to do with anything?"

"'Cause when you've been sucking on a cinnamon stick, and I kiss you, it makes me hungry for apple pie."

He smiled, his eyes lingering on her lips in a way that set her girly parts a'tingling. But she knew better than to expect anything more with half a dozen of his compatriots in the same parking lot—guys for whom mocking and humiliating one another was a life calling.

They both reached for their cell phones at the same moment, then paused and looked at each other.

"Duh," she said. "We should've asked him for his manager's phone number."

"Yeah. I mean, I thought you had it."

"You did not. You forgot, too."

"By then he was all mad at me for asking him to take his shirt off. I didn't want to rile him up any more than he already was, so—"

"Oh, bull pucky. You forgot. I'll call Tammy. She can get it for us."

"Isn't she visiting with her parents?"

"Yes. But something tells me she'll welcome the interruption. I talked to Waycross on the way over here, and I got the idea it's not going well at all."

"That's too bad. Tammy and Waycross are both great kids."

Savannah totally agreed, but Tammy had already answered her phone.

"Hi, Savannah," she said sounding overly bright, far too thrilled, and pretty darned close to breaking into hysterical sobs. "What's going on? Anything new on the case? Anything I can do to help?"

Yes, Savannah thought. *Our Tamitha is in desperate need of a distraction.*

"As a matter of fact, we really need you to work a bit of your research magic for us. If you aren't too busy, that is. I know you have your folks there, and with the baby and all I'm reluctant to ask you to—"

"No, no, no! It's no problem at all. I already told my parents that we have a very important case

right now, and that I might need to work on it with
you. Anything you need, just ask."

Ah, Tammy, Savannah thought, reaching out to
her young friend with her heart and giving her a
hug from afar. *Don't let 'em get to you like this, darlin'.*

"That's great. We need the phone number of
Ethan Malloy's manager, Abel Orman. I think I
heard he lives in San Paulo."

"The manager, huh? Is he, like, your main suspect right now?"

"No. As a matter of fact our main suspect at the
moment is Ethan Malloy."

"Get out! No way! But he seemed so nice in *The
Great Gatsby.*"

Savannah smiled. She'd never known a person
who was quite like Tammy. A golden girl bimbo
one moment, and a computer genius extraordi-
naire the next.

"Do you remember I told you that Pilar had
some broken fingernails, like maybe she had
scratched her attacker?"

"Sure, I remember. That's so sad."

"It is. And guess whose chest is all scratched up?"

"No way! How could the priest who helped that
nun rescue all those orphans do something like
that?"

Savannah had to search her memory banks
awhile before accessing that reference. Last year
Ethan Malloy had starred in *Into the Sunset,* a movie
that had garnered him a Golden Globe award,
and, apparently, the undying trust and respect of
one adoring fan, Tammy Hart.

"He says he got the scratches in an accident on a
set a couple of days ago," Savannah told her. "He

wants us to check it out with his manager. Says Orman will verify it for him."

"Of course, it's a bunch of crap," Dirk mumbled around his cinnamon stick, "but God forbid we don't check it out."

"I'll get right on it," Tammy said. "If there's anything else—"

"I won't hesitate to ask," Savannah assured her. "Thanks, sugar. I don't know what we'd do without you."

"Don't worry about having to 'do without' me, Savannah," Tammy replied with a strength of conviction that Savannah seldom heard in her young friend's voice. "You won't *ever* be without me. The work we do . . . it's too important."

Savannah swallowed hard. "Yes, you're right. It is. Thank you, Tammy. We love you, darlin'."

Savannah heard her catch her breath and then whisper, "You too."

When she hung up a moment later Savannah turned to Dirk with a sinking heart. "Her parents are trying to pull her away from us," she told him. "They're doing everything they can to get her away from here, away from me, and from you and the rest of her Moonlight Magnolia friends. Worst of all, they're trying to get her away from Waycross."

"How can you tell?"

"I just know. I heard it in her voice just now. She's fighting for her life—her life here with us. I thought they were coming to California to see their new grandchild and meet their son-in-law. But they're here to get Tammy, to take her back to New York with them."

Dirk reached over and ran his fingers through the curls at the nape of her neck. "Don't worry, babe. It won't happen. She's stronger than that."

"I hope so."

Tammy was fast. When it came to research—tracking down a bad guy, hacking into his bank account, discovering his dirty secrets through social media, and finding out when he had last changed his socks—nobody did it quicker or better than she.

Only four minutes had passed when Savannah's phone jingled with the merry little tune she had chosen for her sunny-natured, best friend/assistant.

"I've got it," Tammy announced proudly. "Abel Orman's phone number, his address, home *and* business, and his bookie's phone number, too. He gambles too much and cheats at cards."

"Why, thank you, Miss Tamitha," Savannah said with a chuckle. "You've been busier than a cranberry picker before Thanksgiving."

Savannah motioned to Dirk to get out his notebook and pen. "Okay. What's Orman's phone number?"

Tammy rattled off the number, and Savannah repeated it for Dirk.

When Dirk had finished writing it, Tammy said, "You can call him if you want to. But I can tell you right now that Mr. Malloy was telling you the truth about that accident."

Savannah sat upright in her seat, at full attention. "How do you know that?"

Tammy laughed. "You were just telling me a few minutes ago how good I am at what I do."

"That's true. Why should I be surprised?"

Savannah glanced over to Dirk and thought how much fun it was going to be in a couple of minutes when she could tell him he was wrong about Ethan and she was right.

In that instant, life was rich and worth the hassle.

"Actually," Tammy said, "I didn't have to use my Super Duper Sleuther skills. I just googled 'Ethan Malloy' and 'accident on set' and checked for postings within the last three days, and I found several. They were filming the last scene in his latest movie. It's this romantic, sort of cowboy flick, set in Australia—but they filmed it up there in the hills above Simi Valley—about a girl who's falsely convicted of a murder, and she's set to hang for it the very next morning, so during the night she escapes, but now she's out in the desert with no horse and no water, and she's about to die when Ethan Malloy rides up on this big black horse and scoops her into his arms, but they fell off."

Savannah's mind was spinning, but she managed to say, "The horse?"

"No, the horse was okay. It was Ethan and the actress that fell off into some sagebrush and got scratched up. Her not so much. Like a real hero, he kinda pushed her out of the way, and took the worst of it himself. Isn't that romantic?"

"I'm getting hot and bothered just thinking about it." Savannah saw Dirk giving her a funny look, which made her all the more eager to tell him how mistaken he had been about her new client.

She wouldn't bother to mention that, just a little more than an hour ago, she'd been pretty convinced that he was a killer, too.

"They had to take him to the hospital and everything," Tammy was telling her. "It's documented. I checked."

"You're thorough, kiddo. I'll give you that. You've no idea how happy I am to hear this. Dirk's going to be thrilled, too."

Savannah winked at Dirk, and he scowled back at her. He had already heard enough of the conversation to sense the way the wind was blowing. Not his direction.

"I'm glad I could help, Savannah," Tammy told her, her heart in her voice. "I really am. Waycross told me that you guys might be able to join us for dinner at the restaurant tonight."

Savannah felt the familiar tug of torn loyalties. Her client on one side. Her precious friend on the other. Both of them in need of her.

"We'll try as hard as we can to get there, sugar," she told her. "You know we're eager to meet your folks and get to know them. Everyone who's important to you is important to us."

"That's what makes us family," Savannah heard Tammy say, though she had the feeling Tammy might be saying it to someone else, someone other than her.

Maybe she was speaking to her own heart.

"It sure does, sugar," she told her young friend. "Some family we're born with. Some we adopt along the way. But they're all precious. Every one of them."

"That's right. So, you call me if you need me again."

"I sure will."

Savannah ended the call and turned to Dirk. "You've gotta get in that station house and de-detain Ethan Malloy before he gets ahold of his attorney and sues you for false arrest and—"

"Detainment."

"Whatever."

They bailed out of the Mustang and hurried across the parking lot toward the rear door of the building.

"I can just see it now," Savannah mused. "The two of you in court. Him suing you for three million dollars. Him winning because the jury's all female."

"Three million bucks? For fifteen minutes' worth of false arrest?"

"Nope. For forcing him to strip and pose for dirty pictures."

Savannah and Dirk found Ethan Malloy exactly where they had left him, still sitting in the interrogation "sweat box."

But he was hardly "sweating."

Three of San Carmelita's finest station house personnel sat at the table with him: Susie Blaylock, who usually worked the switchboard, but appeared to be taking a break; Kim Johnson from Records; and Patrolman Sherry Harralston.

They were sitting and staring at the actor, unabashedly goo-goo-eyed over him, as he sipped a can of soda. One of three on the table before him.

Next to the soft drinks was a tuna sandwich, obviously a personal sacrifice from somebody's lunch bag, along with a fruit-on-the-bottom strawberry yogurt, and some chocolate chip cookies.

The women were shameless, Savannah decided. What were they thinking?

The chocolate chip cookies were obviously store-bought. She would have offered him home-baked ones, warm from the oven, enhanced with macadamia nuts.

Ethan was the only one who didn't appear to be in a festive mood. He was sullen and tense, gripping the can so hard that Savannah half expected the soda to shoot out the top at any moment.

"What the hell's going on in here?" Dirk demanded, taking in the finer points of the situation. "Susie, go answer the damned phones. Kim, go record something. And Sherry, get your butt out there on the street and patrol, make the world a safer place."

"I'll have you know, Sergeant Coulter, that I *and* my butt are off duty," Sherry replied indignantly.

"Then go home and annoy your husband," he barked. "You'd think you gals were thirteen and never saw a man before."

The disappointed and moderately mortified threesome stood, nearly knocking over their chairs in their haste, and hurried out the door. Dirk slammed it behind them and turned to his detainee.

But before he could speak, Ethan jumped to his feet and said, "Well? Did you call my manager? Are you ready to apologize for holding me here in this . . . ?" He glanced around the tiny room with its gray padded walls and austere metal furniture. ". . . this suffocating broom closet on a day when I need to be out searching for my wife and son or at home waiting for her call?"

Dirk glowered at him and for a moment, Savannah cringed, expecting the worst. Her husband had many skills. The art of delivering a gracious and sincere apology was not among them.

For more than a decade, she had attempted to explain to him that a true expression of heartfelt remorse did not begin with the words, "Well, hell, I'm sorry if that teeny, itty-bitty thing I said got you al-l-l pissed off but . . ."

So, she was both surprised and proud of him when, in a calm and conciliatory tone, he said, "I apologize, Mr. Malloy. Whether you believe it or not, I understand that now's an awful time for you, and the last thing you need is for me to make it worse for you."

But Ethan Malloy wasn't ready to make peace just yet. He walked around the table, straight to Dirk, and leaned forward, well into his personal space.

The two men were nose to nose.

Savannah saw Dirk clench his fists. For a moment, she considered the possibility that she might have to rescue her husband from her larger, younger, overly muscular client.

It had been a long time since she had laid hands on someone who was paying her bills. But she hadn't forgotten how. She figured she could do it again in a pinch.

"Do *not* pretend that you know how I feel right now," Ethan said, his deep voice low and menacing. "If, God forbid, your wife goes missing someday, *then* you'll understand." He turned to Savannah and in a softer tone said, "I'm not wishing anything bad on you, ma'am. Truly. I'm just trying to make my point."

"I think your point's been made, Mr. Malloy," she said softly.

"I don't need your understanding," Ethan said, turning back to Dirk. "I need you to find my wife. I need you to find my baby boy."

His big body began to shake, and for a moment, Savannah thought he was going to burst into tears or start screaming in rage. But he did neither. He fought for control and gained it. "I should apologize to you, too. I wasn't as forthcoming there at first as I should have been. Not with either one of you, and that was a waste of time. Time that we don't have to waste." He drew a deep breath. "I'll tell you anything you want. All of it. Just ask."

"Good." Savannah walked over and stood next to him. "Start with giving me the phone number and address of your wife's ex . . . the guy who cried when the duck bit him."

"But I told you that he—"

"I know what you told me," Savannah said. "But I can tell you that when a woman goes missing it's almost always at the hands of some dude who, at one time or another, held her in his arms and told her that he loved her more than life itself. It's almost always an ex-husband or former boyfriend.

Or whatever guy she was involved with on the day she died."

Ethan appeared thoughtful, then somber. "That's awful. That's about as wrong as it gets."

"Yeah." She sighed and shook her head. "Tell me about it."

Chapter 11

"Once you're on your way home, I'm going to check in with my assistant and before the day is over I'll talk to Ryan and John. I know they'll want to help, too. I don't want you to think that my husband and I are the only ones working on your case," Savannah told Ethan as she drove her Mustang into her driveway, parked next to his pickup, and turned off her ignition. "Then I'll return to your house, later this afternoon. I need to talk to Amy and Luciana, see if they can tell me anything new."

"I doubt they can," Ethan told her as he took off her sunglasses and laid them carefully on the dash. "They aren't nosy by nature, either of them. They mind their own business, and let you mind yours."

Savannah stifled a grin. Ethan didn't know much about women if he thought they weren't curious about other people's affairs. Men either, for that matter.

Human beings were nosy by nature.

When it came right down to it, who on earth wouldn't rather mind somebody else's business than their own?

"Nevertheless," Savannah said, "I need to speak to them. Nobody knows a person better than the one who spends hours and hours inside their home."

"That's probably true. If you think it'll help, Savannah, then by all means, come by."

He winced as he rubbed the back of his neck. She had seen him do the same thing numerous times during the day. She could only imagine the tense muscles and resulting headache he must have.

"I was going to ask your husband something," he said, "but then I got mad at him and forgot."

"Happens to me all the time. What was it?"

"Has he considered putting an APB out on my wife's car? I drove around yesterday afternoon, searching in all her favorite haunts: stores, restaurants, beaches, parks, and play areas where she takes Freddy, but of course, I didn't find her. I was thinking that if the police were all hunting for her . . ."

"What parks did you go to, Ethan?" Savannah stared out her side window so she wouldn't have to look at him when she asked the question.

"Oh, you know. The usual. Paradise Cove, Zuma, El Matador. Then I came up here to San Carmelita and checked out Harbor Cove, Mission Park, and Oak Grove."

Savannah could have sworn that her heart skipped a couple of beats. For a second, she thought she might have to jumpstart it to get it going again.

"Oak Grove?" she said, as casually and even-toned as she could manage. "You told me that you knew the park, that your family went there a lot. But I don't recall you telling me that you'd gone there yesterday trying to find Beth, Pilar, and Freddy."

He shrugged. "It was one of many stops."

"What time were you there?"

"I don't remember for sure. I wasn't really watching the clock. It's hard to keep track of time when you're driving around all over God's creation, worrying yourself sick."

"When you were there, did you drive all the way to the end of the canyon, where the road ends and the foothills and hiking trails begin?"

"Yes. When I got to the end and turned around, that's when I stopped for a minute and texted Beth again. I remember I told her where I was, and I asked her where she was."

"Do me a favor," Savannah told him. "Get out your phone and see exactly what time it was when you sent that text."

"Why?"

"Please, just do it."

He seemed a little worried and maybe even a bit suspicious, but he did as she asked.

A moment later, he shoved the phone under her nose and pointed to that particular text.

She could see that it had been sent at 2:33 in the afternoon. The content was exactly as he had described it: **I'm here at Oak Grove, looking for you. Call me, Beth. Please call me. We can work this out.**

"Why do you care what time I was there?" he asked Savannah. "Is it because that's where Pilar's body was found?"

She saw him shudder. Then he added, "Would I have seen her body from the road? Do you think she was already there, dead? Are you telling me that she was lying there, hurt or dying or dead, and I was just a few feet away? If I'd known, maybe I could've even helped her, but I—"

"No. I don't think it had happened yet."

"Where was she? Where did she die?"

"Down one of the trails, in a stand of oaks. You wouldn't have seen her from the road."

"Then why are you asking me these questions? How do you know it hadn't happened yet if I couldn't have seen her body from my truck?"

She turned to face him and gave him a sympathetic smile. "Because you would've seen the car."

"What car?"

"The white Porsche. Your wife's car. When we found Pilar, it was parked right there in the lot. Toward the end of the road, where the hiking trails begin. You were looking for your family and your friend, for your wife's car. You wouldn't have missed it."

Savannah watched Ethan Malloy's face as what she had told him sank into his consciousness, as the implication contained in her words took hold of his mind and heart.

The silence between them grew thick and heavy. The only sound she was aware of was his breathing—rapid, hard, and ragged.

Finally, he said, "So, what you're telling me is, my wife and child were present when our sweet little friend was murdered?"

"We don't know anything yet for sure, Ethan. But I'd have to say it's possible. I'm so sorry."

Savannah watched her client's face turn as pale as his missing wife's white Porsche.

Once Savannah had Ethan on his way home, she walked into the house, her head down and her heart even lower. She liked to think that with each encounter, she left her clients better than she found them.

So far with Ethan Malloy, she had done the exactly the opposite.

Not good, old girl, she told herself as she unlocked the front door. *You better turn this thing around quick, before things go from horrific to . . . Well, whatever's worse than horrific.*

As soon as she stepped inside, she realized she wasn't alone in the house. While arriving home to find someone there was hardly unusual, what with the Moonlight Magnolia gang coming and going at will, this was different.

Standing in her foyer, Savannah could hear an unfamiliar voice in from her living room, a woman's voice—a woman with an unusual accent that she seldom heard except in movies or on television.

Usually, they were shows set in New Jersey or New York and were about gangsters fitting other bad guys with cement shoes or adorning them with anchor-and-chain necklaces, then dumping them over the sides of ill-gotten luxury yachts.

"I wouldn't waste a dollar in a mall like that," the woman was saying most emphatically in her decidedly "Yankee" accent, dropping *r*'s and adding *w*'s everywhere. Savannah had never heard the like.

"For gawd's sake, you people have a lotta nerve even calling that ridiculous place a mall."

"Mother, please," Savannah heard Tammy reply. "I realize it isn't Fifth Avenue—"

"Fifth Avenue? I've seen better shops in the Village, or even the Bronx."

"Oh, Mother, you've never shopped in the Bronx. Not once in your life."

"I'd rather see you shopping in the Bronx, or anywhere else on the Eastern Seaboard than in this gawdforsaken place."

"I like it here" was Tammy's soft, humble response.

"How can you? The weather is boring with no seasons to speak of. The people here are stupid and shallow. You can't have a decent, intelligent conversation with any of them, because they're—"

"I love them! Mother, you're talking about people I love very much! Please, don't speak of them that way. It hurts me to hear it."

"Yeah? Well, if the truth hurts, that's just too bad. You know I'm right."

As Savannah put her purse on the table near the door, she heard little Vanna Rose start to whimper, then cry.

"Oh, no," she heard Tammy say. "Now we've made the baby cry with our arguing."

"We're just talking. That's all. She's far too nervous, that baby. You're obviously coddling her way too much. The world's a tough place, and you have to prepare children for it. They need a little steel in their backbones."

That was it. Savannah had heard enough. She

reached over, reopened the front door, and slammed it closed again.

Clearing her throat far too loudly, she strode into her living room, ready to do battle on behalf of her friend and her precious namesake, if necessary.

Maybe even if it wasn't necessary. Maybe just for the hell of it, because she felt like it. Listening to bull pucky, not to mention bullying, had that effect on her.

Both Tammy and her guest looked startled to see Savannah's entrance. But little Vanna, who was sitting on Tammy's lap, stopped crying instantly. A smile lit her face, and she held out her chubby baby arms to her aunt.

Savannah wasted no time, but hurried across the room to the desk chair where Tammy was sitting and scooped the child into her arms.

"How's my beautiful girl?" she said, kissing first one soft, round cheek, then the other.

Finally, reluctantly, she turned to the woman sitting on the sofa. "You must be Dr. Lenora Hart." She tried to keep the sarcastic tone out of her voice, but only half succeeded.

Savannah watched as Tammy's mother gave her a slow, evaluating perusal, from head to toe.

Or more accurately, from wind bedraggled curls to scruffy, dusty loafers.

Hiking through the foothills, kneeling on the ground, and spending much of the morning in the sun and wind hadn't done a lot for her appearance.

Although Lenora's gaze had lingered momentarily on the large and elegant engagement ring and wedding band that Dirk had given her—without a doubt, the largest purchase of his lifetime thus far—the doctor's overall perusal of Savannah tip to stern had been critical and disapproving.

Savannah knew she hadn't passed muster.

But then, she hadn't expected to.

"And you," Lenora said, her voice virtually oozing with contempt, "must be the Great and Powerful Savannah Reid herself. You're exactly as I imagined you. I would have known you anywhere."

In her peripheral vision, Savannah saw Tammy cringe and place one hand over her mouth.

Making certain that her own voice contained an equal amount of contemptuous ooze, Savannah replied, "Well, imagine that. And me without my blue tights, red cape, and brassiere made of gas can funnels."

Having scored one for the home team, Savannah took a moment to give Dr. Lenora tit-for-tat— the same of obnoxious, all-too-female once-over she had received.

Unfortunately, it was hard to find anything to criticize.

The woman was lovely, the image of her daughter, plus a few years that had obviously been gentle to her.

Though she lacked Tammy's tan, her skin was smooth and creamy. If she'd had any "work" done by any of those world-famous plastic surgeons on Madison Avenue, they'd done a good job.

Her hair was as shiny and golden as Tammy's lush locks, with just the right amount of gray at the temples, bespeaking worldly wisdom. It was short

and straight, a bit more masculine than any Southern belle would have worn, but Savannah had to
admit it was a stylish and sophisticated cut.

By down-in-Dixie standards, Lenora could have
used a tad more eye shadow and a little more color
on her cheeks, but overall, her makeup was taste-
ful and natural.

Her ivory silk shirt and matching wool slacks, although not overly practical for a typical day at the
beach in sunny California, were as elegant and
fashionable as her small gold hoop earrings. From
a dainty chain around her neck dangled a solitaire
diamond pendant that was far too large to be real.
Except that it probably was.

Savannah had to admit, overall, the woman was
beautiful.

Dr. Lenora Hart was perfect in every way that
counted when shopping Rodeo Drive in Beverly
Hills or the Triangle d'Or in Paris or enjoying a
Manhattan lunch at the Plaza's Palm Court.

Too bad she's a nasty bitch, Savannah thought.

Of course, Granny Reid hadn't raised her to
think such things about her fellow women. Her
grandmother had taught her that, while appearances were vitally important, and a woman should
"Do all ya can with what the good Lord gave ya,"
having a sterling character was essential.

Big, fluffy hair and lash-extending mascara were
extremely important to any true lady, but every
Southern woman was taught that her words should
be soft and kind, indicative of a gentle spirit, even
when she had raccoon eyes and hair as flat as a flit-
ter.

The words "Pretty is, as pretty does" had been

spoken many times in Granny's household with
seven granddaughters.

As usual, Granny's sage advice came to the fore,
even in times of extreme provocation. Savannah
pasted her very best fake smile across her mouth
and said, "Welcome to California, Dr. Hart. We've
all been looking forward to having you and your
husband pay us a visit. It's lovely to finally meet
you."

At first, Tammy's mother said nothing at all. She
just sat there. When she finally did offer a reply, it
was a simple, unpleasant "O-o-okay."

Lenora Hart's eyes locked with Savannah's for a
long time, and it was all too obvious to Savannah
that, once again, she was being evaluated, but in a
whole new way. Like before, she was failing the
test.

In the course of Savannah's life, she had met numerous people from the Northeastern Seaboard.
Some she liked, and some she didn't. As with any
group or classification of human beings, they var-
ied from fantastic, to so-so, to loathsome, with
most flopping back and forth from day to day and
moment to moment.

But the one thing she had observed about folks
from New England and the mid-Atlantic states, the
characteristic they all seemed to have in common
was: they knew a bullshitter when they saw one.

A Southerner might give you the benefit of the
doubt, and a Californian might decide that they
had simply heard you wrong. But East Coasters had
a nose for manure. They could smell a fertilizer
pile, even a small one, from fifty miles away, and
they had no patience or respect for someone who

spread it. As far as they were concerned, everyone should speak their minds as plainly and bluntly as they did.

No sooner was Savannah's little welcoming speech over than Lenora gave her an ugly sneer that told her she saw right through her hypocrisy, her fake-kindness. Rather than give her extra points for attempted civility, Dr. Lenora Hart considered her a coward and thought less of her for it.

That's all right, Savannah told herself. If it weren't for Tammy, she wouldn't have given this woman a moment of her time. If Lenora weren't her best friend's mother, Savannah wouldn't have bothered with kindness—fake or otherwise.

Life was too short to mess with mean people.

But unfortunately, sometimes you have to, she reminded herself. Mean people weren't wise, but they were usually smart, cunning enough to know the value of a hostage.

Their message was all too clear: *Do what I want, or I'll hurt the people closest to your heart.*

Even a superheroine with a cool red cape, blue tights, and a tin brassiere couldn't win in a fight like that.

So, Savannah used the one tactic she had found that worked in this situation. Sometimes.

She ignored the woman.

Turning her back to Lenora Hart, Savannah crossed the room to stand beside Tammy at the desk.

Instantly, her friend pulled an extra chair close to hers and motioned for Savannah to sit next to her.

Savannah did, juggling the squirmy little redhead in her arms. Once settled, she turned to her

assistant and gave her a supportive "don't let her
get you down, kid" smile.

Tammy returned it, but barely.

"I was glad to come home and find you here,"
Savannah told her, loud enough that Lenora
could hear every word. "The clock is ticking, and
I'm really getting worried about Beth and the
baby."

"Me too. Every time I look at Vanna, I think
about Freddy and I want to cry."

Savannah kissed the top of the child's head and
briefly wondered what on earth could be softer
than a baby's hair. Then she pulled her mind back
to the work at hand.

"I appreciate you finding out about that accident
that Ethan had on the set. Especially as quickly as
you did. It saved us from making a fool of ourselves
and a lifelong enemy of Ethan Malloy."

"No problem. I'm glad it worked out. I would
have felt terrible if it had been him that hurt his
own family."

"Me too. But he was the only real suspect we had.
As glad as we all were that there was an innocent
explanation for the injuries on his chest, we're still
back to square one with no viable suspect."

Savannah was about to suggest that Tammy run
a check on Neal Irwin, but before she could even
get the words out, Tammy shoved a report binder
into her hands.

The view cover was even decorated with a photo
of the guy in question. It wasn't a particularly attractive picture. In fact, it was a mug shot.

Savannah couldn't help chuckling at her friend's
sometimes perverse sense of humor.

Glancing over the unflattering picture, the subject's hair standing on end, a deeply disgruntled expression on his bruised, puffy face, the blood clearly visible on the collar of his white shirt, she was impressed. Not to mention, a bit confused.

"Wow," she said. "Looks like he got in a lot of trouble, for a guy who cries over a duck bite."

Tammy snickered, and lowered her voice, as though she didn't want her mother to hear her. "He got caught in bed with some lady. The husband wasn't happy."

From behind her, Savannah could hear Lenora mumbling to herself—but loudly enough to make certain she and Tammy could hear her. "This is what you private detectives do for living? You rake up the muck of people's lives and then wallow in it? They pay you money to do this?"

Savannah turned in her chair and addressed her accuser in a calm, almost humorous tone. "Amazing, isn't it? And to think I wanted to be a go-go dancer or cowgirl and miss out on all this fun."

"I think it's a despicable way to make a living."

"Then it's a darned good thing that you aren't the one doing it, huh?" Just for good measure she added, "If they hadn't had muck in their lives, we wouldn't have found anything to rake. Like when your mom told you to make sure your underwear was clean in case you ever got in an accident. Same principle."

Tammy snickered, covering her face with her hand.

"It's still a dark, dreary way to make a living," Lenora insisted.

"Yes, it is. But when someone's hurt or missing, somebody has to find out who hurt them or took them. It isn't easy. In fact, it's awful sometimes. But someone has to do it."

"And that's us," Tammy chimed in.

Lenora's face settled into a scowl, and it occurred to Savannah that she appeared far less pretty and perfect than she had at first glance.

Savannah turned back to Tammy and said, "Where were we?"

"Discussing Neal Irwin's infidelities and the angry husband who roughed him up."

"Oh, yes. That's right. But you really can't blame the hubby. Most spouses are a mite grumpy under those circumstances. It appears Crybaby Neal got the worst of the fight. Why did he get arrested? Last time I checked, adultery wasn't illegal in the state of California. Bad taste, but not against the law."

"Apparently, he made 'terrorist threats.' "

"*Terrorists?*" Lenora seemed to feel the need to weigh in on this topic, too. "You people deal with *terrorists*? Normal, run-of-the-mill criminals aren't enough for you?"

Tammy sighed and turned to her mother. "According to California Penal Code Section 422, a terrorist threat or a criminal threat is one that threatens to 'commit a crime which will result in death or great bodily injury to another person.' "

Lenora ignored the recitation, but Tammy glowed, nonetheless, when Savannah said, "Well done, Miss Tamitha."

Savannah thumbed through the folder. "What threat did he make, exactly?"

"Apparently, the woman started apologizing profusely to her husband and telling him that she loved him and Neal was just a stupid fling and meant nothing to her. The couple hugged and kissed and made up on the spot, right there in front of him. He took offense and threatened to burn their house down over their heads."

Tammy nodded toward the folder. "There's actually more than one story like that in there."

Scanning the contents, Savannah said, "Wow! I'm surprised the duck got away unscathed."

"Check out page four."

"No way. He hurt an animal? I hate him."

"He went back to the pond and fed the poor thing a jalapeño pepper. Some kids saw him do it and reported him to the park ranger. He pled down to 'misdemeanor harassment of an animal.' They threw out the torture charge and he got community service. Had to pick up garbage around the pond for a month."

"That's it. If there's one thing I can't abide, it's animal abuse. That tallywhacker gets moved right to the top of my suspect list."

Tammy grinned and nudged her. "The suspect list that had nobody else on it."

"The very one."

Chapter 12

When Savannah drove the Mustang up the narrow, curving Malibu road later that afternoon, she felt as though it had been days, rather than hours, since she had first visited the stone castle on the hill.

She was exhausted and hungry and regretted her decision to skip lunch. Although she'd tried to convince her stomach that cinnamon rolls and Gran's apple pie à la mode were a pretty darned good lunch, it rumbled and grumbled its disagreement.

But as she approached the grand mansion on the mountain crest, she couldn't help feeling desperately sorry for the woman who, until yesterday, had lived there in a high standard of luxury that few people in the world would ever be able to enjoy.

How quickly things can change, Savannah thought. Granny Reid often said, "In life, bad changes can happen in an instant. Good changes seem to take a lot more time and work. Life's unfair that way."

Now, even those closest to Beth wondered what sort of life she was living or if, indeed, she was living at all.

What was a missed toasted cheese sandwich and a bowl of tomato soup if she could find that woman and her child and return them to their beautiful home and the arms of their worried loved ones?

Just as Savannah had reached the chateau and was pulling into its cobblestone driveway, the car's new speakerphone jingled and announced that Dirk was calling. She jumped, startled, as she had many times, at having an unexpected voice suddenly manifest in her vehicle. No doubt, someday, she would grow accustomed to it. But not on a day when she was feeling as stressed as she was at the present.

"Answer," she told it.

A moment later, her husband's husky voice filled the interior of the Mustang. "Hi, babe. Where are you?"

"The Malloy mansion. John wasn't kidding about this place. You really have to see it. I'm telling you, it's got everything but the alligator-infested moat."

"Are you gonna squeeze that Amy gal and the maid?"

"Probably not. Thought I'd leave the squeezing up to you. You're better at it. I'll just chat them up, gain their trust, then see if I can get them to spill something good."

"Pansy."

"Honey catches more flies than vinegar."

"Yeah. But they're *flies*."

"Anyway, that's where I am. Where are you?"

"I just blew an hour and change getting a judge to approve a warrant for me to get Beth Malloy's phone records. It took me forever to convince him that she really is missing, her and her kid, and that those records are relevant and material to my investigation."

"Judges. They just don't 'squeeze' as easily as other folks do. I think that robe they wear goes to their head. Or maybe it's the gavel."

"If I had a gavel, I could rule the world."

"You could hammer in the morning," she sang. *"Or you could hammer in the evening. All over this—"*

"Yeah, yeah. Call me as soon as you get out of there."

"I will. And if you can find out where that reprobate Neal Irwin is, and if I get out of here soon enough, we can go shake him down."

"For murder?"

"We'll start with roughing him up for feeding a jalapeño to a poor, unsuspecting duck, and see where it goes from there."

"Ah, something to look forward to. Love ya."

"You too."

She ended the call, turned off the car, got out, and walked up to the big arched doorway that she was beginning to know all too well.

Before she even had time to use the big bear knocker, the door swung open. This time it was Amy there to greet her.

The young woman quickly ushered her into the massive foyer.

"Good afternoon, Ms. Reid," she said with a subdued smile. "Mr. Ethan told me you were coming. He asked me to take care of you, to cooperate with you in any way I could. Of course, I'd be glad to. Anything at all, if it would help us get Miss Beth and Freddy back."

"Thank you, Amy," Savannah said, glancing around. "Is your boss here?"

Amy nodded. "He is. But he's lying down. He didn't sleep at all last night, and I think it caught up with him about an hour ago. He said if you need him, he'd be glad to get up and talk to you."

"He and I have already talked quite a bit today," Savannah told her. "Mostly, I just need to speak with you two ladies. I only have a few questions. I'll try not to take too much of your time."

"Oh, don't worry about that. Anything for Miss Beth and our little Freddy." Amy's eyes filled with tears, but she tried to put on a gracious, hospitable air and said, "I made Mr. Ethan a nice, big ham and cheese sandwich for his lunch. But he was too upset to eat it. I'd hate for it to go to waste. Would you—?"

"I would simply love a nice, big ham and cheese sandwich. God bless your heart, darlin'. You must've read my mind."

Ten minutes later, Savannah was in heaven. Not actual paradise, but about as close as she had gotten so far in this lifetime.

She was comfortably seated on a cushy chaise lounge next to an infinity pool that overlooked the mountains of Malibu and its exquisite, sparkling coastline.

On her lap was a delicate porcelain plate with none other than an artist's rendition of the chateau itself and a graceful 𝕸 scrolled in gold beneath it.

Atop that plate was simply the best ham sandwich she had ever eaten.

Amy had even added a sprig of fresh grapes and some potato chips on the side. On the table next to Savannah, she had set an icy glass of well-sweetened tea.

For the moment, life was well worth living.

Although it was difficult not to be distracted by the breathtaking view and the delectable edibles, Savannah forced her mind back to the critical business at hand.

Amy was sitting in a chair nearby, looking pretty in her sundress, but somehow tense and ill at ease. Her hands were folded demurely in her lap, but on closer inspection, Savannah could see that they were tightly clenched.

"What did you want to ask me about?" Amy asked.

Savannah got the distinct impression that she was eager to get this interview over with as soon as possible.

"I have a few questions about your employer, Miss Beth, as you call her."

"What kind of things do you want know?"

"Personal, sensitive things, I'm afraid," she told her. "Mr. Malloy assured me that you're a faithful, discreet employee. I'm sure that under normal circumstances you keep what you know about the family you serve confidential."

"I try to be. It's important when you have a job like mine. Your employers trust you to keep what you know about them to yourself."

"I'm sure that's true. But this is an extraordinary situation. It may be a matter, quite literally, of life and death. So, Amy, I need you to be completely open with me and try not to worry that you're betraying confidences. That sort of thing doesn't matter right now."

"I understand. Mr. Ethan already explained it to me. He told me that he made a mistake by not telling you everything when you questioned him earlier today. He told me not to make that same mistake, to answer everything you ask me and not to hold back anything at all."

Savannah nodded thoughtfully and set the half-eaten sandwich on the table next to her.

"Then I'm going to ask you one of the hardest questions first, because it may be one of the most important ones."

"Okay." She swallowed. "I'm ready."

"Has your employer, Beth, been having an affair with anyone?"

Amy thought, long and hard, before answering. "I'm not sure. Maybe."

It wasn't the conclusive answer Savannah had been hoping for. But at least, Amy appeared to be open and candid.

"What makes you think it's a possibility?" Savannah asked.

"Miss Beth gets lonely when Mr. Ethan's gone for long periods of time, working. She's still young. She's pretty. Men notice her everywhere she goes, and they flirt with her. She likes that. You can't really blame her. How could she not enjoy male attention?"

"Does she flirt back?"

"She does. I mean she's a classy lady. She's not real obvious about it. Just a little here and there."

"What makes you think she might be having an affair?"

"Sometimes, when Mr. Ethan is away, working on a movie, she asks Pilar to watch Freddy for her while she goes out in the evening."

"Is that unusual?"

"Kind of, because when Mr. Ethan is home, they never go out unless they take Freddy with them."

"Maybe she's spending time with her girlfriends, meeting them for drinks, some girl chat, whatever."

"Maybe. But once in a while, she's gone all night. And a few times, after one of those nights, someone sends her a bouquet of roses. I don't think her girl buddies would do that. Not red roses anyway."

Savannah nodded. "Yellow daisies, maybe. Red roses? Probably from a guy."

Savannah thought of Ethan and felt bad for him. He seemed to love his wife and child, to enjoy being a family man. She was sorry to think that the shadow of infidelity was darkening his door.

"If Miss Beth *is* having an affair, who might she be having it with?" she asked.

"I think it might be Mr. Irwin, her ex-husband."

"Is there any particular reason you think it could be him?"

"She calls him a lot, and they talk for a long time. When she's talking to him she sounds happy, like she used to with Mr. Ethan. She giggles and laughs and gets all excited about the things he says. She hasn't been that way with Mr. Ethan for a long time."

"It sounds like they're having problems in their marriage, apart from her interest in someone else, that is."

"They do have some issues that keep coming up over and over. They argue quite a bit about them."

"What kind of issues?"

Amy shrugged her thin shoulders and crossed her arms over her chest. "It's hard for Miss Beth to see her husband leaving, going off to film some great movie that she's not going to be part of. She was a really good actress, a popular one, when they met. She was more successful than he was back then. Miss Beth, the accomplished movie star, dating the unknown, but up and coming, handsome young actor . . . it was all pretty romantic stuff. The fans sure ate it up."

"I can imagine."

"Actors have to have strong egos, or they'd never make it in such a tough business," Amy said. "And Miss Beth has a strong sense of who she is. Or at least she used to. She hasn't gotten a good job for so long. And since Mr. Ethan won the Oscar, he gets new scripts every day. Good scripts, too. He has his choice of work, while she has none."

"That would be hard for anyone to deal with, I'm sure." Savannah told her. "Is there anyone else other than her ex-husband, Mr. Irwin, that she might be seeing?"

"Not that I can think of. But then, you never really know a person. Not even someone you live with. People are capable of just about anything, aren't they?"

Savannah sighed. "They sure are, sugar. You've got that right."

Amy reached for her own glass of something that looked like an herbal concoction, then toyed with it, running her fingertip around its frosty sides.

Savannah watched her closely. "Is there something else you want to tell me, Amy?" she asked.

"What if there was another person," Amy began carefully, "someone who's really crazy about Miss Beth and, you know, would like to get something going with her, but she's not interested? Would you want to know about that?"

A charge of energy hit Savannah's bloodstream, and it had nothing to do with the caffeine and sugar in her sweet tea. She sat up straight in her chair. "Absolutely."

"I don't want to accuse anybody of anything, because that would be wrong. But I—"

"Don't worry about it. If they didn't do anything wrong, they won't be in any trouble. Who is it? Who wants to get into Miss Beth's knickers, and she's not going for it?"

Amy giggled. "When you put it like that, probably a lot of people. Like I said, Miss Beth's very pretty, and she's nice . . . well . . . to most people most of the time."

"There's nothing wrong with that," Savannah told her emphatically. "'Most people, most of the time' is plenty good enough for anybody. I make a point of never trusting a person who's nice to everybody all the time. Who is it, Amy? Who's in love with Miss Beth?"

"Mr. Orman, Mr. Ethan's manager. He's nuts

about her. Lately, he's really been trying hard with her."

"Trying hard, how?"

"He's been hanging around here a lot more than he needs to, making up excuses to drop by and talk to her."

"Do you have any idea what he's talking to her about?"

Amy nodded. "I haven't been eavesdropping on them or anything like that."

"Of course not. You wouldn't do a thing like that. But a body can't help but overhear some things—"

"You really can't. I try, but . . ."

"What's he saying to her?"

"When Mr. Ethan's home, he just talks about the weather and stupid stuff like that. Or whatever job Mr. Ethan's working on at the moment."

"And when Mr. Ethan *isn't* home?"

"Then he changes his tune completely. He's like one of those little cartoon devils that sits on some-body's shoulder and whispers bad things in their ear. It's like he's trying to turn Miss Beth against her husband."

"What exactly does he say? Tell me his precise words, if you can remember them."

"Okay." Amy concentrated, nibbling on her lower lip, and closing her eyes for a moment. "Three days ago, he was over here. They were ac-tually sitting right here, where we are now. When I came out to ask Miss Beth about some party sup-plies that she wanted me to order, I heard him talking. I don't remember the exact words but this is pretty close. He said something like, 'Beth, you're a much better actor than Ethan will ever be. I could get you so much work, really good roles that you could sink your teeth into. But instead, you have to stay home and take care of the baby, while he's out there, building his career, enjoying more than his share of fame and attention. Especially from women. It's ridiculous how they throw themselves at him.' "

"Nice guy," Savannah said. "You're right. He is an evil influence, whispering crap like that in her ear. Talk about planting the seeds for marital dissension."

"He's got a temper, too."

"How do you know that?"

"He's usually all nicey-nicey when he's around Miss Beth and Mr. Ethan. But one time, I saw him in the formal garden, the one you could see this morning from the library windows."

"Yes, I recall. It's lovely."

"He was on the phone, talking to somebody, yelling at them. Apparently, he didn't like the way the conversation went, because as soon as he finished the call, he threw his phone into the rosebushes and swore like a crazy guy. He used words I haven't heard since my uncle Billy died."

"Uncle Billy had a potty mouth, huh?"

"The world's worst. Well, except for Mr. Orman. I'd say they're tied for the gold medal." She laughed. "You should have seen him after that, bending over, trying to get his phone out of those roses. He was cursing those poor flowers, like it was their fault, and stomping on them so hard that he ruined a Mr. Lincoln bush and a John F. Kennedy hybrid, not to mention his Jimmy Choos."

Savannah reached for the half-eaten sandwich, took one more bite, and washed it down with the remainder of the iced tea. "Best sandwich ever, darlin'," she told Amy as she stood, signaling the end of the interview.

"Thank you very much for this conversation, Amy," she said. "You've been a lot of help, and I appreciate it. I'm sure that Mr. and Mrs. Malloy would, too. You've done well by them."

Amy flushed a pretty pink and smiled, obviously grateful for the compliment and reassurance. "I'm glad. You're very welcome, and if there's anything else I can do . . ."

"Actually, there is one more thing. I have an assistant who's as good at her job as you are. Her specialty is Internet research. I know this is another one of those sensitive questions, but it would help her a lot if she could access Mrs. Malloy's social media pages. You wouldn't happen to know the passwords she uses for those, would you?"

Once again, Amy seemed very uncomfortable, and Savannah knew she had gone too far.

"Like I said before—ordinarily, I wouldn't ask you to violate her privacy. I wouldn't ask *anyone* to do such a thing. But this is an emergency."

"I understand. And I do know some of her passwords. But I feel like I need to ask Mr. Ethan first."

"Fair enough. You ask him and get his permission. But please, don't take too long. Time is of the essence and all that."

Amy gathered up the plate and glasses. "You're going to talk to Luciana now, right?"

"That was the plan, yes. If she's available."

"Oh, she's available all right. She really wants to

talk to you. She loved Pilar very much." Amy choked on her next words, "We all did."

As Savannah followed the young assistant back into the house, she thought of Abel Orman, stomping his employers' rosebushes into the ground and ruining his designer shoes.

She decided to readjust her suspect list.

She moved Orman's Post-it upward, to sit beside Neal Irwin's. Once again, Abel Orman was tied for second place, as he had been with Uncle Billy in the cursing competition.

A rosebush stomper and a duck abuser.

What an ugly pair they made.

Chapter 13

When Savannah and Amy reentered the mansion, and passed through the foyer, Savannah gave the massive bronze statue of Nidhogg the Terrible a wide berth.

She couldn't imagine that any woman would tolerate such a revolting thing in her house. Even worse, since the statue was supposed to represent a critter who chowed down on the corpses of those who had committed adultery, Savannah couldn't imagine that Beth enjoyed passing by him numerous times a day.

If a wife was, indeed, fooling around on her faithful, loving husband, she probably wouldn't appreciate a hideous, mythical dragon-creature reminding her of it every time she shuffled from the living room to the kitchen to grab a cup of coffee.

No sooner had Savannah thought of that particular faithful, loving husband, than she saw him coming down the curved staircase. His hair was wet, as though he had just taken a shower, and he wore a different pair of jeans and T-shirt than before.

But he still looked exhausted and as worried as any person she had ever seen.

He greeted her with a lukewarm smile and a quick nod as he continued down the stairs. "I see you've graced us with another visit today, as promised," he said.

There was a tinge of sarcasm in his tone, but Savannah didn't blame him. She and Dirk were the people who were supposed to be helping him the most at this terrible time. But they had squeezed him through a pretty tight ringer today. She didn't expect to be his favorite person. Or even his favorite private investigator, for that matter.

He glanced at Amy and saw the dishes she was carrying. Giving her a much warmer smile than he had offered to Savannah, he said, "I see that Amy has fed you."

"Yes, one of the best sandwiches I've ever had in my life."

"That's just one of the many kindnesses she does around here, making sure we don't starve to death or get too bogged down with the annoyances of everyday life," he said.

He walked over to Amy and took the dishes from her hands. "I'll deal with these. I'm going to the kitchen anyway." He turned to Savannah. "Are you finished with Amy?"

"I am," she assured him. "She was most helpful, very forthcoming. She helped me a lot."

"I'm glad to hear it, but not surprised. And I suppose you want to talk to Luciana next."

"If that's okay."

"It is with me. But I have to warn you she's not feeling well. She's really upset about what happened to Pilar. I gave her the rest of the day off. She's resting in the maid's quarters. Amy, could you show her?"

"I'd be happy to." She shot a quick glance at Savannah. "And then there's something I have to ask you, Mr. Ethan."

"Sure. When you're ready, I'll be in the library." To Savannah, he added, "When you're finished with Luciana, before you leave, I need a word with you."

"You've got it."

"Thank you. Tell Luciana I'm thinking of her."

"I will."

He left them, heading toward the kitchen, his head bowed, his shoulders slumped—the very picture of dejection.

"I feel so sorry for him," Amy said, echoing Savannah's exact thoughts. "Mr. Ethan is such a good man, an awesome husband and daddy. He doesn't deserve this."

"You're right. He doesn't. No one does. The problem is, we don't even know right now what 'this' is."

Amy's eyes searched hers. "Do you think there's a chance that she might just pull into the driveway any minute, say she's sorry, and give us some good explanation about what happened to Pilar?"

Savannah thought about the white Porsche, sitting in the CSI garage, every inch of it being fingerprinted, scrutinized, and vacuumed. No, she didn't think that Beth Malloy would be pulling it into the driveway any time soon, if ever again.

"We'll just have to wait and see," Savannah told her. "Now, where's the maid's quarters?"

She was surprised when Amy led her not to some designated part of the main house but out the front door and toward the rear of the property.

"Actually," Amy said, "she doesn't live in the maid's quarters. Pilar does—I mean, did. Miss Beth liked having the nanny inside the house at night, in case Freddy needed something, and Mr. Ethan wasn't here to take care of him."

"Mr. Malloy does his share of childcare then?"

"*More* than his share when he's home. Miss Beth likes her sleep, and she figures since he's gone so much of the time, it's the least he can do when he's here."

The longer Savannah listened to Amy, the more she realized that there were numerous troublesome issues in the Malloy marriage. She had seen couples split up for any one of those reasons, and lesser ones besides.

"So, where are you taking me?" Savannah asked as they passed the turret tower, rounded the corner of the house, and proceeded down a cobblestone path toward what Savannah was pretty sure had to be the garage.

Like the mansion, the building was stone and had a steeply pitched slate roof. Its three large doors were arched and its few windows mullioned, like those of the main house.

"She lives in there," Amy said, pointing to the building.

"They keep Luciana in the garage?"

Amy laughed. "No, of course not. She lives in the chauffeur's apartment. It's above the garage. It's actually much nicer than the maid's quarters, which were designed for a single woman. They're just a bedroom and bathroom."

"I'm afraid I'm not very well informed when it comes to this sort of thing. I haven't had a lot of servants in my day."

"Me either. But I was with Miss Beth when the real estate agent first showed her the place. He explained it all. How, long ago, when the house was built, people's maids weren't expected to be married or to have a family, but the chauffeur was. So, his apartment has a living room, kitchen, bathroom, and two bedrooms. It paid to be a guy back then. Now, too, for that matter."

"True. But then, we gals have a few advantages, a few tools of the trade, so to speak, that the guys don't have."

"If you say so."

"I do. Emphatically. Figure out what your tools are, girl, and how to use them to your best advantage. Do it with all of your considerable might. Rock your world, Amy, darlin', and everybody else's around you."

The young woman didn't reply, but she giggled, and Savannah was satisfied that her seeds of wisdom had fallen on fertile soil.

"Just be careful," Savannah warned her. "Female power is potent stuff. Make sure you only use it for good, not evil. You don't want to hurt yourself or anyone else in the process of getting what you want out of life."

"Thank you, Savannah. I'll keep that in mind. I want to be a director someday, so I'm sure I'll need that advice, sooner or later, in this tough business."

They had arrived at the garage and Amy showed her a staircase on the side of the building that led from the ground to the second-story apartment door.

"You go ahead," Amy said. "I'll go back to the house and ask Mr. Ethan about that password business."

"Okay. See you later."

Amy headed back to the main house, and Savannah began to climb the stairs to Luciana's apartment.

She was only halfway up the steps when she heard someone crying inside the building. Crying hard.

Ethan wasn't kidding when he said Luciana isn't feeling well, Savannah told herself as she continued up the stairs.

The upper half of the door was a stained-glass window, depicting a beautiful red rose on a curving vine. Savannah knocked gently on the wood surrounding the glass.

When the crying continued and no one answered, she knocked again, a bit harder.

It took four series of ever more vigorous rapping before the sobbing inside ended.

Eventually, she heard the sound of footsteps, as someone inside approached the door.

Slowly, it opened, but only a few inches.

One tearful eye peeked out through the crack.

"Luciana?" Savannah asked.

"Yes" was the tentative reply.

"My name is Savannah Reid. I believe Mr. Malloy told you about me. He probably mentioned that I was going to be dropping by to speak with you this afternoon. Is that right?"

"Yes, he told me."

"I know this is a really bad time for you, but could I please come in just for a few minutes and ask you a couple questions?"

When Luciana said nothing and did nothing but stare at her with tearful eyes, Savannah added, "I think it might help Miss Beth and Freddy if I could talk to you."

Those were the magic words.

In two seconds, the door was wide open, and Luciana was waving her inside.

"Thank you very much," Savannah said. "I'll try not to take too much of your time on such a sad day."

Luciana was a bit older than Savannah had expected. Her black hair was sprinkled with silver, and her cinnamon-colored skin had a few wrinkles. But Savannah could tell that she had been a beautiful woman in her youth.

She still was.

She moved across the room with an almost regal elegance, even in the midst of her grief. Her back was straight, unbent by the many years of hard work she must have done.

There was something about the woman, an air of strength possessed only by those who had suffered the deepest sorrows and endured the most arduous challenges life had to offer.

Something told Savannah that the loss of her friend Pilar wasn't the first deep sorrow to cross this woman's path.

Luciana waved an arm toward a simple but comfortable sofa. "Please," she said, "sit down. Would you like some water? Some coffee? Some milk?"

"No, thank you. I'm fine. But you have some if you like."

Savannah took a seat on the couch and glanced around the simply decorated room. Almost everything in sight was functional, necessary to daily living. There was hardly anything in the room that could be considered a work of art or even a humble decoration.

Except one thing.

In the middle of the coffee table—a plain, nondescript coffee table—lay a beautiful leather album. The cover had been hand-worked in fine detail, decorated with roses and trimmed with rows of silver studs. In the center of the design was a cabochon of jasper agate, framed with silver.

"What a beautiful book," Savannah said.

She looked up at Luciana and saw an expression of great pride on the woman's face. No one needed to tell Savannah that this book was Luciana's most treasured possession.

"Thank you," Luciana replied. "Miss Beth gave it to me for Christmas last year. She knew I was keeping all of my family's pictures in a shoebox.

She said I needed a special place for them, because they were such special people."

Luciana sat beside Savannah on the sofa, reached over, and touched the album lovingly. "Would you like to see them?"

Savannah nearly said, "No." With Beth Malloy and her child missing, she was reluctant to waste time. Yet, Luciana's heart was shining in her eyes, and Savannah couldn't bring herself to refuse.

"Yes, I would like to see your family, Luciana," she said. "Very much."

"This is my Ecuador family." Luciana pulled the book closer and opened the ornate cover. "Miss Beth, Mr. Ethan, and Freddy are my American family. So was Pilar. But now . . ."

"I know. I'm so sorry."

Luciana drew a deep, shuddering breath, then pointed to the first photos in the album. "These are of my son, Angelo. He is my angel. He was only three years old when I left my home in Ecuador to come to the United States. Now he is a man."

"He's so handsome. *El guapo!*" Savannah said, studying the clear, dark, friendly eyes of the young man in the photo. "How often do you get to see him?"

Luciana seemed surprised at the question. "See him? Not since I left. Not since he was three."

"You never get to go home to see your son?"

"No. It is too far and costs too much money."

"That's terrible."

"But I knew it would be so when I left."

"What a terrible sacrifice for you. That must have been awfully hard to leave your child, your home, and your family, and go to a foreign country."

"It was. But my husband was killed. The bus he was riding to work went off the road and down a cliff. Everyone died. Even my handsome husband."

Savannah winced, thinking that sorrow had knocked hard on this woman's door.

"We had no money. We had no home. We had no food. Someone had to go. It was necessary. But my mother and father were too old, and my sisters and brothers too young, so I went. I came to America so I could work and send money to them so they could live."

She turned the page and showed more pictures of her son, going back in time, a series of over twenty photos. "My mother takes a picture of him every year on his birthday and sends it to me. He is big and strong and is getting married next month. I am so proud of him."

On the next page, she pointed to a picture of an older couple, looking happy and content, sitting on the front porch of a lovely brick home set in a verdant tropical forest. "These are my parents," she said. "That is the house I bought for them."

"You bought them a house?" Savannah couldn't hide her surprise.

"I did." Luciana didn't bother to hide her pride. She smiled broadly and turned the page. Two other pictures showed women closer to Luciana's age, who bore a strong familial resemblance to her. They both stood in front of fine, brick homes.

"These are my sisters, Mayra and Silvia," she said. "Those are the houses I bought for them."

"You bought houses, brick houses, for your whole family?" Savannah was amazed. Apparently, the Malloy family paid their servants most handsomely.

"You are surprised." Luciana seemed to be enjoying Savannah's astonishment. "You think a maid's money is too little to buy houses?"

Savannah was embarrassed by her own ill-informed, preconceived notions. But she decided to be honest about it. "Yes, I guess I am."

"A maid's little money would not buy a good, rich life here in the United States. But in Ecuador, a little money buys much. My family doesn't starve anymore. My family has strong houses that don't fall when the winds blow, and cars that don't break and go over cliffs and kill them. I take care of them, and they send me pictures of my son. Someday, he and his wife will have children. My grandchildren. And they will send me pictures of them, too. I think about that, and it makes me happy."

Savannah thought of all the people she knew, including herself, who found it difficult to be content with so much more than this lady had.

She promised herself that, when she found time—no, she would *make* time—she'd think about the lessons she had just learned, sitting in Luciana's humble living room.

"Thank you, Luciana, for showing me your photos. I'm sure your family loves you very much and are most grateful for all you've done for them."

"It was because of Miss Beth. She helped me." Tears began to stream down Luciana's cheeks. "She sponsored me. She helped me take classes and learn English and learn about the United

States. She helped me study for the test and become an American. I owe her much."

"I'm sure you've been a blessing to her family, Luciana. You can always be proud, knowing that."

"Are you going to find her? Are you going to bring her and Freddy back to us? Or do you think they are . . ." She choked on her words, cried softly for a few moments, then managed to say, ". . . like Pilar?"

"No," Savannah said without even thinking. "Beth and Freddy aren't like Pilar. They aren't. We just have to find them."

"I need to help you," she said. "Pilar was a sister to me. A little sister. I helped her come to work for Miss Beth. I was helping her become a citizen, like Miss Beth did for me. She was studying so hard, night and day. She wanted so much to be an American."

Savannah felt tears burning in her own eyes and a newfound determination to catch the callous, coldhearted killer who would rob a beautiful young woman of her life and her dreams.

She reached over and put her arm across Luciana's shoulders and gave her a hug. Then she reached into her purse and pulled out some clean tissues. She offered them to Luciana, then used a couple herself.

"Let's talk about Miss Beth. How long have you worked for the Malloys?"

"Only three years for Mr. Ethan. After he and Miss Beth got married. But before I worked twenty-five years for her and her family."

"But she's only in her thirties, so . . ."

"Yes, I was her nanny when she was a little girl. Then she grew up and became a lady, I became her family's maid. Then she married Mr. Irwin, and I went with her to her new house."

"No wonder you're close," Savannah said. "You have a lot of history with Miss Beth. You must know her very well."

Luciana nodded. "I do."

"Good. Then tell me this, when she's upset, especially with a husband, where does she go? What does she do?"

"She goes for walks in the hills." A dark expression passed over Luciana's face. "That is where you found Pilar, no? They say you found her in the hills."

"We did. But not Beth and not Freddy. They weren't there, so there's no reason to think the worst."

Savannah paused, framing her words carefully. "Luciana, please don't think that I mean any disrespect to your lady, but I have to ask you something."

"Okay. Ask."

"Some people seem to think that maybe she's been seeing her ex-husband, Mr. Irwin. To your knowledge, is that true?"

"*Seeing* him?" Luciana looked confused.

"Being with him . . . romantically."

"No!"

The response was so emphatic that Savannah jumped, startled. "How can you be so sure?"

"She would never, never *see* him. She would

never touch him. He is a monster, and she hates him. I hate him."

Savannah felt a chill run over her. It was a feeling she often got when a case took a distinct turn.

If this gentle, kind, and humble woman hated a man this vehemently, Savannah was sure he richly deserved it.

"Can you tell me, Luciana, why you hate Mr. Irwin so much?"

"He hurt Miss Beth. He hurt her bad, many times. He is a very bad man."

"How did he hurt her?"

"In every way. He hit her. He said terrible, mean things to her. He took all of her money and spent it on gambling and stupid things. He would . . . *see* . . . other women, many women."

"Then it's a very good thing that she left and divorced him," Savannah said.

A strange expression crossed Luciana's face, one of sadness, and yet something else. Maybe pride? Savannah couldn't be sure.

"She left him because of me," Luciana said quietly.

Yes, there it is again, Savannah thought. Definitely pride and deep satisfaction.

"Because of you?"

"Yes. He was mad at me. I wouldn't do things he wanted me to do with him. Bad things. He hit me. Miss Beth saw that my clothes were torn and my face was hurt, and she told him to leave or she would call police. He did. She got a divorce."

Savannah tried to reconcile this new information with what she had heard from Ethan and Amy. But she couldn't.

"I know that Mr. Ethan thinks she loves her first husband again," Luciana said. "But it is not true. I don't know why he thinks that. I don't know why they argued about Mr. Irwin. He is not a reason for them to argue."

"She wouldn't be the first woman to go back to an abusive husband."

"No. Not her. And not him. Mr. Ethan is a good man. He has been kind to her." She hesitated, then added, "Until now."

"Until now? What's changed?"

"Now he is the one who is *seeing* someone else. Someone he loved before."

"Candace York?"

"Yes. They were going to get married, but he met Miss Beth, and he loved her more. Now he loves Miss York again."

"How do you know that?"

"Miss Beth told me."

"Could she have been wrong about that?"

"No. She had a picture of them, *seeing* each other."

"Did you look at it yourself?"

"Yes. She showed it to me."

"Was it an actual photograph, printed on paper or—"

"No, it was on her computer. Someone sent it to her on the computer."

"Did she say who sent it?"

Luciana shook her head. "She didn't know. They didn't use their name when they sent it. They called themselves 'a concerned friend.'"

"Hm-m-m," Savannah mused. "Sending a person a picture of their spouse *seeing* someone else, including their naughty bits . . . Maybe it's just me, but that doesn't sound like a particularly 'friendly' thing to do. In fact, it sounds to me like something a person would do if they wanted to break up someone's marriage."

Luciana nodded thoughtfully. "That's true. It sounds like something Mr. Irwin would do."

Chapter 14

Her head spinning with the inconsistencies in the interviews she had just conducted, Savannah left Luciana's apartment and made her way back to the main house.

As she rounded the corner near the turret tower, she saw a familiar and beloved vehicle sitting on the cobblestone driveway.

An exquisite silver vintage Bentley.

That could only mean one thing. That two of her favorite men in the world were inside the mansion. And not just any men. Two former FBI agents–turned-bodyguards, offering security to the rich and famous.

They were also co-owners of the best restaurant in San Carmelita.

That alone would have endeared them to Savannah's heart. But at the moment, the idea that they were inside the Malloy mansion, possibly lending their skills to this investigation, lifted Savannah's rainy-day spirits into the sunlit clouds above.

With renewed energy, Savannah practically sprinted to the door. This time it was Ethan who answered her knock.

"How is Luciana?" he asked.

"Not so good," Savannah admitted. "She's grieving for Pilar, and worried sick about Beth and Freddy."

"Aren't we all?" Ethan said softly, as he held the door open for her.

"I saw Ryan's and John's Bentley out front," she told him as they walked into the foyer and passed the snarling statue of Nidhogg.

"Yes. They're in here." He pointed down the hallway toward the library. The door was ajar. "Your husband told them about Pilar, and they called me. I filled them in on what we have—or don't have—so far, and they came right over."

"That's how they are," Savannah said. "They're some of the kindest and most capable men I've known.

They stepped into the library, and Savannah felt the stress that was tying her nerves in knots relax a little just at the sight of their faces.

Ryan Stone and his partner, John Gibson, had been two of her dearest friends almost from the moment she had met them, several years back. Ryan was probably the only man she had ever seen who could give Ethan Malloy competition in the "breathtakingly handsome" department. Tall, with dark hair and bright green eyes, he had only to smile and half a dozen women in his immediate vicinity would swoon.

Savannah didn't mind admitting she was one of them.

So was Tammy.

Even Gran numbered among his swoon-ees.

Part of what made Ryan so gorgeous was the fact that he didn't seem to know it, and if he did, he didn't care. Unlike many beautiful people, he didn't rely on his looks alone to endear him to people. Ryan captured hearts, made friends, and kept them by being one of the most generous and compassionate people she had ever had the pleasure to call "friend."

Then there was John. Older than Ryan by a few years, he had lush silver hair and a thick mustache to match. His pale blue eyes sparkled with humor and mischief, and his thick British accent was a sheer delight to hear. Savannah could listen to him spin tales for hours.

But today, they were less personable, less effervescent. They were concentrating on business, and the business at hand appeared to be something to do with the house phone.

Surveillance, and the equipment required to do it, was only part of the services they offered when providing security to society's most highly esteemed heroes and heroines. Many times, Savannah had been grateful that, as part of her Moonlight Magnolia team, they frequently supplied technological equipment and the know-how to use it.

Apparently, without her even asking, they were doing that for the Malloy investigation.

"Savannah, love," John said, the moment he saw her. "I'm so sorry to hear about the little nanny. Ghastly business, truly." He hurried to her and enveloped her in a tight hug. His mustache tickled her cheek when he kissed it.

Once he released her, Ryan took over with his own affectionate embrace. "Are you all right?" he asked, looking deeply into her eyes and giving her flutters, for which she scolded herself sharply.

This wasn't the time for flutters of any sort.

"What are you fellas up to there?" she asked, nodding toward the big black metal box that sat on the desk next to the telephone. Wires seemed to sprout from it everywhere. A plethora of knobs adorned the front, along with numerous dials and LED displays.

"We're setting up a recording device," John said, "in case your man there gets a ransom call."

"Good idea."

Actually, she doubted that a ransom call would be forthcoming. If kidnappers had been responsible for Beth's and Freddy's disappearances, Savannah would have expected them to have already contacted Ethan and demanded a ransom.

But the recorder was a good idea.

Heck, it couldn't hurt.

Savannah glanced over at Ethan, who was sitting in a chair near the window. He was staring out on the gardens, but she could tell that he wasn't seeing the beauty and serenity there.

Something terrible was going on in his mind's eye. She assumed he was playing some of the same scenarios in his head that she was in her overly active imagination. Her waking nightmares, regarding his missing family, ranged from unpleasant to terrifying.

She walked over to him and sat on a chair near his. "Are you all right, Ethan?"

"No. Probably not," he replied. "How could I be under these circumstances?"

"I'm sure that's true." She glanced over at Ryan and John, who were testing the equipment they had just installed. "It was a good idea, having them come over. I'll be calling a meeting of the members of my agency this evening. But it doesn't hurt to get them started a bit earlier."

"It's a good thing they're here, in more ways than one. While you were talking to Luciana, your husband called."

"Oh? Is there news?"

"Only that things are going to go from bad to worse. He told me he's putting out an Amber alert on Freddy."

"That could be a good thing, right?"

"It could be, if he's found. But it also means that what's happening here is going to be the lead story on the national evening news. Once that happens, things will be very different for all of us, Savannah. Even you."

Savannah doubted that she would be personally affected, but she didn't want to argue with him at a time like this. On the other hand, she was sure he was right about his own world changing, and not for the better.

An A-list movie star and his wife have a nasty argument, she takes off with his kid and the family nanny. Nanny turns up dead, and the wife and child haven't been seen since.

Lead stories didn't come any juicier than that.

"The paparazzi are going to descend on this place like a swarm of hornets," Ethan predicted. "And they'll be about as much fun to deal with. You'll see. People think they'd like to be famous, but much of the time, it isn't all it's cracked up to be."

"I'm sure it isn't. But personally, I'm still hoping that we'll find them, safe and sound—their bodies and their minds."

"From your mouth to God's ears, as they say."

"By the way, did Amy get a chance to ask you about Beth's passwords?" she asked.

"If she could give them to you, the ones that she knows?"

"Yes. I realize it may sound intrusive but—"

"But 'intrusive' is officially off the table now."

"Unfortunately, yes."

He reached into his jeans pocket and pulled out a rumpled piece of paper. Pressing it into her hand he said, "We made up this list of the ones we know. They'll get you into her social media, things like that."

Savannah glanced over the list and was pleased at how many there were. "This may be very helpful. Thank you. My assistant will be able to put these to use right away."

"Can you ask her to be discreet with what she finds?" he asked. "We're big on privacy around here. I know my wife's passwords, almost all of them, as she knows mine. But neither one of us would dream of using them to spy on the other. I feel like I'm betraying her by giving those to you."

"If we use these and find something that winds

up saving her and your son's lives, she'll be very glad you did."

"That's why I'm giving them to you and trusting that they won't go any further than you and your assistant."

"You have my word on that." Savannah glanced over at Ryan and John, but they were chatting and seemed preoccupied as they installed the recorder. She lowered her voice and said, "There's one other thing, Ethan, that I need to ask you for."

He gave her a suspicious look, and she knew he wasn't going to like what he heard next.

"The picture that you have of your wife and Neal Irwin . . ."

"Yes? What about it?"

"Did you send it to my husband yet?"

"No, I did not."

"Would you send me a copy of it? You can send it to my office e-mail. My assistant is a whiz at computers, and she's set it up so that everything we send and receive is encrypted, or whatever you call that. She assures me it's completely safe from hackers."

"I'd rather not. Obviously, it hurt me to see that picture, but she's still my wife. I don't want it out there in the world."

"It won't be. I'll see it, and my assistant will see it. That's all. I promise."

"Why do you need it?"

"For one thing, my assistant can verify its validity. She's an expert at that sort of thing. Wouldn't you like to hear from an expert if it's truly what it appears to be?"

"It's exactly what it appears to be. But if you think you need it, I'll send it to you."

"What I would really like you to do is locate the original e-mail that you received from this anonymous source, the one that had the photo attached to it. If you could forward the actual letter to us, that might be especially helpful."

She took one of her business cards from her purse, turned it over, and scribbled their confidential, secure e-mail address on the back. Handing it to him, she said, "Send it to us there, please. Let the subject line be: 'S&T Only.' Within the hour, I'll alert Tammy that you're e-mailing us something highly confidential and not to open it unless she's alone."

"Okay. I'll wait an hour for you to give her the heads-up and then I'll send it to you."

"Fair enough." She gave him a sweet smile, one that she hoped was encouraging. "You've been wonderful so far, Ethan. You've done everything you can do to help your family. It's important that you know that."

He shook his head. "How can you say that, Savannah? I've been a royal pain all along."

She stood, tucked her purse under her arm, and said, "You've been just fine, Mr. Malloy. I've dealt with people in similar situations who weren't nearly as cooperative and patient as you've been. Heck, I've been working with you nearly an entire day and you haven't cursed me out, hit me, threatened to have me arrested, or spit on me. In my book, you're an absolute gem of a client."

* * *

After saying good-bye to Ethan, Ryan, and John, Savannah left the library and found her own way down the hallway, through the foyer, and out the front door.

That was when she saw it.

The paparazzi swarm.

As Ethan had described, they look like a batch of angry hornets, ready to descend on their unsuspecting insect prey.

There had to be at least a dozen vehicles parked along the narrow road leading to the Malloy home. Mulling about beside those assorted automobiles were men and women with every sort of camera and microphone that Savannah had ever seen, and some she hadn't.

The moment she stepped outside the door, they transformed from bored mannequins into highly animated reporters and photographers.

She saw the flashing of what seemed to be at least twenty cameras, and heard just as many voices screaming questions at her.

"Where is Ethan Malloy?"

"Did he kill his wife and son?"

"The police think he murdered his boy's nanny. Can you comment on that?"

"Who are you?"

"Why are you here? Are you a police officer? Are you investigating the murders?"

"Are you his new girlfriend?"

That last question in particular seemed to spread through the crowd like alcohol poured on a bonfire.

No longer content to stand beside the road, they surged en masse onto the property, heading straight for her.

The rapid-fire questions morphed from annoying to harassing in an instant.

"What's your name? How long have you been sleeping with Ethan Malloy?"

"Did Beth know about you?"

"When did she find out you were having an affair with her husband?"

Savannah hurried toward the Mustang, walking as fast as she could without breaking into a full run. She refused to give them the satisfaction of actually chasing her, but she realized that it was only a matter of moments until they overtook her.

She was still at least ten feet away from her car, and she could hear them running right behind her. She had no doubt that they intended to cut off her escape and continue their bombardment eye-to-eye and nose-to-nose.

"Who is she?" she heard someone ask. "Isn't she that makeup artist he was seeing before Candace?"

Then she heard them. A set of questions so vile that they literally made her sick to her stomach.

"Did you help Ethan Malloy kill his wife and child? Did the two of you murder Beth and Freddy so that you could be together? Did that poor nanny get in your way?"

Images of Pilar's body flashed across Savannah's mind. She thought of Vanna Rose, sweet, innocent, and vulnerable in her arms. Tammy, a young mother with a baby to protect and everything to live for. She thought of Beth and Freddy and the red backpack filled with toys and snacks, discarded like so much rubbish beside the Dumpster.

Thrown away, like that lovely young woman lying dead beneath the oak trees.

She stopped abruptly, then whirled on her tormentors and found they were only a couple of feet away.

"No! No! No! None of that is true. Get away from me, you pack of vultures!"

As though from faraway she heard a woman shouting. She sounded furious and on the verge of hysteria.

It was some seconds before she realized the frightened, angry woman was her.

And that she had referred to a flock of vultures as a pack. She was, undoubtedly, losing her mind.

Then she heard a loud boom very near her and off to her right. Even before the echo of the sound died away, the former cop inside her identified the noise as the firing of a high-caliber weapon.

She turned, was about to dive for cover and reach into her purse for her own weapon, but that was when she saw Ethan Malloy holding a .44 Remington Magnum in his right hand. It was pointed downward at a nearby flower bed. Smoke curled from the end of its massive barrel.

Instantly, the crowd fell silent, though Savannah could hear numerous cameras clicking.

"Get off my property," the actor roared in a voice that would have made even his macho rancher father proud. "Get off *now!*"

"You'd better do as he says," said another deep voice. Ryan Stone stepped up beside Ethan, shoulder to shoulder, and added, "Let that lady pass. Move out of her way right now, and let her get in her car."

"The constabulary has been notified and will be arriving momentarily," John Gibson added as he moved into place at Ethan's opposite shoulder. "If you're still here, molesting that young lady, when they arrive, you'll be taken into custody on the spot."

"Yeah. What he said," Savannah added, wanting to get in on the action. "You'll be arrested for malicious trespass in the first degree."

The reporters stood, momentarily frozen, their mouths agape, staring at the stalwart foursome.

Finally, one of them said, "Malicious trespass?"

"In the first degree," Savannah assured him.

One by one the paparazzi began to file back to their vehicles, get inside, and drive away. But one reporter lingered behind the others, and to her displeasure, Savannah realized she was jotting down the Mustang's license plate number.

She recalled Ethan Malloy's dark prediction that as soon as the news was out about his family, their lives would change, even her own.

"I can see why you don't like the paparazzi," she remarked as she watched them drive away. "I have to admit, that was kind of scary."

"You just wait," Ethan said, sounding tired. Too tired for the fight that was to come. "It's only going to get worse."

Chapter 15

Savannah thought there was a possibility that one of the reporters, who had stormed the Malloy chateau, might have a connection to the DMV, and therefore, could possibly trace her Mustang's plate number and identify her.

One solitary reporter.

That theory came apart like a post-Halloween, dynamited jack-o'-lantern the moment she rounded the corner and headed down her home street.

Not unlike the Malloy mansion, her humble, cozy cottage was under siege, as well.

Apparently, more than one had taken down her plate number and had contacts inside the DMV, or they freely shared information.

She recognized some of the same reporters she had fought off less than an hour before. Plus, their numbers had increased twofold.

Yes, she had to hand it to Ethan. He knew the

"joys" of dealing with the paparazzi far better than she ever would.

She didn't envy him his knowledge or his life experiences that had taught him such wisdom.

She had failed to fully grasp the popularity of the beloved actor and sex symbol. As far as the media was concerned, Ethan Malloy was a hot commodity, and his current tragedy was something to be fully exploited in the pursuit of high ratings for the television stations, and brisk supermarket stand sales for the tabloids.

She nearly ran over half a dozen of the reporters as she tried to pull the Mustang into her driveway.

"Close, but not quite close enough," she muttered to herself as she watched them scurry out of her path.

The mob, which had been standing on the sidewalk and the street, surged onto her lawn, some even trampling her nasturtium flower beds to get to her.

Wasting no time, she parked the car, got out, and shouted, "Hey! Get off my flowers, you pea brains, before I feed you those cameras." When they didn't obey right away, she added, "I'm serious! I'll shove 'em so far down your throats, you won't need no colonoscopy!"

Again, they started shouting the same obnoxious questions at her, wanting to know if she was Ethan Malloy's new girlfriend and if she had helped him get rid of his wife and kid.

She turned to the one nearest her, less than a foot away, who had shoved a microphone at her face and clipped her jaw. "So much for professional journalism," she told him. "You do enough research to find out where I live, so that you can come to my home and harass me with stupid questions. But you don't know that I'm a private investigator and a former police officer."

This created a buzz through the crowd. And a whole new set of questions emerged.

"Are you investigating the murder of Pilar Padilla?"

"Did Ethan Malloy hire you to find his wife and kid?"

"Or are you working on behalf of the police department?" asked a well-dressed, middle-aged woman, who appeared less frenzied and more professional than the others.

Savannah decided to address her and ignore the rest. "I no longer work for the San Carmelita Police Department," she told her. "Not in any capacity. Ever. I don't foresee a time when I will again."

"I understand, Ms. Reid," the reporter replied.

Savannah's instinct told her that the woman did understand, that she knew at least some of her personal history.

The reporter reached into her purse and took out a business card. She pressed it into Savannah's hand.

"I can see that you're busy," she told Savannah. "Since I believe Ethan Malloy hired you to find his family, I won't get in your way as you look for them. But if you ever find yourself in need of a reporter, just call me. I might be able to help, and I would be happy to."

Savannah shoved the card into her purse and said,

"Thank you." Louder, to the others, she shouted, "If the rest of you will get out of my way and off my property, I would appreciate it, and you won't get hurt. That's a win-win for everybody."

Their numbers dropped away as she strode up the sidewalk to her front door. She unlocked it, turned around, and realized they had all not only returned to the sidewalk and street, but most were actually getting into their cars and leaving.

She was relieved, thinking of how Dirk would have reacted if he'd come home to find their yard littered with paparazzi.

"Yeah, you better run, you bunch of roadkill polecats. You'll make tracks, if you know what's good for you," she yelled to the retreating horde. "My husband's on his way, and if he catches you here, you'll be in a world o' hurt! He ain't nearly as sweet-natured and easygoing as I am."

An hour later, Savannah had changed out of her dusty clothes and into a slightly dressier cotton blouse, linen slacks, and wedge heels, which would serve as dining apparel at ReJuvene, should they manage to join Tammy, Waycross, and the Harts.

Dirk had come home, downed a cold can of soda, and persuaded her to be the driver on the way to Neal Irwin's workplace—a used car lot in San Paulo.

An hour later, they had looked for him in several locations and come up empty.

Savannah instructed the car phone to "Call Tammy," thinking she was getting the hang of this newfangled gadget. Far more technically inclined than she, her younger brother had talked her into it, assuring her that it was safer and far more convenient than a regular cell phone.

"Don't you feel stupid talking to your sun visor like that?" Dirk asked as they waited for Tammy to answer.

"No stupider than talking to a little box in the palm of my hand. Besides, it works even if you're stupid. You should get one."

In her peripheral vision, she could see him sticking out his tongue at her. She chose to ignore it.

Ignoring things—she was convinced that was the secret to a happy marriage, the key to matrimonial bliss.

Or at least, less squabbling.

"Hello, Savannah!" Tammy answered. "How's it going? Did you already interview the duck abuser?"

"No. We couldn't find him."

"Did you go by the used car lot?"

"Yes. They said he didn't show up for work today."

"Wooo, that's a sign that maybe—"

"Yeah, we thought of that," Dirk grumbled.

That was the only thing Savannah didn't particularly like about the new phone. Dirk felt free to add his half-a-cent's worth to her conversations.

"Then we tried the home address you gave us," Savannah told her. "Nobody answered the door."

"I gave you the make and model and plate number of his car, right?"

"Yes. It wasn't there, so we're assuming he wasn't either. You wouldn't happen to have any other address associated with him, would you?"

"Give me a minute. I'll call you back."

"Okay. Thanks, sugar."

As they waited for Tammy, Savannah drove up and down the residential streets of the little town of San Paulo. She could recall when she had first driven through the old town, whose economy was based on citrus farming, that the community had been run-down, crime-ridden, and was rapidly deteriorating.

Then some smart city council members had spent a bit more on their police force, cleaned up most of the gang activity, established and enforced some new "quality of life" laws, and property values had begun to rise.

The quaint Craftsman cottages that lined the main street of the town had been decaying, but first one, then another, had been restored to their original beauty.

Now it was a delight just to drive from one end of town to the other.

Unless, of course, one was trying to locate their number one, and only, murder suspect and having no luck.

"We aren't going to find him today," Dirk said. "He did the murder and now he's skipped the country. We're never going to get him or close this case. It just ain't gonna happen."

She pulled up to one of the town's few traffic signals and stopped for the red light. Turning in her seat, she studied Dirk closely. Especially the area right around his head.

"What are you looking at me like that for?" he asked.

"Just wondering."

"About what?"

"Oh, I've heard about mountains that seem to somehow generate their own dark clouds. Then those clouds just sit there, all around them, raining, hailing, thundering with lightning bolts and all."

"What the hell are you talkin' about?"

"I was thinking you're kinda like that. Wherever you go, the sun can be shining to beat the band, but no. You just sit there, generating your own clouds, cooking up your own personal rainstorms, thunder, and lightning."

"Eh, bite me."

Fortunately, at that moment, Tammy's call came through, averting a family flap.

"I've got something for you," she said proudly. Savannah could practically see her bouncing up and down on her chair in typical perky Tammy style. It was good to hear her friend excited again.

"Great. Lay it on us," she told her.

"His mom died six months ago. Her husband passed years ago, and he's her only kid."

Savannah's mind was already racing down the logic path. "Did she leave him the family house?"

"Yes. It's not in great shape, but . . ."

"He might be there," Dirk interjected. "Thanks, kid. Ya did good."

"You're welcome." She sounded surprised, but pleased. "The address is: 251 St. Michael Lane."

"Got it. We'll check there next," Savannah told her. "Thanks a bunch."

"Are you coming for dinner tonight at ReJuvene?"

It hurt Savannah to hear the desperation in her friend's voice. It hurt to have your company wanted so badly, and to know that you won't be able solve your loved one's dilemma, no matter how hard you might try.

So many of life's most important battles had to be fought, won, or lost alone.

Tammy was in one of those now.

Savannah knew it, even if Tammy didn't.

"I'm turning down St. Michael Lane right now," Savannah told her.

"There's 251 up there on the right," Dirk said. "What a rubbish heap. Looks like the grass hasn't been mowed for six months."

"Or the house painted since the Eisenhower administration," Savannah added.

"Hey, free rent," Tammy said. "Somebody gives you a house, you take it."

Savannah smiled to herself, understanding Tammy's covert reference.

"Look at that," Dirk said, sounding moderately excited in a No-Mirth-Dirk kind of way. "There's his car, sitting right under the carport."

"That's awesome! Go get him! While you're at it, Savannah, smack him upside the head once for me and the duck."

"You've been hanging out with me too long." Savannah laughed, then realized that was probably exactly what Lenora Hart had been telling her. "Thank you, Tammy. Once again, you save the day."

"I think I'll wait and see if you nab him," Tammy replied, "before I go taking any bows."

"Whether we do or not, you've done your job, kiddo," Savannah said. "Let us do ours now and see what shakes out."

"Keep me informed. Also about dinner tonight."

"We will, sugar. We'll let you know. I promise."

Savannah ended the call, just as she was pulling the Mustang over to the curb. She parked on the opposite side of the road from the house that Neal Irwin's mother had left him.

As they got out of the car and crossed the street, Savannah gave the old house a thorough look-see. "It could be nice, downright presentable, if someone took the time, money, and hard work to fix it up."

"I remember you saying the same thing about me, when you first laid eyes on me."

"Good point. Never mind then. Too much work."

But in spite of the fact that the house would need a tremendous amount of TLC to bring it back to its former beauty, Savannah couldn't help noticing the charming features of the house that identified it as Craftsman style.

The home's shingle siding and stone details gave it a cozy, natural appeal. Its deep porch reminded Savannah of Granny's old house back in Georgia. Savannah had spent many pleasant hours on that porch, sitting in the swing with Gran as they chatted about everything and nothing.

As she and Dirk stepped up onto the porch, one of the boards beneath her feet wobbled, and she nearly lost her balance

As Dirk grabbed her elbow to steady her, he said, "You may think this sort of place is charming, but to me it's a deathtrap that oughta be burned to the ground before somebody gets hurt."

"Burned to the ground? That's a bit harsh, don't you think?"

"Not at all. The orphanage was an old rickety building, like this one. Us kids were always getting hurt in that rotten, decrepit place. Splinters in our hands, nails in our feet, stuff falling off and hitting us in the head. Years later they discovered lead in the pipes. Pipes that carried our drinking water, no less. No wonder we all turned out like we did."

She slipped her arm through his and gave it a squeeze. "I know at least one kid from that hard place to turn out good. They must've been doing something right."

She was surprised to see him actually blush at the compliment. As a rule, Dirk Coulter wasn't the blushing type.

"Thanks, babe," he said. "For the most part, I don't give a hang what anybody thinks of me. But if one person on earth's gonna think that I turned out okay, I'm glad it's you, kid."

Chapter 16

Dirk and Savannah walked up to Neal Irwin's door, and Dirk rapped his knuckles on the frame around the oval beveled glass that graced the door's center. When no one answered quickly enough to suit him, he knocked again, this time using his loudest, most officious SCPD summons.

Again, no one answered, though they both could hear someone rummaging about inside.

"This is the San Carmelita Police Department," he shouted. "Come to the door."

Savannah stepped to the right and peered through a window into what looked like the living room. She saw a figure scurry across the room, and even though the house was dark inside, she was pretty sure it was a guy in his skivvies.

"Neal," she shouted, "we know you're in there, and we're not leaving until we talk to you. So, come to the door. We don't care if you're dressed or not."

"Well, *I care* if he's dressed," Dirk told her. "I only talk to guys with pants on."

"Oh, please. Like you don't run around the house naked as a jaybird half the time."

"Not anymore, you'll notice. Now that Tammy could be dropping in with the baby any minute, I've been keeping big Dirk and the twins under wraps."

"Sh-h-h. I think I saw him coming to the door now. You don't want our number one murder suspect to catch you talking about your exhibitionistic tendencies."

"I'll have you know that I—"

The door swung open, and there stood what Savannah thought at first was a child. Then she remembered that Ethan had described his wife's first husband as weighing two pounds and afraid of the dark. She decided this had to be Neal Irwin, the Scourge and Enemy of Ducks Everywhere. As she had predicted, he was wearing nothing but some tight red spandex briefs.

"Aw, go put your pants on, dude," Dirk told him. "Can't you see there's a lady standing here?"

Neal sized up Savannah with a lustful eye and said, "That's okay. A lot of women have seen me undressed. Nobody's complained yet."

"Yeah, well, this one's my wife. So, go put your damned pants on before I lose my temper and slug you."

"Are you sure you're a real policeman?" Irwin asked with a smart-aleck grin.

Dirk growled and took a quick step toward him. Immediately Savannah intervened.

Stepping between the two men, she turned to Neal Irwin and said, "Why don't you go get dressed, Mr. Irwin? I'm sure if you do, things will go much better."

Neal started to shut the door, but Dirk stuck his foot in the crack, preventing him from doing so. "Just leave it open," Dirk told him. "And don't take all day getting them pants on neither. We've got business to conduct."

Irwin glanced from Dirk, to Savannah, then back to Dirk. The look seemed furtive to Savannah. She got the feeling he was debating whether or not to bolt.

"Don't even think about sneaking out the back way either," she told him. "We've got a couple of guys waiting in your backyard, watching the back door and the windows, just in case you decide to be unfriendly and leave before you've even had a chance to get to know us."

As soon as Irwin retreated from the door into the darkness of the house, supposedly in search of more substantial clothing, Dirk turned to Savannah and said, "Can you believe the arrogance of this guy? That comment about all the women who've seen him in his underwear and think he's cute. Do you think he's cute, you know, in his red banana hammock?"

She shrugged. "I wasn't really looking at his banana, hammocked or otherwise."

"Good answer."

"Thank you. I thought so, too. Besides, why would I look at him, when I get such a delicious eyeful at home."

"Now you're overdoing it."

"Oh. Sorry. It's hard, you know, striking that delicate balance."

"Between bald-faced, lying flattery, and genuine, affectionate praise?"

"That would be the one."

"But you did notice his legs. I saw you checking them out. You were definitely checking out his legs."

"He's got bird legs, Dirk. Skinny, bony, knobby-kneed bird legs. At home I have big, hairy, manly, tree-trunk legs to look at. Why would I give him a second glance?"

"Gee, thanks." She was surprised to see he looked genuinely pleased about the "compliment."

"You're welcome." She rolled her eyes, stuck her head in the door, and yelled, "Neal Irwin, haul buns, boy. We ain't got all day, you know."

Savannah looked over at her husband. He was still beaming, still grinning like a jackass eating cactus.

All that because I said he had good legs, she thought. *Men are so-o-o easy.*

A few minutes later, Savannah and Dirk were sitting on a sofa that smelled of cat urine, amid stacks of boxes, piles of newspapers and magazines, and bags of garbage that had never found its way to the can, let alone the curb.

Savannah wasn't sure if Momma Irwin had been a hoarder, a lackadaisical housekeeper, or a lot of both.

Either way, Sonny Boy Neal didn't seem to mind.

He tossed a large pizza box filled with empty soft drink cans and ice cream containers off a leatherette recliner and plopped himself down on it.

Savannah decided that Mom might have been a great housekeeper and her son might have managed to trash it so thoroughly in the months since her passing.

Neal's idea of "getting dressed to entertain guests" consisted of pulling on a pair of black, baggy, knit shorts, which Savannah decided must have belonged to Momma. He certainly hadn't bought them in the men's department of any retailer.

She remembered what Luciana had said about him being quite the womanizer, and she found it difficult to believe. While Savannah had never seen Beth Malloy in person, she recalled how the actress looked in *The Great Gatsby*, and she had been lovely. Savannah recalled what Amy had told her about how men found Beth irresistible and flirted with her constantly.

She couldn't imagine a woman like that finding the guy sitting in his mother's chair wearing his mother's shorts attractive.

But then, there was no accounting for taste—or the lack of it.

"What's this all about?" Neal Irwin asked. "You want me bad enough to track me down here? I paid those parking tickets last month. I swear. I can show you the canceled check if you want."

"I couldn't care less about your parking tickets," Dirk told him. "Are you telling me you don't know what's happened?"

"What? What's happened?"

"The business about your ex-wife?"

"Which one?"

Again, Savannah's head spun. He had more than one ex-wife? More than one woman had actually walked down the aisle with this guy? It was hard to believe, but then, maybe he cleaned up good.

She couldn't imagine there was enough soap in the world to do the job properly. An ugly spirit was hard to wash away, and a cruel one impossible to hide.

Dirk gave him one of his worst scowls, the kind he usually reserved for hardened criminals whom he had personally busted more than three times. "Do you expect me to believe that you haven't seen the news or gone on social media or noticed the Amber alerts on the freeway and highway signs?"

"Amber alert?" He seemed genuinely confused. "Why? Is some kid missing?"

"Yes," Savannah said. "Your ex-wife's son. In fact, both she and the child have disappeared."

"Melinda and Jake are missing?"

"Beth and Freddy, you numskull," Dirk said. "Now don't pretend you didn't know that."

"How would I know that?" he asked in a whining tone that grated on Savannah's nerves. "I don't watch TV, and I haven't been on social media all day."

"Well, they're missing, and we need to know a few things," Savannah told him. "Like, when was the last time you saw your ex-wife?"

"I don't know. A long time."

"That's not what I heard," Savannah told him.

"Then you heard wrong. I haven't seen her for

months, years even. Like not since before her kid was born."

"You've seen her since then," Dirk said. "In fact, you've seen a *lot* of her since then. Every single inch of her. I have a picture to prove it."

"I have no idea what you're talking about."

"Have you spoken to her on the phone recently?" Savannah wanted to know.

"Yes. A few times. She's not happy in her marriage, and sometimes she just needs a shoulder to cry on. That's it. That's all that's left of our relationship now—her complaining about him."

"Crying on your shoulder, huh?" Dirk said. "Is that what you call what you two were doing in the picture that I saw?"

"What's this about a picture?" Neal said. "What picture? All of a sudden, everybody's talking about some picture."

"Who's 'everybody'?" Savannah wanted to know.

"You, her, Ethan. She called me yesterday, sobbing her face off, all upset over some picture that somebody sent Ethan. It's supposed to be of her and me getting it on. If it is, it must be an old one. Because she and I haven't done the deed for five years, at least."

Savannah didn't know whether to believe him or not. His facial expressions and tone of voice actually sounded genuine, but then, he wouldn't be the first good liar who managed to sound truthful while lying their backsides off.

Years ago, Savannah had discovered that those who blithely lie their way through life are often quite good at it—practice having made perfect.

Even seasoned members of law enforcement had a hard time discerning whether a suspect was telling the truth or setting their own pants afire with their constant flow of fabrications and deceptions.

"Then you're denying that it's you in that picture?" Dirk asked.

"No, I'm not denying it. I haven't seen the picture. It might be me. I'm denying that I've had sex with Beth since we broke up, and she married that idiot she's with now."

He reached down, grabbed an empty soda can, and squeezed it until it crunched in his hand. Then he threw it across the room.

Temper, temper, Savannah thought. *Not exactly a smart time to demonstrate your anger issues in front of a cop.*

"By the way," Neal continued, "even if I was banging my ex, which I'm not, she wouldn't be the only unfaithful one in that marriage. Old Ethan's getting something on the side himself. There's even a picture of it. A real, up-to-date picture. That's what you ought to be looking at."

"Do you have a copy of this alleged picture?" Dirk asked.

"No, but Beth said she did. Some friend of hers sent it to her. She got all upset about it."

"She probably would," Savannah said, "having been there and done that before. Remember, Neal?"

He gave a derisive sniff and wouldn't meet her eyes. "You just find that picture of Ethan and his former fiancée, and then ask him if he was looking to get rid of his wife so he could get back with her."

"Beth and Freddy aren't the only ones who are missing," Savannah told him. "Their nanny, Pilar, disappeared the same time that they did."

"Yeah, well. That's too bad."

"We found her this morning," Dirk said. "Dead."

Neal seemed mildly interested. "Oh? Wow. Bummer."

"We figure the same person who killed the nanny has Beth and Freddy."

"It wasn't me. That's all I've got to say. Check out What's-His-Face. When a woman goes missing or gets killed, isn't it almost always the husband?"

"Or an ex-husband," Savannah said. "Ethan didn't do it," she added with pseudo-confidence. "If he didn't and you didn't, who do you figure did?"

"I don't know. Maybe that manager of his who's always hanging around their house, trying to get something going with Beth. She told me he creeps her out."

"She told you that?" Dirk asked. "Those were her words?"

"Her exact words."

That was the second time Savannah had heard someone express their distrust of Abel Orman in the past couple of hours. She mentally underlined his name on her suspect board, and moved him a notch higher.

Yet, for all of his protestations to the contrary, she still didn't trust Neal Irwin. She had to be honest and admit that it might have something to do with the duck and jalapeño pepper. But she wasn't ready to peel his name off the board just yet.

She looked over at Dirk, caught his attention,

and began to toy with her right hoop earring. It was a signal they had used for years.

It was time for a "potty break."

"Excuse me," she said brightly to Neal. "But would you mind if I use your little girls' room? I had a big glass of sweet tea at lunch, and it's coming through with a vengeance."

Neal hesitated, frowned, then said, "Yeah, I guess so. If you've really gotta go."

"I really do." She giggled. "My bladder's the size of a thimble. A real nuisance."

She jumped up off the sofa and headed for a nearby hallway entrance. "Is it back here?"

"Yes. Straight down the hall. The door's open. But I have to warn you, it's a little messy."

"I don't mind. Beggars can't be choosers and all that."

She scurried down the hallway. Reaching the end, she saw the bathroom door, open as he had said. She also saw another open door. Glancing inside she saw a bedroom filled with junk and an unmade bed. It was the closed door that caught her eye and captured her imagination.

She listened carefully and heard Dirk chatting away, far more loquacious than the usual Dirk. That was part of the drill. She claimed to need the bathroom, and he kept the subject busy while she snooped.

Of course, nothing she found would be admissible in court, since Dirk had no search warrant, and she wasn't even a cop anymore. But sometimes she found something, some little something, or when she was lucky, some big something that provided a break in the case.

She wouldn't have dared to do anything so under-handed while she was a cop, but now that she was a private detective, she had let her standards slip considerably.

It was part of the charm of being a PI.

Carefully, slowly, she eased the closed door open a crack and looked inside. She could hear Dirk clearly now, his voice louder than before, covering for her, keeping Neal well occupied.

Sticking her head inside the room, she looked around and caught her breath. No wonder he had the door closed. No wonder he hadn't wanted her to come back there.

Neal Irwin had secrets to hide. One very big one in particular.

Chapter 17

"I feel so guilty taking the time to have a nice dinner," Savannah told Dirk as they parked in front of Ryan's and John's restaurant.

"I don't."

She gave him a wifely "look of disapproval," then reached into her purse for her lipstick and brush.

"You have no guilt at all when it comes to anything having to do with food."

"Of course not. Why should I? Food is necessary. Food is good. If it's around, you should eat it. As much of it as you can."

"I totally agree, and having an attitude like that explains my svelte figure and your rock-hard abs."

"Why, thank you for noticing." He looked down at his belly, tapped it, and smiled with genuine pride.

She shook her head and thought how hard it was to insult a male as supremely confident as hers.

With such a high level of self-esteem he seemed impervious to sarcasm.

Leaving him to admire his abs, she reached into her purse and pulled out the beautiful old Stratton compact that Granny had given her for her sixteenth birthday. When she looked in the mirror, she saw a woman who'd had a rough day.

Maybe Dirk was right. Maybe you should grab the opportunity to nourish your body and your spirit with a good meal whenever possible. Even more so if you were in law enforcement or private detection. One could never know when the opportunity to eat might present itself again. Or not.

She refreshed her lipstick, thinking what a perfect lip line Dr. Lenora Hart had when she saw her last. Then she brushed her hair thoroughly, trying to arrange her curls in some semblance of an actual hairdo.

Somehow, she knew that it would take a lot more than this extra grooming to make her presentable to her friend's mother. In fact, she was pretty sure that there was nothing on God's green earth that she could do that would enable her to officially be "up to snuff" in the other woman's eyes.

It seemed to Savannah that Tammy's mother considered her to be competition, and the prize appeared to be Tammy's respect and loyalty.

Savannah knew that no matter what she wore, how she acted, what she said, Lenora Hart would never consider her worthy of her daughter's affection.

So, why try?

Savannah looked in the mirror at the tired woman with great lipstick and silently told her, *Because you're a woman, and you can't help yourself. You can't stand it if everybody you meet doesn't fall in love with you at first sight and think you're the best thing since double-ply toilet paper.*

"Okay," she said, returning her toiletries to her purse. "Let's go eat something amazing, and remember, no talking shop at the table. This dinner is to be about Tammy and her folks, not a business meeting of the Moonlight Magnolia Detective Agency."

"Yeah, good luck with that."

Moments later, when they opened the door of ReJuvene and stepped inside, Savannah could instantly feel her body begin to relax and her spirit to restore.

Walking into this beautiful restaurant, created by her friends Ryan and John, was like being embraced by them.

Both men's exquisite taste was reflected in the decor of the place. John's traditional British upbringing showed in the masculine leather chairs with nail head trim that invited the diners to linger and savor. The antique brick walls and mahogany bookshelves provided the perfect backdrop for the fine old books and interesting artifacts that Ryan and John had collected during their world travels.

Oversized gilt-framed mirrors reflected the contemporary touches that Ryan had inspired. A beautiful water feature behind the bar had been formed from an exquisite slab of green slate. The glittering waterfall cascaded down the stone, disappearing into a line of fire at the bottom.

Yes, ReJuvene had been created to rejuvenate

the spirits of all who stepped over its threshold with good food and drink and a beautiful place to spend time with your loved ones.

As soon as Savannah and Dirk walked into the restaurant, they were met by a lovely and gracious hostess who escorted them to their table. It wasn't just any table but *the* table with the best view of the waterfall.

Savannah was somewhat discomfited to see that she and Dirk were the last to arrive. Tammy and Waycross, Granny, Lenora and Quincy, and Ryan and John were already seated and were, obviously, well along with their before-dinner drinks.

So much for rejuvenation of the soul, Savannah thought, as she and Dirk approached the table. The looks on her dinner companions' faces clearly showed that the evening's fun and festivities had yet to begin.

Even Granny looked glum.

Vanna Rose, who was sitting on her mother's lap, was scowling and grumbling her discontent. But the moment she looked in Savannah's direction, her little face lit with a bright smile and her grumbling turned to coos.

She reached out her baby arms, her eyes glowing with excitement.

It wasn't until Savannah attempted to take the baby from Tammy that she realized it wasn't she whom the child was reacting to. It was Dirk, who stood right behind Savannah.

He scooped her into his arms and held her high over his head. Vanna squealed with delight.

"Sh-h-h!" Lenora said. "Tammy, can't you keep

that child quiet? This is a nice restaurant, for heaven's sake. You shouldn't have brought a baby here if you couldn't control it."

"Please don't worry about such things," John told her from across the table. "No one minds the babbling of a happy baby."

"I love that sound," Gran chimed in. "There's no sweeter sound on God's green earth than the ones that come out of a happy baby."

"John and Granny are absolutely right," Ryan agreed. "This is a family place. A lot of our guests bring their children. It's the adults you have to worry about, making a nuisance of themselves, not the kids."

Savannah noticed that Lenora looked more annoyed than reassured by their words of consolation. Her frown deepened as she saw Savannah sit on the empty chair next to Tammy's.

Yes, Savannah thought, as she watched her from the corner of her eye, *Momma Lenora is a jealous pot. No doubt about it.*

Savannah's first inclination was to maintain a bit of distance between herself and Tammy, to play down the relationship a tad in order to quiet the green-eyed dragon of envy in Lenora.

But that plan was short-lived, when Tammy grabbed her and gave her a tight hug—even tighter than Tammy's usual take-your-breath-away embrace.

One look in her young friend's eyes told Savannah that if ever Tammy had needed to feel their connection, to take comfort in their friendship, this was it.

Lenora would need to deal with her own dragon, or not, as was her choice.

It wasn't until Savannah was settled in her chair that she even noticed the quiet, nondescript fellow sitting beside Lenora. He was a handsome man, to be sure, with thick dark hair accented by silver wings over his temple. He had prominent cheekbones and a strong chin, but his eyes lacked any spark of the life energy his daughter exuded.

Savannah was a bit surprised. She had expected a man with a far more vigorous personality, given that he was the founder and president of a Fortune 500 company.

For the moment, she decided to shove her observations aside and try to enjoy this gentle interlude after such a harsh day.

She reached across Tammy and Waycross, extending her hand to Quincy Hart. "Hello, Mr. Hart. Welcome to California. It's so nice to meet you after all the good things we've heard about you."

"We've heard a lot about you, too," Quincy replied. "All of you, for that matter. The Moonlight Magnolia gang is all my daughter talks about when she phones—you and whatever case you're working on at the time."

"We couldn't solve half of our cases without your daughter's expertise," Savannah said, patting Tammy's shoulder. "She has a real gift for forensic research."

"We're mighty blessed to have her. Both as a friend and on our team," Gran added.

"You certainly are," Lenora interjected. "Very few gifted geniuses are willing to work for free."

"Mother, please," Tammy said under her breath. "You promised. Besides, you don't know what you're talking, I mean, you don't know or understand how it is between Savannah and me and the rest of the team. Please, don't comment on it."

"No, I don't understand how a woman can work as many hours as you do at this 'sleuthing' stuff as you like to call it, and still have to make and sell handmade soap at street fairs."

"Have you tried any of your daughter's organic lotions or soaps, Dr. Hart?" Ryan asked.

"No" was the haughty reply. "I have an excellent cosmetician at Elizabeth Arden. She created my regimen. I wouldn't dream of doing anything else."

"I'm sure she's quite good, considering the glow of your complexion. John and I have used products recommended to us by an esthetician at a Rodeo Drive spa, but Tammy's are so much better, we'll never go back."

"They're the best there is!" Granny exclaimed. "Just look at this face of mine. I'm telling you it didn't look half this young last year, before I started using her stuff. Ever'where I go, folks tell me that I don't look a day over seventy."

"Thank you, Granny and Ryan," Tammy said. "My customers have told me how much they like my products and appreciate the fact that they're all organic." To her mother, she added, "I enjoy making them, Mother, and I have a great time when I sell them at street fairs or the farmers' market. I do it for the pure joy of it, not profit."

"Joy doesn't pay the bills," Lenora replied.

"*I* help her pay the bills," Waycross said, his voice firm but humble. "I'm her husband, and I make sure we get by."

"There's more to life than just 'getting by.' "

"There is, indeed," John said. "There's good food, good drink, and good company! Let's order Savannah and Dirk something to drink, and we'll toast to all three!"

Chapter 18

Having savored a delectable appetizer—roasted figs with honey, goat cheese, and brcsaola—the ReJuvene diners had their entrées placed before them with great aplomb. For the ladies, there was Scottish salmon, grilled lobster risotto, horse-radish-encrusted halibut, and caramelized sea scallops. The men were served sirloin steak with au poivre sauce.

Even Lenora Hart was impressed with her scallops, and at least for the moment, her mood seemed to improve.

Not for the first time, Savannah noticed the power of good food, graciously served in pleasant surroundings. She was encouraged to think they might get through the rest of the meal without any further incoming artillery fired across the table.

But then, someone made the unfortunate mistake of asking Savannah and Dirk how the case was going.

Once those floodgates were open, there was no going back.

"Well, since you asked . . ." Dirk leaned back in his chair and adjusted his belt buckle to accommodate the plate-size steak he was consuming. "Right before we came over here, we were interviewing that Neal Irwin dirtbag."

Tammy nodded excitedly. "The duck abuser. Yes, we hate him."

"We do!" Waycross agreed. "I'd like to hold him down while you shove a big, juicy jalapeño pepper up each one of his nostrils."

Tammy giggled and even Vanna cooed her approval.

Only Lenora was silent, radiating her dissatisfaction with the topic.

"Just guess what Savannah found when she 'used his little girls' room,' " Dirk continued.

"Oh, yes," Waycross said. "My sister and her trips to the bathroom."

Tammy turned to her parents and said, "Savannah excuses herself, saying she's going to the restroom, but in fact she sneaks around to see what she can find that might provide a clue or two."

"Lovely." Lenora dabbed her lips with a napkin. "Once inside a person's house, she lies to them and then violates their privacy by snooping around their home without a search warrant—which, of course, she could never get now because she's no longer a police officer."

Tammy gasped. Waycross shook his head. Granny winced and gave Savannah a quick look of sympathy. Dirk cleared his throat, and Savannah could tell he was about to say something, if possible, even more rude than Lenora's statements.

So, she jumped ahead of him. "That's exactly right, Dr. Hart. Law enforcement officers frequently do lie to those they deal with. Unfortunately, when working with hardened criminals, it's a means to an end. It's a tool that's commonly used, as it is in big business. Isn't that right, Mr. Hart?"

He gave his wife a quick, timid look, then replied, "I wouldn't want to say that it's commonly used, but, well, yes, it is. Lies are part of everyday life in the corporate world. It's unfortunate, but the truth."

Granny could take it no longer. "Enough with the tomfoolery. I wanna hear what Savannah found when she went snooping in that sorry excuse for a human being's house."

Savannah felt a renewed thrill trickle through her system as she remembered what was on the opposite side of the closed bedroom door. "I found a room totally dedicated to Beth Malloy," she told them. "Pictures of her covered the walls—I mean, every available inch was plastered with photos of her. Some of them are from magazines and newspapers. But most of them were candid shots."

"Do you mean to tell us," Gran asked, "that they were pictures he took himself? Like, he's been stalking her?"

"That's exactly what I mean. There were photos of her shopping, playing with Freddy at the beach, and even creepier than that, pictures of her dressing and bathing in her own home."

"Oh, that *is* creepy!" Tammy said. "He's not only a stalker, but a Peeping Tom, too!"

"And get this," Dirk interjected. "Some of those pictures of her playing outside with Freddy—they were taken at the park where Pilar was killed."

Tammy caught her breath. "Then he knew they were in the habit of going there."

"He didn't have a lot of furniture in the room," Savannah said. "But he did have a desk. On that desk, I found a couple of interesting photographs."

"Do tell," Ryan said.

"Yes, love, do," said John. "The suspense is more than we can bear."

Savannah glanced around to make sure no one else in the restaurant was overhearing this more salacious part of the conversation.

Turning to Tammy, Savannah said, "Remember me telling you that Ethan Malloy was going to be sending us a photo, and I promised him that only the two of us I would look at it?"

"Of course, I do, and he did send it. I haven't had an opportunity to examine it yet. Alone, that is."

Savannah turned to the others at the table. "Sorry for being so cryptic. It's a photo that I had to promise Ethan Malloy I wouldn't allow anyone other than myself and Tammy to see. Without going too much into detail, it's supposedly a picture of his wife, Beth, being intimate with her ex-husband. Ethan believes the photo is authentic and was taken recently."

Waycross spoke up. "What does this have to do with the ex-husband's creepy room filled with stalker pictures?"

"Everything," Savannah replied. "That was one of the two pictures he had on the desk.

"What was the subject of the other photo?" Ryan asked.

"Let's just say it was very similar to the former one. Only this time, the, um, participants were Ethan and his former fiancée, Candace York."

"Didn't Ethan tell you that Beth was accusing him of fooling around with Candace?" Dirk asked Savannah.

"Yes, he did. And Luciana told me that Beth showed her a photo she had received anonymously on the Internet. A picture of Ethan and Candace together."

"Let me guess," Ryan said, "someone sent it to Beth . . . also anonymously."

Savannah nodded. "Luciana said that Neal Irwin is the kind of person who would do something like that—send incriminating photos to a married couple with the intention of breaking them up."

"Obviously, from what you saw in that room," Tammy added, "he's obsessed with Beth and wants her back."

"And he just happens to have both pictures in his spare room," Dirk observed, "not on the walls with the other photos, but on his desk. Front and center."

"We don't need to look at those pictures," Ryan said to Savannah, "since you promised only you and Tammy would. But if you want to give us the e-mail address that sent them, we can trace it back to the IP address and find out who they are."

"That would be great." Savannah turned to Tammy. "Get that to them as soon as you can. Okay, kiddo?"

Tammy pulled her electronic tablet from her purse, punched and scrolled on it for a few seconds, and they all heard Ryan's cellphone ding. She grinned. "Was that fast enough for you?"

"A lot faster than we'll be getting the answer to you," Ryan admitted.

"What if it ain't just about Neal Irwin and his obsessions and malarkey like that?" suggested Granny. "Tammy, you said that manager guy, Abel Orman, he's got a gambling problem. People with that kind of an addiction usually find themselves short of cash, a lot of cash."

"That's true, Gran," Savannah agreed, "but what's your point? Do you think Abel Orman did it?"

"I think we need to keep our minds open at this point. If that young woman hadn't gotten killed, then I'd be thinking more about the obsession thing. But she did. And I'm wondering if the person who killed her might have been out to kidnap Beth and Freddy for ransom and poor Pilar got in the way, you know, like she gave her life, trying to protect her mistress and the baby."

Savannah nodded thoughtfully. "That's a possibility, Granny, worth keeping in mind. Luciana spoke very highly of Pilar, and so did Ethan. Apparently, she loved Beth and Freddy very much, so it's quite likely that she would fight to defend them if necessary."

"Then what's next on the agenda?" Waycross asked.

"We have to check out Irwin's alibi," Savannah told him. "He claims he was working all morning and afternoon at the car lot. Then he says he was at a local bar in the evening, where he picked up a chick . . . his words, not mine."

"Whether he was at the car lot or not shouldn't be hard to determine," John said. "Whether he was able to seduce a woman into spending time with him in the evening, that might prove difficult."

"That's for sure," Granny said. "If a woman was to have a weak moment and agreed to keep that dirty dog company for a night, she probably wouldn't own up to it, come mornin' light."

Dirk finished his steak and leaned back in his chair, the picture of misery born of gluttony. "First thing tomorrow, I'll go back over to the mortuary and rattle Dr. Liu's cage again. See if she's done with Pilar."

"You 'rattled Dr. Liu's cage'?" Savannah asked him indignantly. "You know better than to try that. I'm the only one who can hurry her along."

"Yeah, and we know how, don't we?" he snapped back. "If you didn't take chocolate candy or fresh-baked chocolate chip cookies, you'd get thrown out on your ear, too."

"She threw you out on your ear?"

"I don't wanna talk about it."

"Sorry I missed that. Would have been entertaining, no doubt."

Dirk turned his back on Savannah and said to the others, "We've gotta start thinking about organizing a search party."

"Oak Grove Park?" Ryan asked.

Dirk nodded. "It's gonna be murder, trying to get through that thick brush and the prickly pear cactus—"

"And the rattlesnakes," Savannah added with a shiver.

"Oh, we have searchers galore, if we want them," Tammy said. "Didn't you see the fan club's appeal on the five o'clock news?"

"We were interviewing Irwin about then," Savannah told her.

"You should have watched it. Here, let me see if I can find the segment on the news station's website."

Once again, her fingers flew over the tablet as she found what she was looking for. "Here," she said, holding the screen under Savannah's nose. "Look at this. They're so devoted, Ethan's fans. Several of them actually called me today after this story broke, wanting to know if there's anything they can do at all to help find Beth and Freddy. It's surprising how informed they were about Ethan and Beth and how they hold them in such high esteem."

Savannah watched the video on Tammy's tablet. Dirk leaned over her shoulder to look, as well.

A dozen women of all ages had gathered in front of reporters to express their concern about Beth and Freddy. Most were younger, but two of them were silver-haired women, and they were just as fervent in their appeals as their other sister fans. They were begging the public to come forward and report any information they might have. At the end of their appeal, they asked for volunteers to come to the hills above Oak Grove Park.

"Can you get in touch with those gals?" Dirk asked Tammy.

"Sure. Would you like me to?"

"Yeah. I'm sure CSI did a good job around where the body was found, but they don't have enough manpower to thoroughly search those hills. Ask them if they, and anybody else they can get to come, could meet us in the park at noon tomorrow."

"I could go interview Orman," Savannah suggested, "the gambler who's got a secret crush on his most famous client's wife, so secret that everybody knows about it except maybe him."

"You gotta go see Dr. Liu with me first," Dirk said. "Then after we do that, you can go talk to Orman, while I'm poking around in the hills, getting rattlesnake bit."

"Do you think it would be okay if I joined your search?" Tammy's father asked.

Savannah was surprised and not just because it was one of the few sentences he had contributed to the dinner conversation. She was pleasantly taken aback to see a smile on his face and a twinkle in his eyes that she recognized all too well. It was the same sparkle that his daughter's eyes had when she was working a case.

It appeared the apple hadn't fallen that far from the Hart family tree after all.

"Of course, you'd be welcome to join in the search, Mr. Hart," Savannah told him. "The more, the better."

It took only a moment for Dr. Lenora Hart to absorb what had just been said and to raise a complaint. "Quincy, I can't imagine why you would want to join in such a thing."

"Because I think it's fascinating, this work they

do," he replied, showing more boldness and gumption than Savannah would've thought him capable of. "I've been listening to them for the past hour and thinking, *What a wonderful way to make a living.* A lot more exciting than board meetings, that's for sure. There's a mother and a baby missing," he continued. "If I can help find them and return them to their friends and family, what an amazing thing that would be."

"Get real, Quincy, do you really think you're going to be the one to solve this case of theirs?"

"Well, I don't know, Lenora. I might, and I might not. But I could at least try. What have I got to lose?"

"Your dignity. You're too old to go rummaging around in sagebrush. What would your board members think?"

"I don't give a damn what my board members think. We spend way too much time in this family worrying about what other people think, and I'm tired of it."

Suddenly, Quincy Hart stood, reached across the table, and took his granddaughter from Dirk's arms. He held her close to his chest for a while, breathing in the wonder of her delicate baby scent. Then he kissed her cheek and sat down.

He turned the infant to face him, pressed his nose to hers, looked into her big blue eyes, and said, "From now on, sweetheart, if you want to make happy noises, even in a public place, you go right ahead. Like Granny said, it's the sweetest sound in the world."

Quincy looked over at his wife with a strange

combination of affection and sadness. "Starting right now," he told his grandchild, "in our family, we're going to worry a lot less about what other people think about us. We aren't any more important than anyone else. Chances are good, they aren't thinking about us at all."

Chapter 19

The next morning, Savannah and Dirk arrived at the morgue armed for battle. Their weapon: a plastic container filled with chocolate chip/macadamia nut cookies, fresh from Savannah's oven.

No one could say "no" to Savannah's baking. Least of all, Dr. Jennifer Liu, the county's top medical examiner.

She was the only woman Savannah had ever known who craved chocolate as much as she did.

Once they walked through the front door of the drab, depressing building, Savannah steeled herself for what would inevitably come next.

Kenny Bates.

She hated Kenny Bates, the behemoth who manned the front desk with the same ferocity as the Hound of Hades guarded the gates of hell, preventing those inside from escaping their eternal torment.

She wasn't sure why she disliked him so much, though she had a plethora of reasons from which to choose: his taco-chip breath, his flea-infested toupee, his too-tight shirt that gapped open, revealing curly black belly hair. Or maybe it was the fact every time he laid eyes upon her he couldn't resist telling her how deeply in lust he was with her. Although she was quite sure that he behaved just as badly with other woman he met, that knowledge did little to keep her from fantasizing about ways to murder him. Painful ways. Heinous ways.

She often did the math. If she had killed him the minute she'd met him, she would almost be eligible for parole by now.

Ah, twenty-twenty hindsight, she thought as she approached the counter, *you can be cruel.*

When she had Dirk with her, she always thought that Bates would be smart enough not to say anything stupid to her. But she had decided long ago that Kenny possessed absolutely zero self-control. He couldn't help himself, even if it meant taking a beating.

The moment he heard the door close behind them and their footsteps approaching, he flipped off his computer screen and sauntered over to the counter where the sign-in clipboard resided. She watched as the expression on his face went from down-in-the-mouth to drool-out-of-the-mouth.

Apparently, just the sight of her made his day. She supposed she should be flattered to be so adored. But she would've much preferred to have been beaten with a wet squirrel then face Kenny Bates that morning—or any other morning for that matter.

"Hell-o-o, beautiful! I was wondering when I was gonna see you again" was the chipper greeting that awaited her as she stepped up to the counter, in search of the clipboard and its all-important sign-in sheet.

"Shut up, Bates," Dirk warned him. "I'm not in the mood and neither is she."

"I'm just saying hello to the prettiest woman who ever walked through those doors. Ain't nothing offensive about that."

"Bates," Savannah said, "you could recite the Lord's Prayer and make it sound dirty. Hand me the dadgum clipboard."

"I'm not a machine, you know, handing out sign-in sheets like a trained monkey. I keep this place safe, too."

"Yeah, from all those marauding hordes who wanna break in here and steal themselves a corpse."

"I'm a policeman like any other one."

"Frightening thought."

"You should show me more respect."

Savannah pasted the most deliberately phony smile she could summon across her face and said, "Officer Kenneth Bates, defender of Truth, Justice, and the American Way . . . if I have to go back there myself and find that clipboard, I swear I'll beat you to death with it."

Bates gasped and turned to Dirk. "Did you hear that? She threatened me. Your wife threatened me with bodily harm."

"No, not bodily harm. Death. That was a death threat, and I'm pretty sure she means it. You'd better do what she says. She's a scary broad."

"Yeah? Well, you married her."

"I happen to like scary broads. I feel safe when she's around."

"I don't."

"You shouldn't. She hates your guts. If I were you, I'd produce that clipboard pronto."

Bates reached up, straightened his toupee, then squatted down and grabbed a board from somewhere under the counter.

He groaned as he stood and held it out to Savannah. Locking eyes with her, he waggled one eyebrow and smiled.

No doubt, he'd intended it to be a sexy "come hither" look. But he failed by a mile. Rather than getting her hot and bothered, his smarmy, leering grin reminded her of a poor, run-over opossum, lying by the roadside for a week in the Georgia sun.

"Put it on the counter," she said.

"Here it is. Come and get it." He leaned back, holding it close to his chest. When she made a half attempt to grab it, he slid it down to his crotch area.

For a big guy, Dirk could move fast when he wanted to, and apparently, he wanted to. Badly. The next thing Savannah saw was an indiscernible whirlwind of activity. Then she heard Kenny yelping like a hound dog with his nose caught in a hole in the backdoor screen.

Finally, she was able to focus on bits and pieces of the flurry before her, and she realized that her husband was beating the tar out of ol' Kenny with his own clipboard.

When it broke in half, he used both pieces.

By the time Dirk was finished, Kenny's toupee

was nowhere to be seen, Kenny had a bump on his forehead that was visibly growing by the second. His lip had a split, and blood was dribbling down his chin.

"Hey, I was just funnin' with your wife," he sobbed, backing away from Dirk. "You had no call to do that."

"If I'd done what I 'had call to do' you'd be on your way to the hospital right now." Dirk turned to Savannah. "I think we'll just let Bates here sign us in, babe. Let's get goin'."

A moment later, they were walking down the long hallway that led to the autopsy suite.

Savannah slipped her arm through Dirk's and leaned her head on his shoulder. "I want you to know that I appreciate you defending my honor like that back there, but I don't condone violence."

"I have no idea what you're talking about. We just had a little discussion about the proper way to hold a clipboard when you're offering it to a lady."

"You laid hands on him first. Gran says, 'Never put your hands on your fellow man in anger. But if he strikes the first blow, beat the ever-lovin' tar outta him so he'll never even think of doin' it again.'"

"Yeah, you and Gran are real peace-lovin' women."

"We are."

He snorted. "This from the woman who pelted the doughnut gal with her own doughnuts because she grabbed my ass when I was gettin' a fresh cup of coffee."

"I didn't allow myself more than a dozen. Besides, they were just itty-bitty doughnut holes, not apple fritters or anything heavy enough to do any real harm."

"There I thought you were outta control."

"Never."

They arrived at the large, swinging double doors that opened into the morgue's autopsy suite, Dr. Jennifer Liu's domain.

Savannah made sure the container of cookies was in front of her, held almost at eye level. Heaven forbid that the ME should happen to be in a bad mood and not notice the sacrificial offering.

Opening one of the doors a crack, Savannah looked inside. She saw Dr. Liu bending over the stainless-steel table, where she performed most of her work. Inspection, dissection, investigation—all done by the medical examiner to answer the lengthy list of questions society had when one of its members died unexpectedly.

Law enforcement wanted to know, the justice system wanted to know, and most of all, those who loved the deceased desperately needed to know.

Dr. Jennifer Liu was good at finding out what had happened to those who were unfortunate enough to end up on her autopsy table. She knew how important those questions were to those who asked them. She also knew that sometimes the only good thing that could come from a terrible situation was truth.

Before announcing her presence, Savannah paused and watched Dr. Liu as she locked the zipper of a body bag on her table, securing its contents.

From the moment they had met, Savannah had been mystified by this strange woman. Jennifer Liu looked more like an actress or fashion model than a medical examiner. Tall, thin, graceful, she was beautiful in an exotic way. When she was working, her long black hair was pulled back into a pony-tail, usually tied with a colorful silk scarf. Today, it was a print—orange, red, and yellow flames.

Savannah had never once seen her wearing "sensible" footwear. The doctor's shoe closet must have been a wonder to behold, filled with spiky stilettos, strappy sandals, rhinestone-encrusted platforms, and thigh-high leather boots.

The sexy shoes, combined with Dr. Liu's signature miniskirts, caused her to look like anything but a medical examiner from the waist down. The upper half was always professional, covered in a standard physician's white coat. Once in a while, if it was a particularly messy autopsy, she would don disposable green scrubs.

Today she was wearing the white coat, and Savannah was glad. It was bad enough to lose a beautiful young woman like Pilar. But at least her family would be able to view her one last time if they chose.

In her time Savannah had seen far more violent, downright grisly deaths, and she was somewhat relieved that this didn't appear to be one of them.

Dead was dead. But one death could be much worse than another.

As Dr. Liu finished gathering her instruments, she glanced up and caught sight of Savannah. More importantly, she saw the cookies.

She grinned, but only for a moment. Then her forehead wrinkled into a frown. "Is *he* with you?" she asked. "Did you bring *him* with you?"

"I'm afraid so." Savannah pushed the door open a bit farther to reveal Dirk, who was standing just to her side.

"I'm not talking to him." Dr. Liu tossed the tools of her trade onto a steel tray. "He was in here yesterday, noodging me, making a total nuisance of himself. Two days of Coulter in a row is more than I can take."

"But he feels really bad about it," Savannah assured her. "In fact, he was awake most of the night, pacing the floor, and wailing something about offending his favorite medical examiner. He was pert nigh beside himself with remorse."

Savannah turned to Dirk, poked him in the ribs with her elbow, and whispered, "Weren't you?"

"Yeah, yeah, yeah, that's me. Overwrought with guilt." He rolled his eyes.

"A less sincere apology, I've never heard." Dr. Liu took the tray of used instruments and carried them across the room. She placed the assortment in a sink and then began to wash her hands, using a red, strong-smelling soap from a nearby dispenser.

When she had finished, she dried her hands and turned to Savannah and Dirk. "Come in, come in," she said, beckoning them. "But only because you brought Savannah, and Savannah brought cookies," she added.

Savannah handed her the container, then walked over to stand next to the body on the table. "Is this our girl?" she asked sadly.

"Yes. I just finished with her."

"What did you find?" Dirk wanted to know.

"Cause of death: blunt force trauma to the brain. Manner of death: homicide."

Dirk groaned. "Damn. There's no chance it was an accident? Like maybe she fell and hit her head on something?"

"No, I'm sorry, Detective. No chance."

"But how do you know for sure?"

Savannah winced, expecting Dirk to receive a sharp tongue-lashing from the proud and outspoken ME.

But to her surprise and relief, Dr. Liu didn't seem to mind the question. Her voice was uncharacteristically calm and patient when she answered, "Your victim's brain was only damaged on one side, the side where she was hit. When the head is stationary, and it's hit by a moving object, the damage is done on that side only, in the area where it was struck. On the other hand, if the hard object is stationary, and the head is moving, you'll find damage on the side that came in contact with the stationary object and on the opposite side, as well. It's physics, Detective Coulter, and the way the brain moves within the skull upon impact. Understand?"

"Not really," he admitted. "But if you say so."

"Do you have any idea what she might have been struck with?" Savannah asked.

"Yes. A rock."

"You know that for a fact?" Dirk asked.

"Yes."

"How?" Dirk insisted.

"There was residue from the stone embedded in the tissue around the wound. Plus, CSI told me they found it, your murder weapon, thrown into the bushes between where the body was found and the parking lot. It was about ten feet from the path."

Dirk looked at Savannah. She could see the excitement building in him, the same as it was growing in her. Finally, they had a ruling of homicide. They had a murder weapon. It was the oldest weapon ever used by human beings against their enemies. And right then it was at the Crime Scene Unit being processed.

"Is there anything else you can tell us, Dr. Jen?" Savannah asked.

"A couple of things. One, she struggled with her attacker. She has bruises around her wrists and marks, where the killer's fingernails dug into her."

"Did she have any of their skin or blood under her nails?" Dirk asked.

"No. Surprisingly none. However, she did have traces of red fibers. I'll be sending those over to the lab within the hour. I understand there was a red knapsack of some sort found in the scene. Is that right?"

"Yes. A red leather one with a cloth strap," Savannah told her.

"Do you suppose it was the victim's?"

"No," Dirk replied. "It belonged to her employer—the woman who's still missing along with her kid."

"CSI will be comparing the fibers that I found against the ones on that bag, I'm sure. As for me, that's all I have for you."

The doctor reached into the container, pulled out a cookie, and took a bite. She closed her eyes as she chewed, savoring the moment.

When she was finished, she replaced the lid on the container and stood on tiptoe to stash it on the top shelf of the nearby cupboard.

"I'd forgotten how good your cookies are, Savannah," she said. "Anytime you want to bring that guy of yours around here, you go right ahead."

"As long as I've got cookies."

"Exactly."

Chapter 20

"You should've saved at least half of those cookies to bring to Eileen," Dirk told Savannah as they pulled into the CSI parking lot. "You know how she can be sometimes."

Savannah glanced over at Dirk in the passenger seat and saw something on his face that struck terror in her heart. Guilt. She knew the look all too well.

"You've been here already about this case, haven't you?"

"Why would you even ask something like that?"

"You came over here yesterday either before or after you pissed off Dr. Liu. That's why you wanted me to come with you, isn't it? Come on, confess and you'll feel a lot better."

"I plead the Fifth. I wanna lawyer."

She growled and grumbled under her breath as they got out of the car and walked up to the nondescript white door, emblazoned with the county seal.

"If you hadn't annoyed the daylights out of everybody who's supposed to be helping us on this case yesterday, you could be doing this alone, and I could be interviewing Orman. We don't have time to be doubling up on a simple errand like this."

He stopped in his tracks and gave her his "I've got a great idea that you're gonna love!" look. It was seldom a great idea and she almost never loved it, but that never stopped him from employing the tactic over and over again.

Usually when he ran out of other plans.

"You're absolutely right," he said with rare enthusiasm. "Why don't you talk to Eileen here, and I'll go to the park and organize the search team. They'll be arriving there pretty soon, and I really ought to be there."

He turned around as though he was heading back to the car, but she grabbed him by the sleeve and held on tightly.

"Oh, no you don't. We've only got one car. You're not stranding me here and driving my pony. No way."

His face fell, and he muttered something under his breath that she could only half hear.

From the half that she heard, she figured he was pretty darned lucky that she hadn't heard all of it.

"Besides," she said as they turned back toward the building and continued up the walkway to the door, "if Eileen's in a dither over something you said or did yesterday, then you've got to calm her down yourself, face the music, take your lickin', pay your debt to society, reestablish trust with your fellow—"

"That's enough, woman. Any minute now I'm going to fly into a blind rage."

"Yeah, yeah. I've heard it all before, many times before. I live in fear. Trembling, mind you."

"You better. I'm a terror when I'm roused."

She squeezed his arm and gave him a suggestive grin. "Actually, I like it when you're 'roused.' I'd venture to say that 'roused' is my very favorite version of you."

He chuckled deep in his throat and shot her a sideways look that went straight to her nether regions.

Ah, men and their voices. A gal didn't stand a chance.

Nor did she want one.

As they approached the door, she noticed that he was hanging back a bit, allowing her to go first. Usually he did this out of chivalry and old-fashioned good manners. But now she had the distinct feeling that he was hiding behind her skirts. Or her slacks, as the case might be.

It was just as well. Eileen would look at her CCTV monitor screen before opening the door. She might as well see a friendly face first, not the mug of someone she wanted to strangle.

Savannah pushed the buzzer and heard the abrasive sound echo through the building on the other side of the door.

No wonder Eileen and her team are cranky, Savannah thought. *If I had to listen to that all day I would be, too.*

It took quite a while, as it always did, for someone to answer. The building was large, and the team was often in the back, where the evidence was examined. The front half was devoted to offices and all matters computer-oriented.

Finally, the speaker mounted over the door crackled to life, and they heard a testy voice say, "Hello, Savannah. I see he brought you with him this time."

Savannah looked up at the camera mounted beside the speaker and gave it a bright, dimple-deepening grin. "You didn't think I'd miss a chance to come down here and say 'howdy' to my favorite crime scene techs, did you?"

The door opened and a woman in her sixties with long silver curly hair beckoned them inside. "You don't have to kiss up quite that much," Eileen Bradley told Savannah. "He wasn't that horrible yesterday. Just his usual pushy, obnoxious self. Especially since you brought me cookies."

Savannah gulped. "Cookies? Cookies?"

Eileen looked at her empty hands and her expression went from "friendly" to "not nearly so friendly."

"I just got off the phone with Liu, and she said she got cookies."

"Darn you, Dr. Jen," Savannah mumbled. "Rat me out, will ya." To Eileen she said, "I'm sorry. I've had a rough last twenty-four hours, and I only had time to whip up one batch this morning before running out the door."

She held up three fingers in a Girl Scout salute and said, "I swear the next time I come, I'll bring twice as many."

Judging from the scowl on Eileen's face, she

had never been a Girl Scout. The pledge wasn't cutting it.

"Okay," Savannah tried again, "the moment we close this case, I'll bring you the biggest batch you ever saw, and I'll slip them to you on the sly, so that you don't have to share them with anybody here."

That did it. Eileen grinned broadly and said, "Come right in. Tell us what you want, and we'll deliver."

Dirk leaned over and whispered in Savannah's ear, "Those cookies of yours are like magic. One of these days, you gotta teach me how to make those things."

"Next time you get 'roused,' we'll make some together."

"Um-m, that's even better."

Eileen led them past the maze of office cubicles, where lab techs sat, their faces lit a sickly blue from the glow of their computer monitors. Each nodded to Savannah and Dirk as they passed through.

Savannah received a smile with each nod.

Dirk, not so much.

"Except for the DNA tests, which, of course, will take some time, we've finished processing your case," Eileen told Dirk, as they left the office area and proceeded to the back of the building where the hands-on investigations took place.

It was a large, open area with long tables, where evidence could be organized and examined.

Along the walls were benches with all sorts of technical equipment that Savannah didn't recognize. The microscopes were the only things familiar to her.

But she didn't mind the foreign environment.

The members of the CSI were scientists. She was an investigator. They belonged in the lab, and she was at her best in the field.

Every time she worked a case, she was grateful for the truths they uncovered. She couldn't remember a single time that she had solved a crime without their help and expertise.

"You're already finished?" Dirk said, surprised. "Man, that was quick!"

"Not really," Eileen replied. "We only had four pieces to process: the backpack and its contents, the victim's clothing, the Malloy vehicle, and, of course, the murder weapon."

"The rock?" Dirk asked. "Just a plain rock?"

"Yes. Pretty basic. But, unfortunately, for your victim, very effective."

"How can you be sure it was that particular rock?" Savannah asked.

"It had blood on it—her type, A positive, but of course we're waiting for the DNA to be sure. It also had a few long black hairs stuck to it. The color, medulla, cuticle, they all matched the sample taken from her."

"You know, we looked all over for any kind of weapon, including rocks," Dirk told her. "Jake and Mike spent most of the day searching, and they didn't turn up anything."

Eileen shrugged. "They're patrolman. Good patrolman. But they aren't crime scene investigators. They're good at rousting drunks out of bars at closing time and resolving domestic disturbances. We're good at finding rocks with blood and hair on them and finding out whose blood and hair it is."

"Takes all kinds to solve a crime," Savannah said.

"It does," Eileen agreed. "And you should be particularly grateful to the techs who found that one. While pulling it out of a cactus patch, they managed to rub against a large and nasty patch of poison oak. I had to send them home with big bottles of calamine lotion."

"Oh, no," Savannah said. "I got that once, and it was miserable. I wanted to cut my leg off to get away from it. Tell them we appreciate their sacrifice in the line of duty."

"I will. But if you really want to make it up to them—"

"I know. Cookies."

"That's the cure."

Eileen led them to the back of the room, to a long table covered with white craft paper. Lying on the paper was Beth's and Freddy's red backpack, along with its contents.

Just looking at the items brought tears to Savannah's eyes—a small box of miniature cars and trucks, a coloring book and crayons, a few classic children's books, and a Spider-Man cape and mask. Among the toys was a plastic container filled with tiny squares of mango, mixed with fresh blueberries.

Savannah thought of how Ethan had cried when he'd named his son's favorite foods.

"We found something unsettling on the fabric strap of that backpack," Eileen told them.

"Oh, goody," Dirk said dryly. "What?"

"The torn ends of several fingernails," she told them. "It looks like your victim was holding on to it to the very end, and it was ripped out of her hands."

"You're right," Savannah said. "That *is* unsettling."

On the second table lay Pilar's floral print dress. Since Savannah had last seen it on Pilar, the garment had been cut down the front, from neckline to hem. No doubt, Dr. Liu had done the cutting before the autopsy, as it was difficult to undress a body in rigor mortis.

Savannah couldn't help thinking about the young woman who had put on that dress yesterday morning, never dreaming what her day would hold. She would never have imagined that she was living her last hours of life.

At times like that Savannah often had a strange, illogical, but overwhelming desire to somehow go back in time and warn a victim.

"Don't leave the house today, Pilar," she would have told her. "Don't let Beth or Freddy go either. For heaven's sake, please stay home where it's safe, all three of you."

"Where's the rock?" Dirk was asking.

Savannah put foolish fantasies aside and listened to the conversation at hand.

"It's over here." Eileen led them to a nearby workbench, where a large microscope sat beside a white cardboard box about twelve inches square. On the box was a red evidence-identification label, filled out with the appropriate information.

She handed both Savannah and Dirk surgical gloves, and slipped on a pair herself. Once everyone was adequately fitted, she lifted the lid of the box and set it aside.

"I didn't seal the box yet," she said. "I figured you'd be by to look at the rock this morning—bright and early, knowing you."

Dirk grinned. "You know me too well."

Eileen did not grin. "Yes, I do. Far better than I ever wanted to, believe me."

Savannah winced, but as usual, Dirk didn't react to the insult. Whether he had tough skin or didn't realize he was being dissed, she didn't know. Fortunately, she had the rest of their lives to figure him out.

Eileen carefully lifted the rock from the box and held it out to Dirk. "There you go," she said. "Your murder weapon."

At first, Savannah saw nothing but a rock. Yes, it was large, nearly filling Dirk's palm. And it was pointed on one end, making it all the more dangerous. But Savannah saw nothing in the way of blood or hair or anything else biological in nature.

As though reading her mind, Eileen said, "I know. It's hard to tell with the naked eye. But under the microscope you can see some blood, some skin cells, and the hairs I told you about. If you like I'll put it under the scope, and you can see for yourself."

"No," Dirk said quickly. "I'll take your word for it."

Savannah suppressed a smile. Dirk had always been a bit queasy about these matters. He had seen enough in the field to last a lifetime, as had she.

She possessed a certain degree of curiosity about biological and forensic matters that he didn't, and she would've been interested in seeing the evidence magnified.

On the other hand, she was well aware that Dirk was the one here, the only one, who was sanctioned by the state to investigate this crime. She was a civilian, and thereby needed to be careful how much she intruded into his territory.

But she did have one question. "The biological material that you found, was it there on the point, that sharp area on top?"

"Yes, it was," Eileen told her. "However, we swabbed the entire rock for DNA."

"That's good. The killer's palm might've been sweaty," Savannah said.

"Or," Dirk added, "some of his skin cells might've even rubbed off when he hit her. It must've taken quite a bit of force to kill her with one blow."

"That's true," Eileen agreed. "The human skull does a pretty good job of protecting the brain. It's tougher than you think."

"How about the car?" Savannah asked. "Did you find anything that was unusual?"

"No. Nothing at all. The objects inside were only what you would expect to find in a family car. We lifted quite a few prints, inside and out, but they all belonged to the family members and Pilar."

"That bites," Dirk said. "I was hoping there'd be a note from the killer, a full confession with his name, address, and phone number on it."

"Oh, yeah. That happens all the time." Eileen carefully set the rock back in the box, replaced the lid, and then sealed it with four long lengths of tape, bearing the word EVIDENCE in red capital letters. Then she signed the label, and wrote the date and time on it as well.

Dirk sighed. "You be sure to let me know the instant you get those DNA results and not a minute later," he said with an impatient, bossy tone.

Eileen gave him a dirty look. "Do *not* even start with me, Coulter. I mean it. I'll call you when the results come in. If I haven't called you, that means I don't have them. So, don't bug me about them. Got it?"

"It's not like you left a lot of room there for ambiguity," he mumbled, looking down at the floor.

Eileen turned to Savannah. "You should know, I'm not going to give him the results over the phone. He's going to have to come in here and get them in person. Needless to say, he has to bring you, too."

Savannah laughed. "He has to bring me, and I have to bring cookies. A double batch. It's about the cookies, isn't it?"

Eileen grinned and slapped Savannah on the back. "Of course, it's about the cookies. It's *always* about the cookies."

Chapter 21

As Savannah drove into Oak Grove Park to deliver Dirk to the scheduled search, her car phone rang. It was Tammy calling with what she liked to call a "breaking news bulletin."

"Neal Irwin's alibi is solid," she announced with much gleeful enthusiasm—as though she was delivering tidings of joy.

Most of the time, Tammy was a perfect human being in Savannah's estimation. A little too perky in the morning before Savannah had consumed her customary two full mugs of coffee, a little too strict in the dietary department, and a little too outspoken about the virtues of "deliberate exercise." The only exercise that Savannah deliberately participated in was running down a bad guy, hurling him to the ground, pouncing on him, and straddling him, thereby restraining him until Dirk arrived with a pair of cuffs.

The experts said that a person should do an exercise they enjoy. Savannah enjoyed that. Enormously. Since she figured it burned at least fifty thousand calories, she'd decided that doing it once every six months fulfilled those pesky "deliberate exercise" quotas.

But there was this other fatal flaw in Tammy's otherwise sparkling psyche. When one delivered bad news, the deliverer should be mindful of the emotions their news was likely to evoke on the receiving end.

Words that were likely to plunge those who heard them into a deep well of despair should be spoken in a grave, doom-and-gloom tone of voice. Not with the cheerful enthusiasm one would expect from Minnie Mouse, announcing to thousands of eager boys and girls that Disneyland was now open.

"That is *not* good news," Dirk barked at the phone clipped to Savannah's visor. "I did not want to hear that, Tammy. He is the only suspect we have, you know."

"Well, ex-cu-u-use me!" came the testy retort. "I thought you'd want to hear the truth, even if it's inconvenient, but no-o-o. Bite my head off, would you?"

Savannah grinned. It was good to hear Tammy giving Dirk tit-for-tat these days. Since little Vanna had been born, Tammy had experienced a surge of hormones that lowered her sweetness and light level a bit.

That was fine with Savannah. A tad more vinegar to go along with all the sugar was often just what a gal needed to get along more smoothly in the wicked ol' world.

"How do you know he was where he said he was?" Dirk demanded, unable to let the dream die.

"I know because I sent my husband and my dad to his workplace, and they verified he was there all day. He never left, not even for lunch. Then Waycross and Dad went to the bar where he said he went after work. Half a dozen people, including the owner, told them that they saw him there all evening, drinking like he was afraid the tap was going to rust closed. They verified that he picked up a girl named Bambi and took her home. They even gave Waycross Bambi's address."

"All right," Dirk grumbled. "Give me the address. I'll go check out this Bambi broad."

"You don't need to. Waycross and Dad already did it."

"Way to go, Team Tammy!" Savannah said, shaking imaginary pom-poms.

"Well? What did they find out?" Dirk asked, pom-pom-free.

"She told them that she brought him home, they watched a dirty movie, fooled around, ordered pizza, ate it, and went to sleep."

"And how can you be so sure that he didn't pay her to say all that?" Dirk insisted.

"Waycross and Dad aren't dummies. They checked it out."

Dirk still wasn't convinced. "How?"

"My dad asked her if she'd mind showing them on her cable rental menu where she bought the pay-per-view porn. She did, and there they were. They'd ordered two, the first at 9:38 p.m., *Against All Bods*, and at 10:57 p.m., *Frisky Business*."

"I suppose Waycross and your dad checked out

the pizza place, too?" Dirk asked, starting to sound a bit impressed, whether he wanted to be or not.

"Yes, they did. After they left Bambi, they went to the pizza parlor. The manager looked it up on their computer and showed it to Waycross and Dad. They delivered a large pizza with everything on it to that address at 11:28 p.m. Waycross even insisted on talking to the guy who delivered it. A guy named Mel. Mel had no problem remembering Neal. He said he answered the door wearing nothing but some little red bikini underwear. Mel says he's scarred for life."

"Aren't we all," Savannah said.

"Me more than you," Dirk complained. "I just lost my last suspect."

Savannah reached over and squeezed his knee. "That's not true, sugar. We've still got Orman, the degenerate gambler and rosebush killer, and I haven't even talked to Candace York yet."

"That's right, Dirk-o," Tammy said. "Your investigation may be on life support, but it's not altogether dead."

"Gee, with encouragement like that, I think I'll go to the zoo and hurl myself into the tiger habitat."

"O-o-o, I just love tigers," Tammy cooed. "Did you know that no two tigers have the same pattern of stripes? They're kinda like fingerprints with each one being unique and—"

"Good-bye, kiddo," Dirk said. "Thanks for the good work."

"Yeah," Savannah added. "Come down and join the search if you feel up to it."

"I'd like to. But it's not my mom's kinda thing,

and I don't feel like I should leave her by herself, after her coming all this distance to see me. You know what I mean?"

"I know exactly what you mean. Tell your husband and dad I said, 'Thanks a bunch.'"

"You'll probably see them before I do. They're volunteering for the search. They're probably already there now. And by the way, there's another thing about tigers. They—"

Dirk reached up and switched off the phone. He turned to Savannah. "I know she's your best friend, and she's a great gal, good heart and all that. But she drives me crazy sometimes."

"A two-minute ride that'd be, I reckon," she mumbled.

"What?"

"Nothing." She turned off the ignition and started to get out of the car. That was when she saw at least one hundred people standing in a line along the yellow police cordon tape.

Dirk saw them, too. "Wow! What a turnout!"

"No kidding, and look who's front and center."

"Ethan Malloy himself."

"Good for him," Savannah said. "It's his family that's missing. Of course he'd want to be in on the search."

"Come on, darlin'," Dirk said. "Let's go get this unruly mob organized."

As Savannah approached the crowd, she saw another familiar face. One that failed to give her a warm, fuzzy feeling. It was Neal Irwin, standing off to the side of the crowd, well away from Ethan Malloy. He was holding the hand of a woman with a frightening amount of badly bleached blond hair and dramatic cat eyeliner.

Dirk had spotted him, too. "Hey look. Mr. Red Banana Exhibitionist has decided to join us. Oh, well. Could be worse. We can thank our lucky stars that he's dressed at least."

"Why do I have a sneaking suspicion that the woman with him is none other than his pizza-eating friend from last night, Miss Bambi?"

"I suspect you're right."

"Who cares? As long as they're here to search, they're welcome. Especially now that he's no longer a suspect."

"Gr-r-r-r."

As soon as Ethan spotted Savannah walking his way, he headed in her direction. They met in the middle of the lawn, near the swing set. She was shocked and dismayed to see that he looked even more exhausted and depressed than the last time she had seen him, less than twenty-four hours before.

"How are you?" she asked, afraid of his answer.

But he was stoic and gave her a simple "Okay, I guess." He looked around at the crowd, which appeared to be growing by the moment. "I thought it would be a good idea to come down here. It beats sitting at home and feeling helpless, doing nothing."

"I'm sure that's an awful feeling," Savannah agreed.

"But now that I'm here, I realize a lot of my fans

showed up, and I don't know if they're here to help or . . ."

"Or to see you?"

"Something like that."

Savannah saw Dirk getting his bullhorn from the trunk of the Mustang. He was wearing his serious, no-nonsense-allowed scowl.

"Don't worry about that," she told Ethan. "They may have come to catch sight of you in the flesh, but my husband will have them out there among the weeds and the rattlers in two shakes of a lamb's tail. Nobody volunteers to join his search and gets away with loitering."

She glanced around the ever-increasing group and noticed that at least fifty or more of the volunteers were wearing baby blue T-shirts, decorated with a darling picture of Freddy. They stood off to one side and a woman with bright red hair was addressing them. Savannah couldn't hear what she was saying, but her tone sounded urgent and her body language intense.

"I wonder who they are," she said, pointing toward the group in blue.

"That's one of my fan clubs," he replied. "They're probably the most active group of followers I have. They're certainly the best organized. The lady with the ginger hair is Kitty Z., the club president. As soon as she found out there was going to be a search and we needed volunteers, she got right on it. She knows Beth and thinks the world of her. She really wanted to help."

"I've seen her before," Savannah said. "I just can't think—oh, I remember. She and some silver-haired ladies were on the news last night, pleading for anyone who knew anything to come forward."

He nodded. "Yes, the silver-haired ladies are Imogene and Lydia. They're awesome, too. They called Abel this morning to tell him to pass along their love and concern."

"You know your fans by name?"

He shrugged and grinned. "I guess I'm expected to look down my nose at my fans and act like they annoy me. But the truth is, the ones I've met are really great people. I enjoy interacting with them whenever I get the chance. Without them, my audience, I wouldn't be an actor. If they weren't watching my performances, I wouldn't be able to do what I enjoy for a living."

He looked around at all the baby blue shirts, the women, and even men, who were wearing them. "They could be anywhere doing anything right now, but they're giving up their day to come out here and trudge around these hot, dusty hills, to help me find my baby. They are more than just fans; they're friends."

Savannah could see that Dirk was getting ready to address the crowd with his bullhorn. She turned to Ethan. "Come on. Let's get you up there, front and center. If they love you that much, we don't want them to forget who they're doing this for."

Chapter 22

As Savannah had predicted, it didn't take long for Dirk to get the crowd organized. He barked his instructions through the megaphone, they dispersed to their assigned areas. Following his directions, they lined up, side by side, only a few feet apart, and began to move forward, searching, searching.

"What are we looking for?" several volunteers had asked.

"Anything out of the ordinary" had been Dirk's answer. "Even if it just looks like garbage, let us know. If it isn't part of the natural terrain, we want to know about it. Either come and tell me, or talk to one of these fine police officers in blue."

He pointed to a line of cops, most of whom were off duty, but like the other volunteers wanted to help find the missing child and his mother. The off-duty SCPD volunteers were wearing jeans and royal blue T-shirts with the word POLICE printed in large yellow letters across their chests.

She noticed that Dirk had directed the Malloy fans in the pale blue shirts to search the park itself, scouring the perfectly groomed lawn, along with the flower beds and decorative bushes. Some of them were looking inside the restrooms and around the barbecue area. They even crawled inside the children's "fort" and wriggled their adult bodies through the tube slides.

When one group of them, including the red-haired lady whom Ethan had identified as Kitty Z., came close to where Savannah was searching, Savannah used the opportunity to say, "Hello."

"I saw you on television last night," Savannah told Kitty. "You were most eloquent, asking people to help search for Beth and her baby."

"It's the least I could do," the redhead replied. "The Malloys have been really good to me, and a lot of other people I know. Only a few months ago, we were fundraising for the local animal shelter. Beth and Ethan were there, working our booth at the fair, doing everything they could to help us get money—not to mention the very generous donation they themselves gave."

"That's true," said Imogene. "Ethan and Beth are as down-to-earth as anyone you could know. They treat their fans like friends, even family. How could we not come out now and support them when they need us?"

A few moments later the group moved on, leaving no area unsearched, looking for, as Dirk had said, anything that seemed out of place, anything man-made and not part of the natural beauty of the park.

Savannah took out her phone, and scrolled through her contacts until she found the number that Tammy had given her for Abel Orman. Considering that he was a close number two on her mental suspect list, she thought she would be of more use to Beth and Freddy if she spent her time interviewing a viable suspect, rather than continuing the search.

She was just about to call the number when she glanced up and saw a familiar face in the crowd. It was Orman himself, just one among the many searchers.

He seemed less intent about his work than the others. He was walking about, almost as though he were in a daze. It occurred to Savannah that, in his present state, he could have stepped on a body and not even noticed.

She decided to pull him out of the line, take him to her car and, as Dirk would say, "squeeze him" a bit.

But her plan was more easily imagined than executed.

"Do you mean 'leave the line'?" he asked, as though she had just suggested that he cover his naked body with blue paint and dance at a crossroads at midnight in the light of a full moon.

"I just want to ask you a few questions," she said. "I'm working for your client and friend, Ethan Malloy. Surely you don't mind spending just a few minutes with me if it might help me find his wife, Beth, and their little son."

When he still resisted, she added, "I hear you're fond of Beth. In fact, I hear you're *extremely* fond of her. I'm surprised you wouldn't do everything you can to try to help her."

Just when Savannah thought it was a lost cause, an unexpected ally came to her aid.

Quincy Hart walked up behind Orman, leaned close to him, and said, "If I were you, I'd do as she asks. Before the day's out, you're going to be talking to either her or him." He pointed to Dirk, who stood a few yards away, bellowing into his megaphone. "I've had dinner with them both, and I can tell you right now, she's not only a lot prettier than he is, but she's much better company, too."

"Plus," Savannah added, "if you talk to me, you can do it sitting in my gorgeous, red, fully restored Mustang. If you don't talk to me, you'll wind up having a little chat sitting in the back of his squad car. I guarantee you, 'the cage' as they call it, isn't nearly as comfortable as my bucket seats."

"Okay, okay, okay." Orman the Rosebush Crusher threw up his arms in surrender. "Here I think I'm doing a good thing, volunteering to search for a missing kid and his mom, and I wind up being harassed by the cops."

Savannah slipped her arm through his and walked along beside him companionably.

"You aren't being harassed by the cops. I'm not a cop—not anymore, anyway. I'm just a nosy lady who wants to spend a little time with you and ask you a few personal questions."

"Like what?"

"Like . . . what does it feel like to be in love with

a woman, when that woman is married to the hottest actor in Hollywood?"

Abel stopped dead in his tracks. "I beg your pardon?" he asked, his voice dripping with indignation.

She gave his arm a squeeze and an affectionate little pat. "Just keep walkin', darlin'. Just keep walkin'. If you think that question's a doozy, you just wait. I've got worse ones than that."

A few minutes later, they were sitting in her Mustang. Savannah was asking him questions, and he was refusing to answer most of them.

"I have no intention of discussing how I feel about Beth with you," he was saying, "other than to tell you that I have the utmost respect for the lady. She's smart and beautiful and kind, and extremely talented."

"Is that why you signed a contract with her recently? You're going to be both Ethan's and her manager?"

He looked startled to find out that she knew.

"Oh, you thought that was hush-hush, right? Does Ethan even know?" she asked.

Still there was no answer.

She decided to press a bit further. "Does Ethan know that you're in love with his wife?"

"You need to not say that again. It's insulting to her and to me."

"But it's true. It's not like it's a secret. Love is a hard thing to hide, Abel. You've been so transparent about it that everyone knows."

"I asked you not to say that again."

She could see his fingers clenching into fists. She reminded herself to be careful. Sitting in a car with a man who had a reputation for possessing a foul temper, who might have killed another woman less than twenty-four hours ago, asking him infuriating questions, might not be the smartest thing she had done all day.

"Okay. I won't. But I do need to ask you where you were the day before yesterday, when she disappeared."

He gave her a smile that was anything but warm. In fact, it gave her the creeps, much like he did.

Something was askew with this man, and she wasn't sure what. All she knew was that she didn't trust him. Deep in her gut, where it truly counted, she wouldn't put anything past him.

When he didn't answer her, she repeated her question. "Where were you, Abel, when Pilar was killed and Beth and Freddy went missing?"

"I have an alibi, if that's what you're asking."

"Okay. Phrase it anyway you like, but Mr. Orman, you need to account for your whereabouts during that time period."

Again, he gave her the sinister smile that did nothing to reassure her.

"I was in China."

That was a new one. She couldn't recall ever having someone use China as an alibi.

"Seriously?"

"I have a passport stamp to prove it. I didn't reenter the country until yesterday morning, right before I came over to the Malloy home. This car we're sitting in was in their driveway, so I assume you were there and know that I was, too."

Savannah felt her stomach drop, much like it did on a giant roller coaster when it hit the first big dip.

Another suspect Post-it fell off her mental suspect board and fluttered to the ground.

Two in less than an hour. That had to be some kind of record, even for her.

"What airline?"

"Air China. Beijing to LAX, arriving in LA at nine o'clock a.m. I landed here after a twelve-hour flight and headed straight for Malibu and the Malloys' home."

"Why the rush?"

"I had been there for eight days, discussing a new movie deal for him. The financiers green-lighted the project, and I couldn't wait to tell him. Beth, too. They wanted her to be the leading lady. It would be the chance of a lifetime for her. A role worthy of her talent."

He paused and turned his face away from Savannah to stare out the passenger-side window. "I wouldn't hurt Beth for anything, Ms. Reid," he said, his voice tremulous. "You're right. I do have a great deal of affection for her. But mostly, I just want to do well by her as her manager and her friend. If you don't find her, if she misses out on this, she'll never get over it."

Savannah believed him. She didn't want to, but she couldn't help it. Dirk would be able to find out with one phone call whether or not he had been on the flight. He wasn't a stupid man, and he had to know that.

So, he was probably telling the truth.

Dangnation, she thought.

"All right, Mr. Orman. I'll tell Detective Coulter about your trip to China and your return flight. I have no doubt that what you told me is true. I apologize for offending you with my accusations. Also for my indelicacy when questioning you about personal matters. It was insensitive of me, and I'm sorry for upsetting you."

He turned back to face her. His eyes searched hers deeply before he finally answered. "Thank you, Ms. Reid. A sincere apology is a rare thing in this day and age. I appreciate receiving one from you."

They sat silently for a while, as the tension inside the Mustang gradually subsided.

"Before I get out of this car," he said, "and begin to search again for my friend, my client, and her child, is there anything else I can do for you that might help her?"

"As a matter of fact, Mr. Orman, there is. Thanks to you being in China at the time Ms. Malloy disappeared, I'm now running very low on suspects. Could you tell me if you know anyone else who might consider Ms. Malloy their enemy? Anyone who might wish her harm?"

"There's only one person I know of who hates Beth. One person who despises her so much that they would want to see her dead."

"And who is that?"

"Candace York. Candy never got over the way Beth and Ethan made a fool of her. Her career has never been the same. Her confidence was shattered. When Ethan jilted her for Beth, Candace lost more than a fiancé. She lost part of herself that she'll never get back."

Savannah tried to hide her excitement, but she couldn't as she filled out an imaginary Post-it with Candace's name on it in big, bold black letters, and stuck it at the top of her otherwise empty board.

"Before you start getting all excited though," Abel Orman said, as if reading her mind, "I think I should tell you something."

"What's that?"

"Candace didn't kill Pilar or abduct Beth and Freddy."

"Begging your pardon, sir, but how can you be so sure?"

"Because Candace was with me in Beijing. In fact, she's still there. The financier wants her in the movie, too. And get this, he wants her to play the villainess."

Once again that ugly smile played across Abel Orman's face, and it occurred to Savannah that he could easily play a convincing villain himself.

"Just picture it, if you can," he said. "Ethan the hero, Beth the heroine, and Candace the black-hearted villainess. The fans will go wild!"

Savannah tried to picture it, as requested. She tried to be happy for him. But it was a little hard to get excited about a movie, because a nasty wind had just blown her remaining Post-it away.

Once again, she was staring at an empty board.

Chapter 23

Savannah couldn't remember a time when her rose chintz chair looked more comfortable, her ottoman more inviting, her cats more welcoming. What a wonderful thing "home" was when you were feeling exhausted, frustrated and like a total failure.

"I'm sure I've been more bummed than this at some point in my life, but right now, I can't recollect exactly when," Savannah told Granny, who was sharing the sofa with Lenora.

One glance at Lenora told Savannah that the woman was taking a certain amount of perverse pleasure from seeing her so down in the dumps.

Knowing it made Savannah feel the need to walk across the floor and box Lenora's ears soundly for her.

But she was too tired.

That alone should have told her she was in desperately bad shape.

"You didn't get a lot of sleep last night, darlin'," Gran said gently, as she shifted Vanna Rose on her lap so that the baby could see her Aunt Savannah. "It's no wonder you're frazzled around the edges with all the obstacles you've come up against."

"I hear your search and rescue effort in the park was a waste of time," Lenora said.

Savannah just stared blankly at her for several seconds, not trusting herself to reply in a civil manner. She wasn't in the habit of doing violence to guests under her own roof—with the exception of Marietta, the second oldest of the Reid siblings, who had totally deserved that pillow beating and more—and she didn't want to start beating visitors just yet.

Though Lenora did try her patience sorely.

Momentarily, she entertained a vision of having both Marietta and Lenora on the sofa and her pounding the everlovin' daylights out of them with her best accent pillows.

The pillows would be ruined, no doubt, lace and rosebud ribbon embroidery torn asunder. But it would be worth it. She'd feel so, so much better.

"No, Mother," Tammy said from her seat at the desk. "They didn't find anything during the search. But when you consider that what they were mostly looking for up there in those rugged hills were the bodies of two people, then not finding anything would be classified as 'good news,' no?"

"It's a bittersweet feeling, to be sure, Tammy," Savannah told her. "Of course, we're mighty grateful we didn't find any bodies, but it would've been nice to uncover some sort of clue about what happened to Beth and Freddy. Or find out about the person who may have taken them. Or find something that would lead us to Pilar's killer. *Some* little something. *Any* little something."

"It's a bad break, Savannah girl," Gran said with genuine sympathy, "but don't go thinking you're defeated. Tomorrow's another day."

"All I know," Savannah replied, "is that I started the day with at least three suspects, and now I don't have a single one. That feels like three giant steps backward and right off a cliff."

"Have you ever considered another form of employment?" Lenora suggested. "Something a bit more mundane, perhaps, but that paid better and was actually a boon to society?"

I'll give you a boon, Savannah thought, *a great big boon, right up the rear end.*

"Would you like some refreshments, Dr. Hart?" she asked her unpleasant guest.

She said it with just enough sugar and spice in her voice to sound like the perfect hostess. But she was silently wondering if she still had that box of rat poison under the kitchen sink.

Would it mix well with apple pie? Or would it be detectable? she asked herself.

You can't be careless about these things. You only have one chance to get it right. If you blow it, it's forty years to life.

Will it show up on the tox screen during the autopsy?

If it does, can I buy off Dr. Jennifer with a lifetime supply of chocolate chippers?

"No, nothing for me," Dr. Hart replied. "All you people eat around here is sugar. It's appalling. And I thought Southern Californians were known for their health consciousness."

"I reckon that's the problem," Granny said softly. "We're a bunch of Georgians, and, though some have learned to do better, most of us still like our pecan pie, peach cobbler, and sweet tea."

"You'll pay for it in the long run."

"Yes, ma'am, that may be so. There's a day of reckonin' for everybody sooner or later, and on that day, I 'magine most of us will wish we'd done things different."

Tammy turned away from the computer and said, "If you don't mind me changing the subject—"

"Heavens, no," Savannah told her. "Please do, as quickly as possible."

"I was just looking at Ethan Malloy's fan pages. I thought *I* was smitten with him, but some of these women just live for him! They make fan-vids, videos where they take clips from all of his movies and put them to music. Some of them are very romantic and nice. Some are funny. They even dub his voice over other actors and create little story lines where he's saying and doing stuff. I mean, they're obsessed with him."

"You should have seen the turnout for that search today," Savannah told her. "They were even wearing matching T-shirts with little Freddy's picture on the front. How did they even get those made so fast?"

"They need to get a life of their own," Lenora said. "Grown women acting like adolescents about a guy with a pretty face."

"And a deep voice," Gran added. "Not to mention muscles galore just poppin' out ever'where."

Tammy sighed. "He's sweet and kind and brave,

too. He plays all those noble characters so well because that's who he is inside."

"Okay, okay," Savannah said. "My blood sugar is going up just listening to y'all. Dr. Lenora just told us the dangers of livin' life too sweetly."

Tammy turned back to the computer and said, "There's something I need to do, and I'm sorry, but I need the room to myself to do it."

"Are you telling us to leave?" Savannah asked, hoping that wasn't what she meant, because, when she had sunk into that chair, she had promised her body that she would never force it to move again.

"Not telling, exactly. But . . . well . . . do you remember that picture you had someone forward to me, and I was only supposed to open it if . . ."

Savannah jumped to her feet. "Oh, right. I forgot all about that." She turned to Gran and Lenora. "How's about you two ladies join me in the backyard for some black coffee or unsweetened tea or—"

"Is everything you people drink full of caffeine?" Lenora gave a derisive sniff. "Because caffeine isn't—"

"*Water!*" Savannah said, trying not to scream. "Anybody want a glass of plain ol' unsweetened, decaffeinated, *cotton-pickin' ice water?*"

"Is it filtered? If it isn't filtered, I—"

Savannah stomped away into the kitchen, muttering, ". . . still under the sink . . . I'll bet it is . . . but how much would it take to . . . ?"

Ten minutes later, Savannah was sitting in her chaise lounge under the wisteria arbor, listening to the bees abuzz in her roses. At least, she was trying to listen to the soothing sounds of nature, but *someone* kept distracting her. Apparently, Lenora found Southern Californians far too casual in their attire. She had seen several diners at ReJuvene the night before who were wearing jeans, and as much as she had liked Ryan and John, she couldn't fully respect any restaurateur who didn't enforce a suitable dress code.

"It's a different culture here," Savannah finally said. "Isn't there something rather sophisticated and worldly about having a flexible attitude about these things when traveling? You know, like 'Live and let live'? 'When in Rome . . . '?"

"No. There is nothing whatsoever sophisticated about wearing jeans to a fine restaurant or granting permission for others to do so."

"Okay. Never mind. It was just a thought."

Savannah looked at Gran, and they both performed perfectly synchronized eye rolls.

"Now that I have the two of you alone," Lenora said, leaning forward in her chair, an intent gleam in her eye, "I have something I need to discuss with you. It's vitally important."

"Of course, Dr. Hart," Gran said. "Do tell us what's on your mind."

"My daughter, of course. Her happiness. I'm very concerned about her."

Savannah thought that her day couldn't have been much more stressful. But she decided it could, and was probably about to become so any moment now.

"We're all concerned about Tammy and want to see her happy," Savannah said, forcing her voice to be soft, her words gentle.

Something told her this wasn't a heart-to-heart that she could afford to get wrong.

"Yes, but your idea of her being happy and mine appear to be very different."

"That may be so," Granny said, "but your opinion or Savannah's or mine don't mean much a'tall. It's Tammy's opinion that counts."

"I think my opinion counts." Lenora raised her chin a few notches. "I *am* her mother. But even if what you say is true, she doesn't appear to be happy to me in the least. She's tense and short-tempered and not at all herself."

Savannah bit back the words "She was fine until she heard *you* were coming, and she's been a nervous wreck since."

She couldn't speak that way to Tammy's mother, and for the life of her, she couldn't think of a nice way to say it.

"She never should have come to this place," Lenora continued. "I told her not to, I forbade her to, but she defied me and did it anyway. Now look where she is."

Lenora started to sniffle and wipe at her eyes.

Savannah reached for the tissue box on the table beside her and quietly, slowly, slid it under her chaise and out of sight.

"She was such a beautiful girl," Lenora said. "She used to have such a lovely figure and—"

"She still does," Savannah returned.

"She's gained weight. At least ten pounds."

"She just had a baby!" Savannah could feel her last nerve fraying. "For heaven's sake, Lenora. Your daughter is gorgeous. She's the picture of health, and so is her beautiful little girl. Why can't you just accept Tammy as she is?"

Lenora looked up and down Savannah's ample figure, then Granny's. "Some families are more accepting of fat than others. We don't tolerate it."

"Well, bully for you. Must be nice to be perfect. Or, maybe just think you're perfect."

Lenora gave her an ugly smirk, then said, "You have anger issues, Savannah. I think you're jealous because you know that, as Tammy's family and people of means, we can offer her a much higher standard of living than you ever will with this ridiculous business you have here, if one can even call what you do a business. It's no secret that my husband and I are wealthy, and you're jealous."

"I'm not jealous of your wealth, Dr. Hart," Savannah told her. "Not at all. I've known far too many wealthy people to believe that their money allows them to live charmed lives. Every torment that visits the poor can knock on the rich person's door just as quickly. Sickness and death, betrayal and infidelities, unexpected calamities that no amount of money can set straight. Look at Ethan Malloy right now. His wealth can't shield him from the pain he's going through. He told me so himself. Money only gives the illusion of control."

"Maybe wealth can't buy happiness," Lenora returned, "but being poor can cause a *lot* of suffering. I know that for a fact, and I don't want that for my daughter. Or my granddaughter either."

Savannah looked into the woman's eyes and saw tears. Real tears. Real pain. Real memories welling up, bitter and hurtful.

"You haven't always had money," Savannah said softly to herself. She was starting to understand Lenora Hart. Maybe better than the good doctor wanted her to.

When Lenora didn't reply, Savannah forged ahead. "You were poor once, and you suffered. Badly."

"You don't know what you're talking about!" Lenora said, almost shouting.

"Yes, forgive me, but I think I do. I think there was a time in your life when you had very little and during that time you went through a lot of pain. But the poverty wasn't the most painful part, was it, Doctor?"

Lenora began crying in earnest, tears streaming down her face. Savannah reached under her chair, pulled out the box of tissues, and handed her several.

"It's okay," Savannah said softly. "I understand. When I was a kid, I lived with my mom. She drank and neglected us, and I always blamed our misery on the fact that we didn't have enough money. Then the courts took her kids away from her, all nine of us, and gave us to Granny here."

Savannah paused to give her grandmother a long, loving look.

It was returned threefold.

"Gran was poor, too," Savannah continued. "There were days when we had no idea where our next meal was coming from, but we were happy. We were loved. We were nurtured, and that made all the difference."

Gran moved from her chair to one next to Lenora's. She reached over and laid her hand on the crying woman's arm. "I feel real bad about whatever happened to you back then, Dr. Hart," she said. "I'm glad it got better, and you found happiness. Leastwise, more than you had before. But Savannah's right. It wasn't about the money. It was about the love. And your sweet daughter is much loved here. Much loved. By Savannah, by Waycross, by Ryan and John, by me, and even by Dirk. Though he has a hard time showing it, 'cause he wasn't loved enough either when he was growin' up, and that sorta thing stays with you, whether you want it to or not."

Lenora Hart pushed Granny's hand away. Savannah half rose from her chair, ready to do battle, but Gran gave her a simple look that stopped her.

"You don't know me. You don't know anything about me," Lenora protested. "Neither of you do, so don't pretend you've got me all figured out."

Then a look of horror crossed her face, and she said, "Did you run some kind of background check on me? Have you been prying into my private business the way you pry into everybody else's?"

"No, ma'am," Granny said. "We most certainly did not. But if you took offense at anything we said just now, then I apologize to you. More than anything, we want you to be happy, and we want Tammy to be happy, 'cause you both deserve it."

"If you want her to be happy then let her come back home where she belongs. She wants to. I can tell. But she's too proud to admit that she made a mistake."

Savannah felt a deep anger growing inside her. The last thing she wanted to do was explode all over Tammy's mother. But there was only so much of this she could take.

"How can you say that your daughter made a mistake? All you'd have to do is look at that beautiful little granddaughter of yours and know that Tammy's life here was meant to be."

"Okay, so the baby's cute. All babies are cute. But that doesn't mean that bringing her into the world was the smart thing to do. Especially with a father like that. For heaven's sake, his grammar is atrocious, and he has no table manners to speak of whatsoever. I'll bet he didn't even graduate from high school, did he?"

"That's my grandson you're speaking of there, Dr. Hart," Gran said. "He's always been a fine boy, and he's grown up to be a truly good man. I'll ask you to speak well of him in my hearing, or not at all."

"Yes," Savannah interjected, "and he's my brother, too. Don't you—"

All three women heard a sound behind them, a small cry, like that of an animal caught in a painful trap. They turned in unison to see Tammy standing there, her baby in her arms, pain and horror in her eyes.

Savannah jumped to her feet and rushed over to her friend. "Oh, Tammy," she said. "I'm sorry. So sorry."

Tammy said nothing for a long, torturous time. Finally, in a surprisingly calm voice she said, "I came out here to tell you something, Savannah. Something important."

"What's that, sugar?"

"I was examining those pictures, the one that

Ethan Malloy sent us, and the one you found of Ethan in Neal Irwin's spare room. I zoomed in on them really tight, and I studied the pixels. They're fakes. Both of them. Composites of other pictures, skillfully photoshopped together."

Tammy looked from Savannah to Granny and back to Savannah, avoiding her mother's eyes.

Tears flowed down her cheeks as she said, "I thought it might be important. That's why I came out to tell you."

"It *is* important, Tammy," Savannah said. "Very important. Like you."

"How important can I be," Tammy replied, her tears falling faster, "if my own mother thinks my whole life is a mistake? My marriage. My career. My draperies. What I wear, how I speak, what I eat and drink. Oh, yes, and my hair. My hair that everyone in the world seems to think is pretty, except you, Mother."

For the first time since she had stepped outside, Tammy looked into her mother's eyes. "I've tried my whole life to please you, to live up to your standards. Just before I moved to California, I realized something—that I never could, never would please you.

"So, I did something to please myself," she continued. "I moved to the other side of the country, as far away from you as I could get without falling into the Pacific Ocean. I built myself a new life. A wonderful life with friends who love me, and approve of me. Then I met a man who thinks that I'm an angel that God sent to him. He really does believe that. But he doesn't realize that *he's* the god-sent angel. He's taught me how to love, and how to trust, and he gave me this baby. This perfect, wonderful baby. If you can say that she was a mistake, then there's no point in me ever trying to do anything that you will approve of again."

Her speech given, Tammy walked slowly but purposefully back into the house.

Savannah looked back at Lenora Hart to see the effect her daughter's words might have had on her. But Dr. Hart's face looked like a wall of ice to Savannah. Cold and unyielding. Her tears were gone, her jaw clenched, her chin raised.

Savannah walked over to Granny and held out her hand to her. "Let's go, Gran," she said. "I think we've done all we can here."

"I'm afraid you're right, darlin'. Words don't mean much if they're falling on hard-packed soil."

Chapter 24

Gran retired upstairs to catch a nap, as Tammy settled down in the living room, at the desk.

Savannah could have used a nap herself, but she sensed that Tammy needed to talk, so she pulled up a chair and sat down beside her.

"When Waycross gets here, I'm going to ask him to take my parents to our house to get their things and then drive them to the hotel by the pier."

Tammy flipped on the computer, then held her baby close and nuzzled her neck.

"I understand," Savannah said.

"Something tells me that you do. You, of all people."

Savannah noticed that Tammy wasn't crying anymore. In fact, she didn't look as wounded as she had in the backyard, when she had first heard her mother's condemning words.

Something had changed in Tammy. Savannah could feel it.

"Are you okay, sweetie?" Savannah asked her.

"Strangely enough, I am. I'm better than I've been since the moment I heard my parents were coming to visit." She turned to face Savannah. "I feel like a huge weight has lifted off me, the burden of trying to please my mother. I never saw her, our relationship, the way I do now. So clearly."

"What do you mean, darlin'?"

"The one thing I've wanted most in my life was to win my mother's love, to earn her respect and her approval. Now I know for certain that I'll never receive those things. Actually, I've known it all along. But today I realized that she can't give me what she doesn't have."

Savannah nodded. "I think you're right about that. Her withholding her approval is about her, not you. You aren't lacking anything, Tammy. You are *enough*. You're *more* than *enough*. If she can't see that, then she has a blindness that only she can cure."

"I'm not even sure that *she* can," Tammy said. "I don't think she knows how she is, how she treats people. How can she fix something she doesn't acknowledge or even see?"

"I agree. I think you're wise to have figured that out."

"I've put up with her hurting me for my entire life, Savannah. I thought it was the right thing to do, to honor my mother, my flesh and blood."

"It's important to honor your family, especially your parents, but . . ."

"Yes, it is. But when I heard what she said about you, about Waycross, and worst of all, about Vanna,

I realized I've given some of the best parts of my-self to someone who doesn't value them. That isn't virtuous. That's just foolish."

"I can see how you would feel that way."

"I won't do it anymore. It's bad enough that I al-lowed her to abuse me. But I will *not* let her harm Waycross and Vanna the way she has me."

"I don't blame you, darlin'.."

Tammy reached over and grabbed Savannah's hand. Holding it tightly, she said, "I used to won-der how anyone could walk away from their own mother. Now it seems like the easiest thing in the world. The right thing to do."

"I've done much the same with my mother," Sa-vannah told her. "It wasn't easy, but sometimes it's a matter of self-preservation."

"It's as if I'm protecting my family from my fam-ily. But Vanna is the innocent one here. As long as she's a child, her world will be whatever I make it. My mother's an adult. She chooses her own path, and that's her right. But I won't walk it with her anymore. I won't force my husband and my baby to walk it with her."

"How does that decision feel to you, Tamitha?" Savannah asked, searching her friend's eyes.

"Like I have peace deep in my heart for the first time in my life."

"Then it sounds like the right thing to do. I al-ways feel that way when I've made a decision, even a difficult one."

Tammy nodded, then returned her attention to the screen. She typed and scrolled and a moment later, the image of Neal Irwin and Beth Malloy appeared on the screen. "I need to move on, Savannah. At least for the moment. I want you to see what I did," she said. "How I know it's fake."

"Okay. Good. Show me."

"The picture of Neal and Beth together is probably real, unaltered for the most part," Tammy said. "But then, they were married for quite a while. It's not surprising that they might have taken some naughty pictures of themselves for kicks."

"True, but the caesarian scar . . ."

"That's the part that's been photoshopped. Here, watch this and you'll see what I mean."

Tammy began to zoom in, tighter and tighter, on Beth's belly and the scar that showed so prominently, low on her abdomen.

"Someone cut that area out of another picture and pasted it on there," Tammy explained. "Sometimes when you create a cutout from one picture and paste on another, they don't have the same resolution. Pixels, the little squares that make up a digital photograph . . . see them now?"

Tammy had zoomed in so closely that what had once looked like a photograph now resembled a quilt made of tiny squares.

"Yes, I see them," Savannah said.

"Look at these squares over here, the ones that make up her thigh and his hip. See, they're much smaller than the squares where the scar is."

"That shows that they're from two different pictures, photos with different resolutions?"

"It sure does."

"Wow."

"Yeah, wow."

"How about the picture of Ethan with Candace?"

"Oh, that one's just a mess of cutting and pasting. It looks to me like they stole bits and pieces from a number of photographs to come up with that one. It wouldn't be hard, if you think about it. Ethan and Candace have both been photographed a million times or more. Those pictures are out there on the Internet for anyone to capture and use."

"Like the way his fans make those videos?"

"Exactly like that."

Suddenly, Tammy turned to Savannah, her eyes bright with excitement. Savannah's were sparkling, too.

"The fans!" Tammy said.

"Or one of the fans. You said they're obsessed."

"They are! You should hear some of these women talk about Ethan, like how he's the man of their dreams, their soul mate, if only he wasn't married . . ."

"Any one fan in particular?"

"No one who stands out. They're all crazy about him. Young women, old women, girls, even guys. He has that effect on people."

"He's kind, too," Savannah said thoughtfully. "At the search today, he was interacting with his fans like they were friends, family even. I talked to him about it, and he sees them that way. At least some of them, ones he's gotten to know well."

"You have to call him right away," Tammy said, practically bouncing on her chair—an activity that Vanna was enjoying. She was waving her arms, as excited as they were. "Call him, tell him we think it might be a fan, and ask him if that rings any bells for him."

"Someone who's especially close to him and Beth. A fan they consider a good friend. Maybe *too* good."

"Perhaps someone who's worked on some of these fan-vids of him."

Savannah reached for her cell phone, but the moment she did, it rang.

"It's Ryan," she said, looking at the caller ID. "Let's run this new theory of ours by him and see what he thinks."

"Yes, good idea!"

"Ryan, I'm so glad you called," Savannah said. "Your timing's perfect. Tammy and I just came up with an idea that we'd like to bounce off you."

"I'd love to hear it," he replied, "but you might want to hear mine first."

"Sure. Let 'er rip."

"We were able to trace the origin of that e-mail, the one that someone sent to Ethan. The one with the image that you wouldn't let us see."

"That's because I promised Ethan I wouldn't let anyone see it but Tammy. It's private in nature."

"A nude shot? Somebody or bodies getting it on?"

"Um, yes. As a matter of fact, it is. But Tammy examined it, and there's no doubt it was doctored."

"How about the one with Ethan and Candace?"

"That one has more pieces patched together than Frankenstein. We think it might be an obsessed fan. Heaven knows, he has enough of them. And they like to make up these elaborate fan videos of him in movies he was never in, doing things he never did, dubbing his voice and his image over all sorts of things. If they could do that, it wouldn't be any problem at all to alter a couple of photographs."

"I completely agree. I don't know anything about that, whether the person who sent the e-mails was a fan or not. I'll give you the name, and you can take it from there."

"Sure. Who is it?"

"Her name is Katherine Zeegers. She lives here in San Carmelita. Interestingly, she moved to this area only a couple of weeks after Ethan and Beth bought the castle there in Malibu. Coincidence?"

"Maybe. Or an obsession?"

Savannah turned to Tammy. "Tams, when you used Beth's passwords, the ones I got from Amy and Ethan . . ."

"To look over her social networking pages."

"Exactly. Were you able to read some of the letters between Beth and her fans or Ethan's fans?"

"Yes, but they were all friendly, the fans telling her how much they enjoyed her and her husband's performances. Her thanking them. Just standard stuff."

"Do you recall anyone by the name of Katherine Zeegers?"

Tammy thought for a moment. "No. I don't recall anyone by that name. But I could check again."

"Would you?"

"Sure."

Savannah returned to Ryan. "Tammy's checking Beth's social pages now, looking for that name. Do you have an address?"

"Of course." He chuckled. "When John and I do a job—"

"I know, I know. You do it right."

"She lives at 224 Wolf Road. It's on the outskirts of town, a run-down area."

"I know the place. We raided a lot of meth labs around there, back in the day."

Meanwhile, Tammy was flipping from one computer page to another, searching. "I don't see any Katherine Zeegers, but I do see a lot of correspondence between Beth and a woman named Kitty Z. Isn't Kitty sometimes a nickname for Katherine? I think it is."

"It absolutely is." Savannah could feel her excitement growing by the moment. "And I know that woman! Well, I don't know her personally. But I met her this morning at the search in the park. He said he knew her well, that she's like a friend of the family."

"Is this her?" Tammy had pulled up a profile picture of Kitty Z.

It was Savannah's turn to bounce up and down on her chair. "It's her. That's the woman I saw in the park today. But is it Katherine Zeegers?"

"I just sent you Katherine Zeegers's driver's license photo," Ryan said.

Savannah's phone dinged. "Got it," she said. "Let me look."

She opened his message and there she was, Katherine Zeegers aka Kitty Z. "No doubt about it," she said, showing the DMV shot to Tammy. "They're the same woman."

Savannah sank back in her chair, weak with excitement. "Thank you, Ryan," she said into the phone. "Thank you, thank you! I owe you any kind of pie you want."

"Bourbon pecan."

"You got it, boy, and a big hug and kiss to go with it."

"That'll be the sweetest part. Keep us posted."

"Oh, I will. I most certainly will. Bye, darlin'."

She ended the call, then turned to Tammy, who was beaming as she cuddled her baby close.

Even little Vanna seemed to be in a celebratory mood, smiling and playing patty-cake.

"I have a feeling about this gal," Savannah said.

"Me too. While you were talking to Ryan, I checked, and she's one of the fans, the main one, in fact, who's posted those fan-vids. She's got the know-how, that's for sure."

"I'm thinking of how she showed up for that search. How many times does the killer mingle in a crowd of searchers or mourners after he's done his dirty work? Enough that the FBI and even savvy local law enforcers videotape searches and funerals, then identify everyone there."

"Did Dirk do that this morning?"

"He had both Jake and Mike filming the whole thing." She shivered with delight. "I can't wait to tell him! We've finally got an honest-to-goodness suspect!"

Chapter 25

"I've gotta tell you, I have mixed emotions about this," Dirk said as he reached into the glove box and pulled out the bagful of cinnamon sticks.

"I don't see what's 'mixed' about it," Savannah replied. "Your wife and friend solve your case for you, and all you have to do is go scoop up the perp. Sounds pretty peachy to me."

Savannah turned the nose of the Mustang toward the east, heading for what was not so affectionately called the "East End."

The easternmost area of San Carmelita was the part of town where tourists rarely ventured, unless they wanted to score a recreational, illegal substance of some kind.

The buildings that lined the main streets were old, and not in a quaint, picturesque way. Storefronts seldom got painted, potholes rarely got filled, and crimes were hardly ever solved, mostly because they were infrequently reported, for fear of retaliation.

"Don't think I don't appreciate it," Dirk said, poking the cinnamon stick in his mouth. "It just feels like I missed out on all the fun."

"You also missed out on a lot of gut-wrenching family drama in our backyard," she said. "I'd gladly trade my day for yours, if you're up for it."

Dirk looked shocked. "You had a fight with Granny?"

"Of course not. The only thing we ever fight about is who gets to make the Christmas fudge. No, unfortunately, this was between Tammy and her mom."

"Who won and who lost?"

"That's a good question. I'd say that, in the long run, Tammy won, though I doubt she feels victorious. Her mother lost, big-time, but I don't think she realizes it yet."

"I don't care much for her mother. Seems like everything out of her mouth is some sort of complaint about somebody. I don't like being around negative people like that."

Savannah nearly laughed aloud. Most folks who had met Dirk Coulter might have said that he was the most negative person they had ever met. Funny, how a person's flaws were always the ones that irritated them the most in other people.

Granny Reid always said, "If you want to know what a sneaky person is up to, just listen to what they gripe about the most, when it's somebody else doing it."

"I'm sure we were up here a million times during our meth lab–raiding days," Dirk said as he looked around, trying to find familiar landmarks. "But everything's changed now. It actually looks worse, and I didn't think that was possible."

Unlike her husband, Savannah couldn't work up any curiosity about the area and its changes. She was too busy wondering if they would find any signs of Beth and Freddy Malloy at Kitty Zeegers's house on Wolf Road.

More importantly, was it too much to hope that they might actually find them alive and well?

Yes, she supposed it was. But so what if she was a bit of a Pollyanna? The world needed more dreamers, more believers in happily-ever-afters.

"Do you think they're there?" she dared to ask Dirk. When he didn't reply, she added, "Beth and Freddy, I mean."

"I know who you mean. I doubt it. I don't want to get my hopes up, you know?"

"Yeah, I know. It would be nice though."

"It would be wonderful," he said softly, his voice soft with emotion.

Sometimes, with his rough exterior, Savannah forgot that her husband was, at heart, a gentle man. Even more so when it came to children. Other than the baby's own father, Savannah doubted there was anyone on earth who wanted to find little Freddy, safe and sound, more than mean, crusty ol' Dirk Coulter.

"I'll tell you one thing," he said, "if that gal knows where those two are and holds out on me . . ."

"Yes, I hear you. If ever there was a time to lean on a suspect, this would be it."

Savannah saw the house ahead, its numbers

painted with what must have been a kid's brush, dipped in cheap red paint.

Two broken-down cars littered the front yard of the ramshackle house. The building had gray shingles for siding, but most of them hung loose from one end. Narrow and deep, it reminded Savannah of the shotgun house where she had been raised. Except that Gran's house, old as it was, had always been neat, clean, and cheerful, with geraniums spilling from its flower boxes, white lace curtains at its windows, and a lush garden growing behind.

But Gran's house had been loved.

This property was not.

A dog of mixed breeds was running in circles, chained to a spike driven into a lawn that was little more than brown weeds.

"It's a good thing Gran isn't with us," Savannah said. "She'd forget all about the missing people and rescue that dog. She has strong feelings about dogs being chained outside, away from their family."

"I don't like it either," he answered. "A chained-up dog reminds me of how I used to feel."

"Growing up?"

"Yes. Later, too. Until I met you."

"That might be the most romantic thing you ever said to me."

"I'd better get some new material then."

Savannah parked the Mustang across the street end of the driveway. Just in case someone wanted to make a run for it and peel out, tires smoking, there was no reason to make it easy for them.

"Ready?" Dirk asked her as he checked his weapon—a Smith & Wesson that he kept in a shoulder holster, concealed beneath his bomber jacket.

She did the same with the Beretta 9mm under her sweater.

The redhead she had seen in the park hadn't looked like a particularly tough girl. But someone had pulled a backpack out of a young, strong, healthy woman's hands with enough force to break off her fingernails. And probably, the same person had smacked her victim with a rock hard enough to kill her.

Obviously, the killer—whether it was Katherine Zeegers or not—was no pushover.

"Who's got this?" Dirk asked. "You or me?"

"I talked to her already. She might be under the mistaken impression that I'm nice."

"We can't have that."

"Definitely not."

"Okay, I've got it," he said. "Let's go."

Fortunately, as they walked up the cracked cement sidewalk to the house, the dog couldn't reach them. He snarled, barked, and bared his teeth to them as they passed.

"I don't blame you, fella," Savannah told him. "If all the space I had in the world was a four-foot circle to run around in, I'd be cranky and want to bite somebody, too."

As they walked up to the house, Savannah took in every detail of her surroundings, looking for any sign that Kitty might be "entertaining guests."

Other than some rusted bicycles and a swing that was hanging from the tree by one rope, there were no signs of children.

They walked up to the door and stood, quietly

listening for sounds inside the house. Hearing none, Dirk knocked on the screen door's frame, loud enough for Savannah to fear the thing might come loose from its hinges.

It took a long time for Kitty Zeegers to answer the door. When she did, she had a strange look on her face that Savannah couldn't quite interpret. Fear, to be sure, mixed with something like guilt?

Savannah took that as a good sign, along with the woman's shaking hands.

She didn't even know that Dirk was a cop yet, and she was already nervous?

"Hello," Dirk said, taking his badge from inside his jacket and flipping it open in front of her nose. "I'm Detective Sergeant Dirk Coulter with the San Carmelita Police Department. This is Savannah Reid. May we come inside? We need to have a word with you, Ms. Zeegers."

"Well, uh, I'm very busy at the moment," she stammered.

"It's important," he said. "We can either talk inside your home, or you can come with me now to the police station. It's up to you."

"I . . . um . . . okay. If it's really important."

"It's about the missing mother and child that you were looking for earlier today," Dirk told her. "I'm sure you would consider that important."

"Oh. Of course, that's important. Come on in."

She led them into the living room and moved some dirty clothes off the sofa. "There. Have a seat." She tossed the clothes onto the floor in the corner. "Sorry about the mess. It's laundry day," she explained.

O-kay, Savannah thought. *The conversation has just begun, and she's already told her first lie.*

"This is about Beth and Freddy?" she asked.

"Yes," Dirk said, watching her with predatory eyes.

"Have they, you know . . . been found?"

Savannah felt a shot of adrenaline hit her bloodstream. That was, without a doubt, the most transparently misleading question she had ever heard.

Kitty Z. knew full well that Beth and Freddy hadn't been found. It was all over her face, in her defensive body language, in her quavering voice.

Savannah knew there was only one way that Kitty would ask the question in that way. The false cheerfulness, the fake hope that all might be well. She would only have to pretend if she knew full well that they couldn't possibly have been found . . . because she still had them.

"No," Dirk told her. "They have not been found. We only hope that nothing terrible has happened to them."

"Oh, of course not. They're probably okay." She sat on a chair across from them and began picking at her hangnails. Savannah noticed they were badly infected and her nails had been bitten down to the quick.

"I certainly hope so," Dirk told her, "because if they aren't okay, if someone has harmed them, that person will be in a world of trouble."

"I'm sure they would be. I mean, if they hurt them."

"If they're holding them against their will, that's kidnapping," Savannah told her.

"If someone is killed—like that sweet little

nanny was—during the commission of a kidnapping, that's a special circumstance," Dirk added. "You know what they do to people convicted of murder with special circumstances, don't you?"

"Yes, but . . . but what does that have to do with me? I'm a friend of Beth's and her husband, Ethan. I know Freddy, and even their nanny was friendly to me. Why would I hurt them?"

"You tell me," Dirk said, standing and walking over to her chair. "Why would you do something so awful? I guess when sending them fake, dirty pictures of them fooling around with other people didn't work, you had to come up with another plan."

Savannah's eyes strayed from the conversation in front of her to a nearby bookshelf. Lined up on the middle shelf were DVDs. Many DVDs. They were all Ethan's movies and TV guest appearances.

She looked over to an end table and there was a pile of cut-up paper, articles from every newspaper and magazine that had announced the kidnapping of Ethan Malloy's family.

Kitty Zeegers had cut out every story and was pasting them in a scrapbook. It was an enormous scrapbook, and something told Savannah it was filled with Ethan Malloy memorabilia.

Kitty had ceased to chew her nails for a moment and was scratching furiously at her ankles. Savannah could see that they were actually bloody from all the scratching.

Poison oak, she thought. *The CSI techs had to walk through poison oak to retrieve the rock left by the person who killed Pilar.*

As Dirk continued to grill Kitty, Savannah stood

and walked around the room. She could see in her peripheral vision that Kitty was watching her every move.

When Savannah stepped closer to the kitchen, Kitty cried out, "Stop! What are you doing? You can't just walk around my house like that. I didn't give you permission!"

Savannah stopped, but from where she stood, she continued to look.

On the kitchen counter, she saw some food that appeared to be half prepared. Mangos. Mangled mangos, at least half a dozen of them, had been awkwardly cut by someone who had no idea how to get the most of the seemingly difficult-to-prepare fruit.

There were also blueberries. Two boxes of fresh ones, next to the mangos.

Savannah turned to Dirk, a grim smile on her face. "They're here," she said. "At least, Freddy is."

He looked at her as though he wanted to believe her, but wasn't sure. "She's got them, I tell you! They're here!"

Dirk reached into his rear jeans pocket and pulled out a pair of handcuffs. He quickly secured Kitty to the leg of a heavy table.

"Beth?" Savannah called out as loudly as she could. "Beth, where are you?"

Both she and Dirk began to look under the bed, inside cupboards, behind chairs.

"Beth? This is the police," Dirk shouted. "We're here to help you. If you can hear me, answer."

Within seconds, they heard a crashing sound, as though something metal had been pushed over.

Eventually, they found it, a door, which opened

to a steep flight of stairs, reaching downward into the musty darkness of a cellar.

"We're coming, Beth," Savannah yelled. "We're coming."

Savannah gave Kitty a quick look to make sure she couldn't escape, then plunged down the stairs with Dirk right be-hind her.

Once in the cellar, it took Savannah's eyes a few moments to adjust to the almost complete absence of light. Only dimly could she make out the outline of a woman, crouched in the corner of the small, dank room.

"Beth?" she asked, hurrying toward her.

All she heard in response was a feeble grunt.

Suddenly, a light illuminated the dark scene. Dirk had produced his ever-handy penlight and was showing its small but powerful beam on the corner.

What Savannah saw nearly made her sick.

Beth was sitting in the corner, on the wet cement floor. Her mouth was covered with duct tape. Her wrists and ankles were also bound with the silver stuff. She was filthy, her eyes wild with fear.

Clinging to her arm was her child, as dirty and terrified as she was. When the light hit his face, he began to wail piteously.

"Oh, you poor darlin's," Savannah said, rushing to them. "You poor, poor things."

She and Dirk eased the tape off Beth's mouth and peeled it from her wrists and ankles. At the captive woman's feet were the awful, spilled contents of a bucket, the bucket she had overturned to alert them to her presence.

Beth was crying, as loudly and as hard as her child.

Savannah pulled Freddy to her, wrapped her arms tightly around him, and held him close. "Don't cry, sweet boy," she told him. "You're all right. You and your momma are going to be all right."

Dirk helped Beth to her feet, but she was so weak, she could hardly stand. Like Savannah had with Freddy, he pulled her into his embrace and held her as she sobbed against his shoulder.

"Don't cry, Ms. Malloy," he said. "We've gotcha. You don't have to worry anymore. You and your son are completely safe. We've gotcha now."

Chapter 26

Many, many nights, the members of the Moon-light Magnolia Detective Agency had sat at Savannah's dining room table, basking in the glow of good companionship, good food, and the light of her dragonfly stained-glass lamp, which lent its cozy gold-and-red light to the setting.

This particular night, the mood was a bit less jovial than usual.

They weren't as festive as they might have been after closing a case, but there was a quiet sense of deep satisfaction in the air.

They were all the better for being there and sharing the moment.

"Thank heavens above that nasty woman didn't do any major harm to Mrs. Malloy and her baby," Granny said. "I don't think I could have borne it if they'd wound up in the same condition as Miss Pilar."

"None of us could have borne an outcome like

that, Granny," Waycross said. "While that baby was missing, I felt guilty ever' time I picked up my own child and hugged her."

"Ethan must have been thrilled to death when you called to give him the news," Ryan said to Savannah. "I can't even imagine the relief he must have felt."

"He made record time getting to the hospital once we told him they were there," Dirk said.

"He must have just been thrilled to death to see them," Tammy said.

Savannah and Dirk exchanged an awkward glance, which Granny's sharp eye caught immediately.

"Okay, what's that all about?" she wanted to know. "Was he happy to see them or not?"

"He was tickled pink to see them," Savannah told her. "I'm sorry to say that Beth wasn't happy to be reunited with her husband."

Granny was scandalized. "Why in tarnation not? You must've told her that stupid picture was fake, just like the one of her and her ex-husband was false as Aunt Josie's teeth."

"We did," Dirk said. "But she has in her head that she and the boy got kidnapped because crazy women all over the world are in love with her husband."

"That's hardly the lad's fault," John observed. "He's exceptionally talented and extraordinarily handsome. What can she expect?"

Savannah sighed. She felt a weariness in her bones, just thinking about the Malloy family. "I reckon she expects to have her husband all to herself in every way. But considering his occupation, which is also his passion, that isn't likely to ever happen."

"Maybe she's just in shock, from all she went through," Tammy suggested.

"Could be." Savannah took a cookie from a plate that was being passed around. "Seeing Pilar killed like that had to take a toll on her. Even if she recovers from the shock of it all someday, I wouldn't bet that her marriage will."

"I still don't get what that Kitty woman thought she was going to accomplish by kidnapping Beth and the baby," Waycross said.

"She's obsessed with Ethan," Savannah told him. "Her diaries show how sick and out of touch with reality she was. She created those pictures and e-mailed them to the Malloys and Irwin and Candace, thinking that would break them up. When it didn't as quickly as she'd hoped, she decided to kill Beth and then pretend she had rescued Freddy from the evil person who had killed Beth. She thought that would cause Ethan to fall in love with her, and with Beth out of the way . . ."

"That's crazy, not to mention cruel," Tammy said.

"Yes. It is crazy and cruel. She's both." Savannah continued, "She hadn't intended for Pilar to be there, or for Pilar to put up a fight. But Pilar did, and Kitty murdered her. Kitty took Beth and Freddy to her house and kept them in that basement, waiting until she got the nerve to kill her."

Granny said, "Maybe after taking someone's life, Kitty realized it was harder to do than she'd thought."

"You may be right, Gran," Ryan told her. "I'd

like to think it would be hard for most people to do such a thing."

"How did Pilar's parents take it," Tammy asked, "when you told them you had their daughter's killer in custody?"

"They were grateful," Dirk said. He looked down at the table, at his hands, which were clenched. "It really gets you, when people are so thankful under circumstances like that."

"They should be very proud of their daughter," Tammy said. "She fought to protect her family." She closed her eyes for a moment, and tears spilled down her cheeks. "They *were* her family, you know. Not bound by blood, but by love."

"I'm sorry, sugar," Savannah said, reaching over and patting her hand, then stroking the baby's head as she snuggled up to her mom. "I know it was rough, saying good-bye to your parents today. Considering, well, your mother's last words to you."

"It's okay," Tammy said. "My dad was nice. Said he was glad to see me and the baby and to meet Waycross. He promised to come back again soon. As long as I'm all right with him, the rest is okay."

"No, it isn't." Gran took a long, shuddering breath. "It's a cryin' shame's what it is. But what could you do, Tammy? The Good Book tells us to live in peace with all men, as much as is within our power to do so. But sometimes, some people . . . you just have to let 'em go."

Tammy nodded as tears rolled down her cheeks. "I did. I let her go. She asked me one more time, as she was getting into the airport taxi, to go back to New York with her and leave my family behind.

I told her I would never, never do that. So, she walked away, and I let her. I think she believed I'd run after her, because I always have before. But not this time. No. Not this time."

"You did the right thing," Gran said. "The noble thing. I'm most proud of you."

"Thank you, Granny." Tammy took a moment to look around the table, at each person sitting there. "Pilar died defending her family," she said. "Her *family*. And I would for you, too. Any one of you. You *are* my family, the one my heart adopted. I'll never let you go."

Savannah dropped to her knees beside her friend's chair and enfolded her and her child in her arms. She kissed Tammy's wet cheeks. "We'll never let you go either, kiddo. You're *ours*!"

Tammy nodded and laughed through her tears. "I hear you, loud and clear. There's no family I'd rather belong to than this one right here."

As the Moonlight Magnolia Agency revisits old memories on Christmas Eve, Granny Reid takes the reins back thirty years to the 1980s—back when she went by Stella, everyone's hair was bigger, and sweaters were colorful disasters. But murder never went out of style . . .

Christmas has arrived in sleepy McGill, Georgia, but holiday cheer can't keep tempermental Stella Reid from swinging a rolling pin at anyone who crosses her bad side—and this season, there are plenty. First an anonymous grinch vandalizes a celebrated nativity display. Far worse, the scandalous Prissy Carr is found dead in an alley behind a tavern. With police puzzled over the murder, Stella decides to stir the local gossip pot for clues on the culprits identity . . .

Turns out Prissy held a prominent spot on the naughty list, and suspects pile up the presents on Christmas morning. Unfortunately, the more progress Stella makes, the more fears she must confront. With a neighbor in peril and the futures of her beloved grandchildren at risk, Stella must somehow set everything straight and bring a cunning criminal to justice before December 25th . . .

Please turn the page for an exciting sneak peek of G.A. McKevett's first Granny Reid mystery MURDER IN HER STOCKING now on sale wherever print and e-books are sold!

Prologue

"This has to be the absolute best Christmas ever."

"With Granny here in California and the new baby, too, it doesn't get better than this."

"Just don't get between me and that plate of fudge. I'm warnin' y'all!"

Stella Reid settled into her granddaughter's most comfortable chair, which sat beside the glittering Christmas tree, and propped her feet on the overstuffed footstool, between a couple of warm, purring black cats.

Ahhh, her spirit whispered. *Nothin' quite like a kitty foot massage.*

Hugging the latest addition to her family close to her heart, Stella listened to her loved ones chattering among themselves.

She breathed in the familiar holiday fragrances: the rich pine smell of the tree, the spicy bouquet of the gingerbread house on the kitchen table, the lingering aroma of chocolate from the fudge making that afternoon, and, most importantly, the sweet scent of the infant in her arms.

Baby Vanna Rose snuggled against her chest, the child's tiny fingers wrapped tightly around her great-grandmother's thumb. Her eyes glistened, reflecting the splendor of the tree's twinkling lights and shiny ornaments.

Stella looked around the room, adoring each friend and family member in turn. Her grown grandchildren, Savannah and Waycross, were nibbling on generous squares of her famous fudge, while their spouses, Dirk and Tammy, helped themselves to a punch bowl of eggnog.

The family's closest friends, Ryan and John, had just arrived and were placing gifts, wrapped in elegant silver and gold foil papers, on the glittery, fluffy "snow" beneath the tree.

But as deeply as Stella Reid loved everyone present, she had to admit that her favorite, at least this year, was Vanna Rose, Tammy and Waycross's tiny, red-haired imp and Stella's youngest great-grandchild. There was nothing quite as beautiful as a baby at Christmastime, a reminder of the reason for all the celebratory uproar.

As Stella listened to her family members express their joy and appreciation of the holiday, she had to agree with them. Christmas *was* a wonderous time, and *this* was the best one yet.

Well, the *second* best.

As delightful as this one was, there was another Christmas that held a special place in Stella Reid's heart and that none could ever eclipse.

"The night is darkest just before the dawn" was a quote Stella had often heard and had frequently recited herself. That year had been especially dark, its night long and deep, filled with trials and worries galore.

When the dawn had finally broken, its warming light was badly needed and most welcomed by all.

No Christmas, no matter how bright the tree, fragrant the food, bountiful the gifts, or merry the fellowship, would ever be as sweet, as soul satisfying, as that one had been more than thirty years ago. . . .

Chapter 1

"**A**in't Christmas just the best, Gran? It's like the magic in fairy tales, only *real!*"

Stella Reid looked down at her eight-year-old granddaughter Alma, whose eyes sparkled with holiday wonderment as she gazed at the same old battered tinsel stars and ragged streamers that were strung across Main Street every year in tiny McGill, Georgia. Since it took so little time and money to decorate the dinky three-blocks-long town, Stella wondered, not for the first time, why the town council didn't splurge and shell out a few bucks for some new ones once every quarter of a century or so.

But the glow on her grandchild's lovely face gave Stella reason to rethink her position. Magic, the real kind, was born in innocent, open hearts, who sought it everywhere. And found it. Even in tattered tinsel decorations.

"Yes, Alma sugar, Christmas *is* the best," Stella told the child as she squeezed her small, warm hand. "It plumb dazzles the eyes and the heart alike. A time when most anything can happen."

"Good," piped up Marietta, the restless eleven-year-old who was tugging at Stella's other hand. "Maybe I'll finally get them sparkly dress-up high heels I been asking for. Ever' year I write Santa a letter and tell 'im I want 'em, but when I look under the tree . . . nothin'! Diddly-squat! I don't know why. Lord knows, I'm always good as good can be."

Stella heard a throat clearing behind her. Her oldest grand-angel, Savannah, whispered, "Yeah, Miss Contrary Mari's good, all right. Good for nothing."

The third oldest, Vidalia, clapped her hand over her mouth to stifle a giggle. She almost always agreed with Savannah about Marietta's shortcomings, but she knew a reprimand was forthcoming.

Casting a disapproving look over her shoulder, Stella said, "I heard that, Savannah girl. If you can't say something nice, then—"

"I know. Sorry, Gran."

Marietta stuck out her lip and whirled around to face her accuser. "What're you saying sorry to Gran for, Vannah Sue? I'm the one you insulted! Gran, make her say sorry to me, too. I'm the one who was wounded."

Stella halted the entire entourage of her seven grandchildren in the middle of the sidewalk and cringed a bit to see her fellow McGillians having to walk around the blockage.

Stella had just collected her grandchildren from their mother's house and hadn't had a chance to give them baths or wash their hair and clothes, as she usually did once she got hold of them, a time or two per week.

She saw the disapproving looks of some of her neighbors as they passed the Reid gang, and she couldn't blame them. From the chocolate that was smeared on the face of the youngest, little Jesup, who had just turned six, to nine-year-old Waycross's wild mop of dirty red curls and second grader Cordelia's torn blouse, they were a motley mess, to be sure.

The oldest, twelve-year-old Savannah, did her best to keep them clean and neat, but it was a heavy burden and a losing battle for any child.

Stella's daughter-in-law, Shirley, had surrendered long ago—if, indeed, she had ever fought at all. She possessed a talent for bringing children into the world, at the rate of one per year, and she had a knack for naming them all after towns in Georgia where she had lived at one time or another. But that was where her mothering skills and maternal interests ended. No one who knew her could say they had ever seen her pick up a hairbrush, a bar of soap or a bath towel, or, heaven forbid, an iron.

Shirley's time and life energy were spent sitting on a barstool at the Bulldog Tavern on Main Street in downtown McGill, beneath a picture of Elvis, listening to sorrowful jukebox songs and bemoaning her perpetual rotten luck.

Stella tried to keep the anger she felt for her daughter-in-law to a minimum. After all, Stella's own son, the children's father, did even less for his brood than his wife. A truck driver who came home only a few times a year and stayed just long enough to impregnate his extremely fertile wife, Macon Reid wasn't the sort of son that Stella bragged about at church socials. She was fine with him driving a big rig. It was honest, hard, skilled work. But she'd be a lot prouder if he hadn't stashed a girlfriend or two in every port of call. Or if he'd put out at least a little effort to be home for the important stuff. Like Christmas.

Wondering how Macon had turned out so badly when he'd had such a fine daddy kept Stella Reid awake at night. It also kept her from judging her daughter-in-law too harshly.

Stella liked to think that most people tried the best they could. Some came up a mite light on the All Things Virtuous side of the scale, but Stella refused to believe that anybody started out in life determined to be good for little, if anything, to their fellow man.

At least, that was what Stella told herself when she collected her seven grandkids from Shirley's filthy house, with its empty refrigerator and unused washing machine. When she was carting the youngsters out the door and wishing Shirley well with the brightest fake smile she could muster, Stella was often enjoying the fantasy of snatching her daughter-in-law off that barstool, shaking the daylights out of her, and then finishing the job with a smack upside the noggin.

Stella felt guilty about entertaining such violent imaginations, but just a little. She figured it was better to *think* it than *do* it.

Hey, whatever works, Stella frequently told herself while indulging in those satisfying daydreams. Resisting temptation was an art that took many forms.

Stella drew a deep breath, summoning her patience, and told Savannah, "Tell Marietta sorry, too, darlin'. Nobody should ever be called 'good for nothin',' because the good Lord made ever'-body good for somethin'." She added under her breath, "Though it's sometimes more obvious what certain folks are good for than others."

She turned to Marietta, whose lip was back in place and curled into as ugly a sneer as Stella had ever seen.

"Miss Marietta," she told her second oldest, "you wipe that nasty look off your face. If you don't cotton to bein' called 'good for nothin',' you might try bein' good for *somethin'* come dish-dryin' time. Hear me?"

The lip shot out again as the child gave her grandmother a hateful glance that could have peeled the paint off a freshly polished fire engine.

"You stick that lip back in, girl," Stella added, "before a crow flies overhead and poops on it."

Demanding sparkly plastic high heels and showin' a heap o' disrespect to her elders, indeed, Stella thought. *Lord, have mercy. That young'un's not even a teenager yet, and she's already giving me fits. I can see trouble comin' a mile off.*

With some effort, Stella got her troops reassembled, and they continued their march down the Main Street sidewalk, toward the drugstore.

History had taught Stella that taking her grandchildren from their mom for an "overnight" usually meant a week's worth of Grandma babysitting, at least. The medicine chest was low on Merthiolate, castor oil, and bandages. In a house filled with active, accident-prone children, a well-stocked bathroom cabinet took precedence over holiday shopping.

The army of Reids rounded a corner, and too late, Stella saw him.

Elmer Yonce. One of her least favorite McGillians.

He was between the Reids and the drugstore, blocking their path. Something told her that he had been waiting there for quite a while, intending to do exactly that.

It wasn't the first time she had tangled with Elmer.

She noted with some amusement that his hands were on his hips in what might appear to be a grandiose and authoritative stance. But Stella had known Elmer since elementary school, and she could tell he was taking the opportunity to hold up his britches, which were in danger of heading south, due to him sucking in his belly overly much.

For her benefit, no doubt.

An unsettling thought.

Any guy in the habit of pullin' in his gut and puffin' out his chest to impress womenfolk should probably invest in a pair of suspenders, she decided as he approached their group.

"Merry Christmas, Sexy Stella. You're lookin' ever' bit as sweet and tasty as a plate of your best fudge," he said, waggling his right eyebrow in what was, no doubt, an effort to appear flirtatious and irresistible. "Got plans for Christmas Eve? If not, I could slide down your chimney and leave a little something in your stocking, if you know what I mean."

Stella bristled. This was a bit over the top even for the town degenerate. If she weren't surrounded by her wide-eyed grandkids, ol' Elmer's left cheek would be glowing red and her palm would be tingling.

"Reckon I know exactly what you mean, Elmer Yonce, you filthy-minded peckerwood," she told him. "You best watch what you say to me. Specially when my grand-young'uns are within earshot." She reached out and pulled her brood close, like a hen gathering her chicks when a hawk soared overhead.

"Yeah!" snapped Savannah. "Her name's not Sexy Stella. It's Gran or Granny, or Sister Stella, or Mrs. Reid."

"That's right," Marietta chimed in. "She's pretty, but she ain't sexy. She's our *grandma*!"

"Well, I . . ." Elmer coughed and stared down at his mud-caked boots. "I knowed your grandma for years, kids, and I always thought she was mighty, um . . . Oh, never mind. I didn't mean no disre—"

"Our gran's strong, too," nine-year-old Waycross added, equally indignant. "If she decides to smack you upside the head with her big ol' black skillet, you'll know you've been beaned one for sure!"

"Yeah, Granny's fierce. She'll work you over good fore she's done with you," threatened little Alma, with the fury of a much-riled second grader, "and we won't lift a finger to save your mangy hide when she does it, neither."

In her peripheral vision, Stella caught sight of a figure, a large figure in a sheriff's uniform, moving toward their sidewalk assemblage.

"Have we got a problem here, folks?" asked a deep, rich male voice—the voice of law and order in McGill, Sheriff Maniford Gilford. Though, the citizens whom he protected and served knew better than to call him Maniford.

Born as he was on Saint Patrick's Day, rumor had it that his daddy had been deep in a bottle of Irish whiskey when he saddled his innocent baby son with that awkward handle. Those whom Sheriff Gilford arrested on a fairly regular schedule opined that this might be the source of his contrariness.

Though, Stella had never thought of her old schoolmate as difficult. Quite the reverse. For as long as she could remember—which was her entire life, since both of them had grown up in McGill—Manny Gilford had treated her with only kindness and respect.

Since Stella's husband had passed away six years earlier, the sheriff had developed an almost uncanny talent for appearing out of nowhere the moment she needed a friend. Especially one with a badge.

"No, Sheriff Gilford. We got no problem a'tall," she said, deciding to cut Elmer some holiday season slack. "Mr. Yonce here was just wishin' us a Merry Christmas. He'd 'bout wrapped it up and was fixin' to move along."

The sheriff fixed his pale gray eyes on Elmer, causing the older guy to squirm. Under the lawman's suspicious, unwavering gaze, Stella's wannabe suitor withered like a well-salted slug and slithered away. He limped slightly from an old war wound— a battle that had raged many years ago between himself and a mule he had attempted to harness. Elmer had consumed the better part of a six-pack. The mule, on the other hand, had been stone sober, so he'd won the fight with one well-placed kick, which Elmer was too inebriated to dodge.

Gilford watched Elmer until he disappeared around the corner, then turned back to Stella. "If that knucklehead brings you grief, Mrs. Reid, you just let me know, and I'll put a stop to it right away. I know how he is. I get complaints on him all the time."

"He called Gran 'Sexy Stella,' " Alma piped up. "That's *not* her name!"

"But we fixed his wagon," Waycross added proudly. "I warned him how good she is at skillet smackin'."

Sheriff Gilford's gray eyes twinkled. "Yes, son, your grandmother's skill with a cast-iron frying pan is pretty much legendary in these parts. If I could do what she does with a skillet, I wouldn't need to carry a gun."

Savannah stepped forward. Her bright blue eyes glowed with admiration and something akin to infatuation as she looked up at the sheriff, who, even though he was in his fifties and had silver hair, was still an attractive man who cut a handsome figure in his sharp, crisply pressed uniform. "He said something downright disrespectful to my grandma," she said solemnly, "but we stuck up for her."

"I'm glad you did," Gilford replied, with a sober expression that matched the child's. "We have to look out for each other, and especially our kinfolk. What did he say that was outta line?"

"It doesn't matter," Stella interjected. "You can't take anything a weasel like that says to—"

"He said something not nice about coming down her chimney and leaving something in her stocking," Savannah replied with a knowing look that, sadly, was beyond her tender years. "We don't have a chimney, and I'm pretty sure ol' Elmer knows that. So, I reckon he meant something naughty."

It hurt Stella's heart to think of the environment her granddaughter was being raised in, one where she would understand a double entendre at her young age. The girl was growing up far too fast, thanks to her mother and the characters Shirley exposed her children to on a daily basis.

A look of anger crossed the sheriff's face, and it occurred to Stella that he was thinking the same thing.

Gilford reached over, placed his big hand on Savannah's shoulder, and gave her a quick reassuring pat. "Thank you, young lady, for reporting that offense to me. Now that you've given your statement to a law official, you don't have to worry about it or even think about it anymore. I'll deal with it now, and I assure you that Mr. Elmer Yonce will regret that he showed your grandma any disrespect. In fact, after I get done givin' him a proper talkin'-to, I reckon he'll be scared to say boo to a fine lady like your grandmother anytime in the near future."

Satisfied and happily reassured, Savannah slipped back in place behind her precious gran.

Stella was about to thank Sheriff Gilford when she saw a familiar figure sprinting up Main Street in their direction.

"Pastor O'Reilly," Gilford said when the out-of-breath runner reached them. "What's going on? Is the church on fire?"

"Worse than that," replied the minister, trying to catch his breath as he leaned on one of four municipal garbage cans evenly distributed for shoppers' use along the three-block-long city center.

"Worse than the church bein' afire?" Stella said, trying to even imagine such a thing.

"Reckon it's not quite as bad as that," Hugh O'Reilly admitted, wiping an overly abundant amount of perspiration from his brow, considering the chilly nip of winter that hung in the air. "But it's a sacrilegious felony that's been committed. That's for sure! You've gotta come see for yourself!"

The pastor and the sheriff took off down the street toward the town square two blocks away. Stella could see that a group of her townsfolk had gathered near the gazebo, with more joining by the moment.

Whatever felonious mayhem had been committed, the much-revered town square appeared to be the scene of the crime.

She felt one of her grandkids tugging at her sleeve. When she turned to them, she saw a look of nearly rapturous excitement and curiosity on her oldest grandchild's face.

"Please, oh please, can we go see what it is, Granny?" Savannah begged. "Pastor O'Reilly said it's felonious! We don't hardly ever have anything *felonious* to look at here in McGill!"

"No!" Waycross shouted at his sister, his ruddy face flushing red. "We was on our way to get Merthiolate and bandages. Gran said so."

Savannah gave her brother a suspicious look and said with all the grim authority of an FBI agent questioning a suspected serial killer, "Since when, Mr. Waycross Reid, did you get all hot 'n' bothered about buying Merthiolate?"

He scowled up at her. "Ain't hot 'n' bothered 'bout nothin'. Just sayin' we should tend to our own bizness fore we go tendin' to other people's."

At that moment, Stella saw one of her two best friends, Elsie Dingle, join the knot of lookie-loos gathering in the square. She could tell by the way feisty Elsie was elbowing her way through the crowd to get a better view that she considered the sight to be worth the effort. The diminutive black woman might be only five feet tall, but Elsie knew how to use her otherwise abundant proportions to her advantage in a rambunctious crowd.

Anything Elsie took an acute interest in was something Stella had to see firsthand. Elsie Dingle might be the second nosiest woman in town—or *inquisitive,* as Stella preferred to call it—but Stella Reid was the Queen of Curious.

"Okay. We'll go take a look at whatever it is," Stella told her brood. Other than Waycross, who had developed that newfound hankering for medical supplies, they were eager to investigate the commotion. "But," she added in her sternest grandmother voice, "if it's somethin' awful and not fittin' for young'uns' eyes, I'll tell you to close 'em, and y'all better snap 'em shut then and there. Understand?"

Heads bobbed in eager acquiescence.

In an instant, the Reid clan was off and running, with Stella and Savannah leading the charge and Waycross bringing up the rear.

As they neared the crowd, Stella caught bits and pieces of the gossip flying about.

"Blasphemy!"

"That's what it is, all right. Plain and simple."

"A crime against Christmas itself. I can't stand it."

"Whoever would do such a thing?"

"I can't even imagine, but when the sheriff catches them, they should be horsewhipped right here in the town square, in front of everybody."

McGillians by the dozen were gathering in a tight semicircle in front of the new gazebo, their eyes wide, mouths gaping at the carnage before them.

Stella reached the front of the crowd a few steps behind Savannah, who was smaller and nimbler at darting among the sightseers.

Stella heard her granddaughter gasp. The child

whirled around and looked up at her grandmother with a mixture of horror and mortification
on her face.

"Oh, no! Oh, Gran," she whispered as Stella put
an arm around the girl and pulled her close.
"Lord help us. We're in deep doody now!"

Stella looked past her granddaughter to the
town's pride and joy, the new gazebo and, more
importantly, the recently acquired nativity scene,
elegantly displayed for all to enjoy, with real hay
and everything.

The sacred depiction of the first Christmas had
been bought with monies raised by schoolchildren
selling candy, teenagers washing cars, moms baking and selling cakes and cookies, and dads con-
tributing their Christmas bonuses, and with the
generous donations of members of the McGill
Chamber of Commerce. All six of them.

The display was an old one, its paint faded, a
few figures chipped, a couple of shepherds' fingers broken off. But without those minor flaws, the
people of McGill could never have afforded such a
luxury. The town council had decided that since
the sheep had a broken leg and was, therefore,
well behaved, the shepherds didn't need ten fingers to corral it.

Stella's next-door neighbor, Florence Bagley,
had once taken a correspondence art course that
she'd found advertised in the back of a magazine,
so she had been given the chore of restoring the
figures to their original glory. Other than one of
the wise men being decidedly cross-eyed and the
Virgin Mary having a downturned mouth, which

made her look more disgruntled than "blessed among women," Flo had done a pretty good job.

Overall, McGillians had been thrilled with their lovely acquisition. No other town in the county had anything to rival their beautiful, darned near life-size, nativity scene.

But now . . . the unthinkable had happened.

Vandalized!

No wonder everyone was in a dither.

As Stella gazed upon the destruction wrought by desperately perverse roguery, she thought her heart had surely stopped.

Every figure, from the Virgin Mary herself to Joseph, from the shepherds and wise men to the sheep and the donkey, and even the angel hovering above them all—every single member of the holy entourage was sporting a mustache.

And not just a simple under-the-nose dusting of whiskers, either.

The elaborate, long, sweeping black mustaches curled upward at the ends, then around and around in a series of ever-tightening spirals.

It was truly a sight to behold.

Even baby Jesus himself was thus adorned.

"I wanna know who did this!" Sheriff Gilford exclaimed as he stood next to the manger, pointing at the ruins. "Whoever you are, step forward and own up to it right now. If I have to come after you, you'll be in a whirlwind of trouble."

Stella could scarcely breathe. She could almost feel the mustachioed Virgin gazing at her with painted eyes that were filled with disappointment and sorrow.

Having been born with the divine gift of Preeminent Nosiness, Stella had solved many crimes in McGill. Single-handedly, she had uncovered the villain who had plundered Miss Abigail's fine flower garden on the evening before the county rose competition. She had solved the cases of the Ex-Lax-laced brownies at the church social of '69 and the unsettling appearance of outhouses on the tops of barns on homecoming night in '78.

But Stella Reid didn't need to use any of her finely honed detecting skills to solve the crime at hand.

Far too many times before, she had seen this particular artist's distinctive work. Facial hair adornment was his stock-in-trade. His signature flourish—mustaches with tightly wound spiral ends.

His artwork had adorned the newspapers and magazines in her home, a few books and, one dark night, even a page in her precious family Bible. Yes, Adam and Eve's wardrobe of fig leaves had been accessorized by these unique spiraled cookie dusters.

Much to Stella's and the young artist's distress.

Her distress when she had discovered the unwelcome adornment. *His* when she had taken him behind the henhouse and introduced the seat of his britches to a freshly cut switch.

Not because of his art, but because he had lied about it when questioned.

There was one thing that every Reid kid knew: Granny didn't abide lying.

As Stella looked down at Savannah, she could tell by the look on her granddaughter's face that she, too, had solved this mystery in an instant.

In fact, all her grandchildren had turned and were staring at their brother, whose face was flushing nearly as red as his mop of curly hair.

He looked like a fox caught in the corner of a henhouse, with a flapping chicken in his jaws.

Stella took one step toward the nine-year-old culprit, and a second later, all she saw was a copper streak as he wriggled through the crowd and darted down the closest alley between the tavern and the pool hall.

Someone grabbed Stella's arm. She turned to see Elsie standing next to her, a look of concern on her round bronze face. But her coffee-colored eyes sparkled with good-natured humor as she said, "Go tend to your scoundrel of a grandson, Sister Stella. I'll haul the rest of your crew back to your house and get some supper on the stove for 'em."

"Would you mind much?" Stella asked, knowing the answer. When it came to helping her fellow man, Elsie didn't mind a bit. She'd do anything for a friend, and if Elsie had an enemy in the world, Stella was sure she'd do right by him, too.

Elsie Dingle was one of the few people Stella had met who actually worked hard at living the life everybody talked about in church.

"Wouldn't mind a bit," was the generous answer.

Elsie expertly herded the Reid youngsters into a manageable huddle. Stella wasn't surprised at her skill. Elsie had been present the day Savannah was born, and although she had never been blessed with children of her own, she had performed the services of a surrogate grandma for the gang more times than Stella could count.

Elsie glanced toward the now-empty alley in

which Waycross had disappeared. "I recognized your little booger's handiwork the minute I saw it," she said with a wave of a hand toward the nativity scene. "You best go grab him before he reaches the Mexico border."

"Naw," Stella replied with a soft chuckle. "I know right where that child's headed. 'Tain't as far as all that."

Chapter 2

During the more than half a century of her life spent in McGill, Georgia, Stella had often wondered why her hometown had more cemeteries than grocery stores, schools, churches, or even taverns.

At first glance, it might seem that people did more dying than living in McGill. But in the end, Stella had decided that she'd seen far more people leave McGill than arrive. It wasn't the sort of town that people relocated to, seeking a better way of life for themselves and their families.

When the population of McGill wavered, it generally dropped rather than rose.

To the consternation of parents and grandparents of grown children, most of their offspring moved away after graduating from high school. Either they escaped to college campuses out of the area or they designed more anonymous lives for themselves in the cities of Atlanta, Chattanooga, or Nashville.

Then there were the others who left McGill by
establishing a permanent residence in one of several cemeteries outside of town.

The oldest of those graveyards was St. Michael's,
situated just out of town, on a hill overlooking the
river. St. Michael's was established before the Civil
War, and its population included soldiers who had
died fighting in that bloody conflict and their wives
and children who had died when Sherman cut his
bloody path through Georgia. Those tombstones
showed the gradual but inevitable ravages of time,
their inscriptions becoming less readable with
each passing decade.

Even as a child, Stella had walked the rows of
that cemetery, smelling the rich mustiness of the
place, feeling the too seldom groomed grass swish-
ing against her ankles, reading the names on the
stones, most of which she eventually memorized.
Entire families had perished during those dark
years, and smaller towns, like McGill, had never
fully recovered.

The gnarled oaks dripped their gray Spanish
moss onto the weathered stones, adding a feeling
of graceful melancholy to the place. The lacy moss
softened the hard look of the tombstones, as
though lending a maternal, feminine touch to the
otherwise cold and forbidding setting.

The elegant draping graced every tombstone,
ancient and recent, without partiality, sharing its
gentle beauty with all who rested in that peaceful
place. It touched the large, imposing statues of
weeping angels and those of soldiers brandishing
their battle swords, as well as the simple head-

stones of the poor, less celebrated, but just as loved sons of Georgia.

Like Arthur Reid.

The sun was beginning to set as Stella passed through the wrought-iron gates and entered the graveyard. She gave her customary brief nod to the statue of Michael the Archangel, who, for as long as she could remember, had been fighting and subduing the mighty dragon serpent at his feet by piercing its head with a sword that was longer than the angel was tall.

In her time, Stella had seen far too many acts committed by the likes of that old serpent. She figured that any being, like Michael, who could keep Satan under control—even for a season—was all right in her book.

With a heavy, troubled heart, she headed toward the rear of the cemetery, where the dates on the gravestones were the 1900s rather than the 1800s.

Where her Irish father and Cherokee mother were buried.

Where her husband, Arthur, had been buried six years ago.

Where Stella knew she would find her grandson.

The small-for-his-age, copper-topped boy was right where she knew he would be, in front of the simple tombstone that bore the inscription:

ARTHUR REID
AUGUST 7, 1928–OCTOBER 26, 1976
BELOVED HUSBAND, FATHER, AND GRANDFATHER
AT LAST, A WELL-DESERVED REST

The child sat on the dew-damp ground, his knees drawn up to his chin, his thin arms wrapped around his shins. He was shivering from the cold, and from more than a little fear, Stella suspected.

A curious, energetic, and highly creative child, Waycross had pulled off some doozies in his life. *But no doubt about it,* Stella thought as she approached the boy, *this one plumb beats all.*

Her heart softened when she realized he was crying. Sobbing, even. His small shoulders were heaving hard and fast. His face was pressed against his knobby knees.

He wasn't even conscious of her presence until she knelt on the grass beside him.

When she touched his shoulder, he jumped and pulled back, then looked up at her with eyes the same shade of brilliant blue as her own and wide with alarm.

"Don't worry, little one," she said. "We're just gonna talk, you and me. We've got us a problem, and between the two of us, we're gonna figure out the best way to solve it. Okay?"

"Okay, Gran."

Stella watched as relief took the place of fear on his delicate features.

After sitting on the ground, she pulled him onto her lap and began to gently rock him. As he snuggled in, she couldn't help thinking of her husband, six feet beneath them, and how sad it was that he was the closest thing to a male figure that this little boy could turn to in a time of trouble.

Six years ago, Arthur had left them, taken in a

terrible tractor accident while working their small farm on the other side of town. Stella and everyone who loved him had thought their lives had ended along with his.

The townsfolk of McGill had never seen a funeral with so many attendees or so many tears shed. It had been an enormous outpouring of grief for the gentle man who had quietly touched so many lives with his acts of kindness.

"Art Reid pulled my car out of a ditch with his tractor one cold night in the pouring-down rain. Wouldn't take a dollar for it, neither," one mourner had said.

"He spent a whole Saturday helping me pull the automatic transmission outta my old Buick, and you know what a hateful, backbreaking job that can be. Didn't even cuss when it slipped and danged near tore off three of his knuckles, neither."

"He's the 'friend that sticks closer than a brother' that Proverbs talks about," another said. "He gave me five dollars for gas when I needed it bad. Found out later it was the last money he had in the world. What's more, when I tried to pay him back, he wouldn't hear of it."

"Didn't tell ever'body in town he gave it to you, neither," someone added, "like some do. They help you out one time, and you never hear the end of it. But Art 'tweren't like that. He wasn't the sort to do you a favor, then throw it up to you later on."

Indeed, Arthur Reid had been well loved, respected, and missed. But his chief mourners, by far, were his wife and grandchildren.

Little Waycross had been only three years old when his grandfather passed. But, although the boy had no distinct memories of him, he cherished every good word, every kind story he had ever heard spoken about Gramps. Waycross Reid was fiercely proud of the man who had been his grandfather.

Perhaps, Stella surmised, his attachment to his grandfather was because he had so few reasons to be proud of his own father. Sadly, the boy and all the Reid family members were reminded of Macon Reid's shortcomings daily. Such were the trials of living in a small town filled with people who had plenty of opinions but precious little common sense about when, where, or how to state them.

She brushed the auburn curls from the boy's forehead, placed her hand beneath his chin, and forced him to look up at her. "You out here talkin' to your grandpa?" she asked.

He sniffed. "Yes, ma'am."

"I thought so. Bendin' his ear 'bout all your problems?"

Waycross shook his head. "No. That'd take way too long. I was just lettin' him know 'bout this last one. The worst one."

"What'd he have to say 'bout it?"

"Not much. I'd just got done fillin' 'im in when you showed up."

Stella suppressed a chuckle. "Sorry. Didn't mean to interrupt an important conversation like that."

"It's okay. Gramps don't mind. He likes it when you come to see him. He misses you somethin' fierce."

At first, Stella thought her grandson was teasing. But when she looked into his eyes, she saw a level of sincerity that shocked her.

Could there be more to Waycross's graveside visits than she had considered?

"He told you that?" she asked. "Gramps told you that he misses me?"

The boy nodded vigorously, setting his curls abob. "All the time."

Stella gulped, trying to swallow the lump forming in her throat. "Well, ain't that interestin'. What else does your grandpa tell you?"

"He said he likes your new hairdo. It reminds him of the way you wore your hair back when you and him was courtin'."

A shiver skittered down Stella's back, and it had nothing to do with the damp earth she was sitting on or the brisk twilight air. She had, indeed, worn her hair in much the same fashion when she and Art had first started keeping company. Back then, she had worn it long and loose about her shoulders, because that was the way he preferred it. Now the carefree style was born of necessity and a lack of time to primp and crimp while providing part-time care for a herd of grandkids.

But there was no way for little Waycross to have known that. Only a couple of old black-and-white photos remained of that era of her life, and she was pretty sure her grandson had seen neither of them.

"I didn't know you came here to have actual conversations with your grandpa," she said. "I thought it was just so you could be close to him."

"That too," he replied. "But Gramps is a smart guy. He gives good advice. You should try it yourself sometime."

Stella tried to get her mind around the idea that her grandson had some sort of spiritual connection with her departed husband. But she reminded herself that she shouldn't be surprised. Art had always put his family above everything, helping them in every way he could. It wasn't so hard to believe that he would continue to do so from the other side.

"What sort of advice does Gramps give you?" she asked.

"Mostly, he tells me to mind you and always do what you say, 'cause you're smart and won't lead me wrong."

"That *is* good advice."

"But he tells me I shouldn't do everything that Mama says to do, 'cause some of it's against the law, and I could wind up in the hoosecow."

"I think that's *hoosegow*. It means 'jail.'"

"I know what it means, and I don't wanna go there."

"Why would you go to jail for doin' somethin' your mama tells you to do?" she asked, suddenly quite concerned.

"'Cause Sheriff Gilford takes a dim view of stuff like snatchin' cigarettes at the service station."

"Your mama told you to . . . what?"

"She told me to act like I need to use the station's toilet, and then she'd pretend she was having problems pumpin' the gas so that ol' Mr.

Warren would come out to help her. Then she wanted me to go in and take some of her favorite cigarettes out from behind his counter."

Stella felt her blood pressure rising by the second. She ached to get her hands on her daughter-in-law and, at the same moment, was thankful she couldn't. How dare that woman involve this innocent child in her own illegal shenanigans!

"Have you actually done that, sweet cheeks?" she asked the boy. "You can tell me the truth. It's okay. Have you gone and snatched cigarettes from ol' Mr. Warren? If you have, I won't hold it against you, 'cause it weren't your idea."

"Nope. I told her a little fib. Pretended I couldn't find her brand. She was mad, but at least I didn't get a whuppin' for not doing what she said."

"She would have whipped you for not doing it?"

He nodded.

"How do you know that?"

"'Cause she told me so, and she had that look in her eye. The kind she gets when she means business."

For the child's sake, Stella fought to keep her temper under control. The last thing he needed was to have the adults he loved at each other's throats. But that was exactly what she wanted to be. At Shirley Reid's throat, strangling her until her eyes bugged out on stems like those of some cartoon character who had just seen something startling.

"I know it's a sin to lie," Waycross said, continuing his confession, "but I figured it was better than stealin'. I could've got in bad trouble for thievin', but all I got was one smack on the head for not doin' what she told me."

"You done good, darlin'. Real good. I'm proud of you." Stella fought back tears as she pressed a kiss to his forehead and promised herself that she would deal with this problem as soon as she settled the issue of the Holy Family's unsightly facial hair.

She drew a deep breath and said, "Speakin' of wrongdoings, we need to address the problem at hand. The one you created when you decided to take a paintbrush to—"

"A marker."

"What?"

"I used a marker. Paint works okay for beards, but a marker's better for mustaches."

"I shudder to think of how you became such an expert."

"You said it was okay to draw them. You said it looked funny."

"I said it was okay for you to draw them on magazines and newspapers after I'd done read 'em. But, as I'm sure you remember, I draw a line at Bible folk. Remember the Adam and Eve incident?"

"Yes, ma'am." Tears filled his eyes.

"Then why did you do it, punkin? Those figures belong to the whole town. Why would you think it was okay for you to deface public property like that?"

He shrugged. "I didn't know I was defacin' nothin'. I just wanted to make people laugh. You laughed when I put mustaches on the president and Queen Elizabeth."

"Yes, but that was in my magazine, not the town manger scene. What do you reckon we oughta do to set this situation straight?"

He looked up at her with wide, frightened eyes. "We gotta *do* somethin'?"

"Sure we do. We can't just pretend nothin' happened, and that we don't know squat about it."

Tears began to stream down his face, and she could feel his small body trembling against hers. "Do we have to tell them, Gran?" he asked. "Do I have to fess up?"

"That's usually best under circumstances like these."

"But it wouldn't be the best. Not this time. It would be plumb awful."

"I don't think it'd be so bad. Most folks hold a body in high regard if they admit they did something wrong and want to set it right."

"Not me," he said, shaking his head. "Nobody in this town is ever gonna hold none of us Reids in high regard, no matter what we do."

Stella felt like someone had just shoved something cold and sharp between her ribs. "Why would you say such a thing, Waycross?"

"You know," he said, with eyes too old for his years. "Because of my mom and my dad. Because of . . . the way they are."

"How's that, darlin'?" she asked, dreading the answer. Of course, she knew better than her grandson what her son's and daughter-in-law's reputations were, but she needed to know how much he knew and understood.

"They say," he began, "that my mom's afraid that

arstool—the one under Elvis's picture—is gonna float away if she ain't holdin' it down night and day."

"What do you think of that, sugar?"

"I think it's dumb, 'cause that stool's bolted to the floor. I checked myself one night, when I went in there to tell her to come home."

"I see."

"And they say my dad's always keepin' the road hot in his truck, drivin' all over the country, 'cause he'd rather be away from his wife and kids so's he can chase skirts."

The feeling of something sharp and cold stabbed even more deeply into Stella's chest. She was sure it was piercing her heart. "What do you reckon that means," she asked him, "when they say that?"

He shrugged. "I don't know. That sounds dumb, too. He's a guy. What would he want with a skirt? Besides, skirts don't run down the road on their own, now do they? Why would anybody need to chase one?"

"I agree, sweetheart. In all my born days, I've yet to see a skirt of any kind hightail it down a street." She kissed the top of his head, breathing in the precious boy smell of him. "It sounds to me like whatever folks in this town are sayin' 'bout us Reids is a bunch of hooey and not worth gettin' ourselves in a dither about. Okay?"

"I just don't want to confess my crime to anybody, 'cause it'll add to all the hooey."

Stella thought it over long and hard, weighing the value of teaching the child the consequences of a transgression versus adding to the burden shame he already carried.

Finally, she said, "I think I've got a solution to this problem. A way you can atone for your crime without the town gossips gettin' all in a tizzy."

He looked up at her, painfully hopeful. "What way's that, Gran?"

"You'll see. It requires you putting that artistic flair of yours to work, and some old-fashioned sneakiness on both our parts. Reckon you're up for it?"

Grinning broadly, he said, "Yes, ma'am. Let's git 'er done!"

Connect with

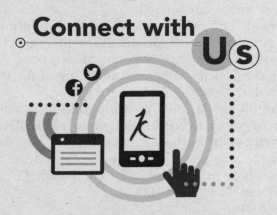

Us

Visit us online at
KensingtonBooks.com
to read more from your favorite authors, see books
by series, view reading group guides, and more.

Join us on social media

for sneak peeks, chances to win books and prize packs,
and to share your thoughts with other readers.

facebook.com/kensingtonpublishing
twitter.com/kensingtonbooks

Tell us what you think!

To share your thoughts, submit a review,
or sign up for our eNewsletters, please visit:
KensingtonBooks.com/TellUs.